The Avenue

by Andrew C. Cecere

RoseDog  Books

PITTSBURGH, PENNSYLVANIA 15238

The contents of this work including, but not limited to, the accuracy of events, people, and places depicted; opinions expressed; permission to use previously published materials included; and any advice given or actions advocated are solely the responsibility of the author, who assumes all liability for said work and indemnifies the publisher against any claims stemming from publication of the work.

This novel is a work of fiction. Names, characters, places, and incidents are either the product of the author's imagination or are used fictitiously, and any resemblance to actual persons living or dead, events, or locales is entirely coincidental.

RoseDog Books
585 Alpha Drive
Suite 103
Pittsburgh, PA 15238
Visit our website at www.rosedogbookstore.com

ISBN: 978-1-4809-6336-8
eISBN: 978-1-4809-6358-0

Prologue

He was at ease, and he was conscious. It was like lying in the too-tall, browned grass of an August afternoon looking up at the cloudless sky, falling in and out of remembrances. An effortless exercise without forcing any sequence to the thoughts that filtered through the lethargic screen. And it was good. Because there was no sense of recrimination, no feeling of lost opportunities, and, above all, no desire to do it all over again. The star in the sky that had shone so brightly at one time was beginning to fade, soon it would be cooler, and then it would slip over on the other side. It would pass away to return anew. Would he, too, ever again be as bright and invigorating, as alert, as intolerant, as caustic, as relentless as a new sun on a new day? But it was not pursued, not because it was too enervating or uncomfortable to contemplate. It was simply unimportant now.

The room was spartan — painted white walls and curtainless window. The times and costs dictated that a hospital bed, was simply a place to lay a body, removed from others, as if death could be contagious. Disturbances to the living from those who were departing to the realm beyond were thus minimized. It was comfortable though, the sheets were clean and crisp, the mattress firm, and the hueless covering was warm enough.

What a shabby way to finish. Evidently, it was going to be like passing off to sleep, all adventures over, and no possibility of dreams.

It was unfair. There should be a fanfare of blaring trumpets, the striking sounds of percussion instruments, a stentorian voice, fireworks, loud music and dancing. But no, it was to be otherwise. It was so unlike birth, the thrusting, the force, the struggle and pain, crying and then liberation. Now that he was resigned, what the hell difference did any of it make? The intravenous feeding of morphine was the rope that was lowering him into the cave from which there would be no rescue. And then, when the light failed to reach the lower levels of the cavern, there would be the slow retreat into the state of forgetfulness ...but not yet.

Chapter I

The old man had lived at least thirty years before he had consciously tried to reconstruct his first recollection of being alive. How far back could he go based on his own independent memory? He strained to find facts to sustain knowledge of an event or a happening or even an individual before he was five and one-half years of age. The first reproducible picture of his being was an extremely cold winter forenoon. He was standing in front of an unclear windowpane in a basement which overlooked a steep gorge traversed by a stone and steel bridge. A slate gray fog in a sunless sky seemed to flow serenely under the span of the bridge as streams of gusty winds surged over the guardrails. It was almost noon, but it appeared to be dusk. Oily soot balls, the size of a pencil point, swirled and danced on the windowsill. It was 1926, he learned later. He was to start kindergarten that afternoon. All he could remember being told was that he was going to school. What was "school"? Other kids would be there, too. No mothers or fathers, just teachers, his older sister told him.

"Come on, Danny, it's time to go. Put your sweater on. It's cold outside. I've got your hat."

He remembered the knickers, long socks, and sturdy shoes with a metal strip guarding the toe and a tie up to the ankles. He could not recall feeling any fear that day.

Sis took his hand, and he remembered saying, "Bye Mama," as he marched out into the cold, his hat over his ears and covering his brow. He walked his hand in her hand, for the three blocks. He was more concerned with the blustering cold blast of air when they turned the first corner past the block of frame houses that provided a break from the wind sweeping up from the chasm.

The school building was red brick, with concrete pavement surrounding it on all sides, all enclosed within a black wrought-iron fence. It was one of the few brick structures in the neighborhood, most of the other buildings were made of wood, and all painted different colors. The houses looked old and tired. They were close together, sometimes only two or three feet apart, no side yards, and all fronting on public sidewalks. They seemed to lean toward each other for support and comfort, closing together when the heavy winds blew up from the valley. They seemed to rely on each other, like the people who huddled inside.

His short legs marched up the concrete steps to the heavy oak door. They stopped at the top of the stairs. He looked down toward The Avenue. Across The Avenue was a chain link fenced-in dirt playground. It really was only an open field about 200 yards by 100 yards wide. The Club Yard was to be the most important piece of earth that he was to know for the next twelve years.

Before they went in, Sis said, "Can you remember how we came? You're going to have to come back without me. Be careful when you cross The Avenue. You can do it."

They went into the school and then into a big room where there was a lady so big, such a round face on such a round body, fatter than Mama.

She asked his sister, "Are you the mother of this child?"

Sis's face reddened. He lowered his head to hide the grin creasing his face.

Sis told her that Mama was home with the baby and that Mama didn't speak English too good. This lady was different than Mama; she had light hair and talked without Italian words. Her face was round like Mama's, but it was almost red and she had a lot of brown spots all over her face, mostly on her nose. But she smiled like Mama, both faces opened wide.

She asked questions. And he remembered Sis told her when he was born, where they lived, and Papa and Mama's name. Then the lady took his hand and they started walking into the hallway. Sis waved good-bye. Then he and the lady walked into a large room where there were about twenty kids — boys and girls. She told another lady, "This is Donato," and when Danny looked back, the fat lady was gone.

When he was seated, he looked around the room and saw some kids he had seen before on the streets of the neighborhood. The teacher was talking about books, stories, and toys. He had never had a book before, no one ever had told him a story. And he had no toys, except the smashed tin can that he would hit with a broom stick in the street, and the "pushie" made of an orange crate attached to a two by four under which was nailed a pair of roller skates.

He walked home after school with Ronnie, another boy who lived on his street. Ronnie said he didn't like school because you couldn't talk anytime you wanted to, or run or hit people. Danny would only say it was "OK"; he liked the stories. He liked the story about the girl with the funny sisters who met a prince who had his own horse.

It was always dark when Danny's Papa came home from work in the wintertime. He worked on the railroad, an outdoor laborer.

He always seemed cold, but he took off his shirt and the upper part of his underwear and washed his face, chest, and arms in the sink in the kitchen. Danny could tell that the water was cold, Papa's face always got red, especially as Papa rubbed it hard to dry it. Papa always put on a clean top. Then they ate at the big table, in the kitchen in the basement, Papa, Sis (who quit school at 16 to work part time at Lombardo's grocery store), Danny's older brother Salvatore ("Sal") twenty-two years old, who left school to work on the railroad), and little brother Armando ("Arman", who was two and one-half). Mama hardly ever had time to sit down to eat with the family, she was always busy getting the food, cleaning and washing. She ate in-between. No one talked too much, everyone just ate. Papa was hungry.

Danny remembered Papa asking that night, "School, it was OK? Listen to your teacher and be good. OK?"

Danny nodded.

No one left the table until after Papa wiped the last of the tomato sauce in his dish with a piece of Mama's bread. In the summer, Danny would run out the back door, up the steps, into the street, hoping to find someone to play with. In the winter, he went up to the first floor living room and sat there until time to go to bed. It was warmer there than where Arman and Danny slept. They shared an iron bed with a rolling mattress on one side of the attic, which was separated by a stair well. Sis had her own bed on the other side of the stairs. There was no central heat up there. Danny slept in long underwear under heavy blankets. The only warmth came from the heat coming to the second floor where there were two bedrooms — one for Mama and Papa, and the other for brother, Sal. It was almost warm on the second floor in the winter. In the summer time when smog covered the city and there was no wind, it was always hot. But it was better when it was hot than cold, even though Danny would wake up sweating in the summertime, his shorts and sheets wet like he had peed in the bed.

The summertime was good because he could run to the playground, everyone called it the "Club Yard." No one knew how it got its name. Maybe it was because everyone met there to talk, to choose up sides, and play football and baseball. Someone had a football. It really wasn't a football except the cover. The insides were filled with old newspapers. And they played "fumble the ball". Someone would toss the football into the air. The one who caught it would run in, about and around the others, until tackled and then the least aggressive would pile on. Everyone ended on the ground or on top of someone else. He later wondered about the purpose of the game. There were no goal lines to cross — no scores to keep. There were no teams, no winners, and no losers. Maybe it was to show how tough you were, or how long you could stay on your feet, but no one kept time. Maybe it was to touch, to be close to someone. That could have been the answer.

Chapter II

Danny would always remember the sixth grade because of two separate incidences, both of which involved his friend, Frankie. They were considered to be buddies. But now that the years had passed, Danny could not understand what had been the tie that bound them. They were opposites in most ways. Frankie swore frequently and loudly, every other word, it seemed. Frankie liked hitting the other kids, which he did often and harshly. Danny tried to be conscious of the use of his language, he rarely swore. They had certain similar physical characteristics which may have been the bond that made them appear to be friends. Each had fairer skin than most of the boys on the Avenue. Danny's hair was tightly curled, a shade lighter than brown, but not a towhead. And Frankie's hair was almost red. They were both square shouldered, and taller and fairer than the other kids. Although Frankie was older, they were both in the same grade. Frankie had been held back, he had started late and missed too many school days.

It was a Spring day rich with the promise of the coming Summer, warm with cloudless skies. Frankie and Danny were sitting on the outside stairs looking longingly at the abandoned playground across The Avenue. The afternoon class bell would ring momentarily. Frankie poked Danny on the upper arm and laughing said, "We should be playing ball, Danny, you don't like music, like me. We can't sing worth a shit, so why don't we screw off, cut Miss Wood's music class. We don't sing no how, so no-body's gonna miss us. Whatta ya say, Danny?"

Danny had never skipped a class. He enjoyed listening to the class singing together, although he did not participate. Frankie thought going to school was a "waste of time," and all the teachers were "pansies." Frankie thought that any boy who liked going to school had to be a "sissy" or a "queer."

"Whatta you say, Danny boy? You gonna run out on me?" Frankie yelled, slapping Danny on the top of his head as he ran down the stairs toward the rear of the building.

Danny rose slowly and followed.

Frankie had found some white chalk and began marking the smooth red brick. He drew some lewd stick men and women. He printed, "Miss Bartel is a fat ass fatso". They giggled as they stepped back and admired the bold white letters on the red background. Danny looked backward as he felt a strong pull at the nape of the neck. Frankie did the same. They had been collared by the strong hands of Mr. Jackson, the janitorial and security force of the school, who marched them up the stairs, through the hall to the principal's office. No words were spoken.

Miss Bartel, the principal, could not have been more than five feet tall, and she surely weighed over two hundred pounds, and had the arms of a longshoreman.

Mr. Jackson pushed them into the office so that they stood immediately in front of her desk. She was sitting in a high chair, just nodding her head, almost smiling, without saying anything when Mr. Jackson recited where he had found them. He told her about "some printed matter" on the outside brick walls.

She took her time getting up out of that chair — very slow, very deliberate. Maybe because there was so much to lift.

She stood in front of Danny. He wondered why it was now cold in that room. How could it be? Her eyes seemed inflamed. Danny was frightened.

"Donato, this is a surprise. You seem to like school. Your grades have been very good." She looked past Danny toward Frankie, turned back to Danny, and said, "Following that character is going to lead to reform school. Mr. Jackson, hold on to that bad one, Danny is coming with me." She took Danny's hand and led him into a large closet-like room with some bookcases, a wooden bench and several chairs. She closed the door and went to the bench, where she picked up two yardsticks.

"Now, Donato, I know this will never happen again, but so you don't forget this meeting, I want you to bend over, rest the palms of your hands on that bench. Then relax, and always remember the why of this exercise," Miss Bartel said, as she picked up the wooden yardsticks.

Danny puckered his lips tightly; he didn't want to cry out. The five blows stung, but his mouth stayed tightly shut.

"You may stand up, Daniel. Remember, you will never cut class ever again. Mr. Jackson will provide you with a bucket of water and some rags, and you will wash all the markings off the bricks. Is that clear?" she spoke tensely.

He nodded and said dejectedly, "Yes, Miss Bartel," and as he started to retreat, she said, "And another thing you must do, you must bring you father or mother with you before you can return to school."

That blow hurt the most, much more than the thrashing. He didn't want his folks to know, they must never know.

He pleaded, "My father can't come. He works every day, and if he misses a day he'd lose his job. He works from six in the morning until six at night".

"Then you will bring your mother," Miss Bartel answered decisively.

"Mama don't speak English," he replied.

"Don't worry, we will understand each other." She opened the door and led Frankie into the back room. He could hear Frankie yell as he left the building with bucket and rags.

That night at the supper table was the worst. He was tight. Like a robot, Danny moved his spoon from the plate to his mouth, which would not open completely. His chin was close to his chest, as if in prayer. He would not look at Papa, but he could hear him gulp the hot soup down, and crunch the two-day-old homemade bread. Danny was saying to himself, "If this guy beats me, I'll show him how bad I can really be. I'll be worse than Frankie". He was a prisoner in the lock-up of his chair. No one had spoken during the entire meal. He knew he must have been breathing but he couldn't hear anything. Finally, Papa pushed himself away from the table and started to get up. Then he put his two big hands on the table. The veins turned purple as he leaned toward Danny, and in a rather strained voice said, "I hear you get yourself into some kind of trouble in school today, eh".

Danny's response was an almost inaudible, "Yes, Papa". Danny's insides became more knotted as he anticipated the rain of blows that would follow the harsh rasping sounds from Papa.

"Well, I'll tella you," Papa said slowly, "if you wanna work like a jackass like I do every day, you'll do what you do today. If you wanna make something out of yourself, you'll go to school and learn," and then he walked out into the backyard.

Danny didn't move or breathe. The will to fight was all gone. It was as if someone had stuck a pin into an inflated balloon. There was nothing inside Danny; he was empty. He ran upstairs to the attic.

Danny did not miss another class that year, and he was never tardy. And he tried to avoid Frankie as much as possible. But Frankie had become the most popular boy in the school. There was always a crowd around him in the halls, many of them girls, giggling and talking. Frankie was the best-dressed sixth grader, sweater, and matching slacks, and shoes that fit. It was confusing to Danny. He knew that Frankie's father worked in The Mill, when the doors were open. The Mill was working only three days a week, except when it was shut down. Frankie was the big spender, buying milk and crackers for some of the girls and two or three of the boys who followed him wherever he went.

Danny was late leaving English class one day; he had stayed to ask Miss Lyons a question. As he pushed out the door, three or four bodies that were circling Frankie in the hallway had to step aside. As Danny shrugged a shoulder, in apology, and started to move toward the restroom, Frankie caught his arm and laughingly, almost shouting, "Hold on, buddy. How come you've been making yourself so scarce? Kinda funny, ain't it, when you and me is supposed to be pals?" The band of followers spread out and moved away from Frankie and Danny.

Frankie reached into his jacket pocket, pulled out a quarter-pint of milk, took two graham crackers from the hand of one of the hangers-on, thrust the prizes into Danny's hand, and said, "Have a drink on me, my treat. You're too damned serious, Danny Boy, have some fun." and there were smiles from Frankie's clique. Frankie continued, "Anyhow, I probably owe you one. I guess you never told Miss Bartel nothin about who started that business about cutting class and writing on the walls. And I didn't hear you cry when she whacked your ass."

Frankie knew that Danny had heard Frankie's vocal reaction to the ruler meeting his backside. And Danny had never spread that word. Frankie would always brag that he always paid his debts.

Danny soon discovered how Frankie was getting all that money. Somehow, Frankie picked up some dirty little books, cartoon figures in cheap booklets, showing guys and girls making out. They showed everything. Frankie was charging the boys two cents a minute to view the pictures. Some of the boys were going without their milk and crackers; Frankie had re-directed their hunger. Frankie was known as an operator, a wheeler-dealer. All the kids believed that he would make it big. Frankie became a believer; too, you could see the swagger in his walk. And he looked older than the other kids. He was a boss even then.

Chapter III

The summers were a joy, except during the hot, muggy months of July and August. The soiled atmosphere seeped through the porous walls of the house, coating the ceiling of the attic with fine, gray soot. Sleeping during such nights, two a-bed, was an adventure in tossing, turning, exhaustion, and awakening in dampness. But the days were glorious, baseball in the Club Yard, and swimming at the City Pool, a three-mile walk from home. The guys generally met at The Bridge and, en masse, crossed to the other side of the chasm. It really was almost like walking into a new world on the way to the City Park. The houses were different, mostly brick facades, manicured lawns, elm and oak trees, dogwood and flowering shrubs. And space. Open areas between houses — One mile, two miles, a different world. And the air seemed purer and the sky appeared bluer. It was as if one had passed through a dimly lit tunnel into the searing noontime sunshine of summer. And the thought always was how do you pass from here to there? Even the people on the other side of the bridge looked different. They all seemed taller, fairer in complexion, with a predominance of lighter straighter hair. Danny always had a feeling of being a trespasser when he crossed the bridge.

But it all changed when they entered the free municipal swimming pool.

The Avenue boys marched in together, swam together, but had no association or talked with others in the pool. There was no mixing. The Wops were tolerated but not really accepted. Everyone recognized there were various shades of whites. Most of The Avenue boys were olive complexioned, perhaps the Sicilian descendants carried too much of their Moorish ancestry — dark skin and tight black, curly hair. One of Danny's buddies was called "Black Boy".

But there were no Negroes in the city pool. It was simply understood, "No Niggers allowed". There had been rumors for several years that they were going to make a push some day, the uninvited guests were going to make an appearance in force. And Danny was led to believe (there had been Club Yard talk) that counter-forces had been formed and were always available to repel any invasion by those "primates".

It was a scorching day in mid-August, and Danny noticed them first as he started for the men's locker room, a toilet break. It was then he encountered what most kids on The Avenue called "burr-heads", a lanky adolescent, tightening his bathing trunks, and looking over his shoulder as eight other huge, black, shiny bodies sulked toward the pool. As if on signal, the white bodies emerged from the pool. It seemed that in a matter of minutes, two hundred swimmers had decided to retire from the pool. And the Colored dove in, shouting, splashing each other, and seemingly enjoying the exclusiveness of the cool wet waters. They now owned it.

Danny gathered his buddies, Tony, Hugo, Mario and Paul, Black Boy and Ronnie, and walked toward the water fountain.

"How in the hell did they get in?" someone shouted.

"Where the hell are The Avenue Boys? Maybe someone should call down at the Joint. There's always a group there," yelled Black Boy. Ronnie was Danny's age, fourteen, he was a tough kid, loved contact sports, a hard hitter, and agile. "We're younger and smaller than these boogies, but we can take them on. Who wants to go with me?" Mario nodded, but no one moved.

Then Danny saw them coming. Frankie was in the lead with a baseball bat trailing behind, bumping the pavement. Behind Frankie there were at least a dozen more guys from The Avenue, all armed with bats and clubs. The shimmering sun outlined some brass knuckles. All, except for Frankie, were in their late teens. But Frankie strode up to the edge of the pool, slammed and banged his bat on the aluminum ladder, and screamed, "Get out, you fucking niggers, or we going to have to drain the pool to clean out your blood and your black sweat and stinking piss." He jumped onto the diving board, swinging the baseball bat, and yelling that they had a minute to get the hell out of the water.

The Negroes circled around the biggest, the obvious leader, and surveyed the scene. And their option became apparent — stay in the pool and stay together. In a fight they would be separated, and they were not armed. Evidently, a decision had been made because their leader spoke out loudly, but the words came out tremulously.

"This is a free country and we got the right to go any place we wants. This here pool is for everybody, we is taxpayers, too. We is gonna stay, and there is more of us where we come from. We don't want no trouble. We just wanna swim, see?"

And from the white group someone shouted, "All we see is you got less than ten seconds to get out or get the shit kicked out of you."

As if on signal, four more Negroes emerged from the dressing room. Frankie led the charge, screaming, "Kill the bastards." Followed by eight or nine of his compatriots, bats swinging, they drove into the astonished and bewildered newcomers. Almost immediately, three of the four were down, crawling to the wall, hands over their heads as the blows descended. Blood colored the pavement, mixing with the chlorinated pool water. Cries could not mute the harshness of wood striking bone and cartilage. The Negroes in the pool clambered out and charged to save their fallen comrades, and they, too, were met by crashing bats and the screaming, shouting, yelling mob of the bystanders. The shrill screaming from the girls joined the frenzy.

Frankie was at the forefront, striking each of the colored boys as they stopped to rescue the fallen. Soon there were eight on the ground and four trembling with their backs against a wall, hands up to protect faces and heads.

The lifeguards sat, legs crossed, whistles hanging, eyes lowered, but not moving. Danny heard sirens in the distance. The armament, clubs, bats, sticks, went flying over the chain link fences surrounding the pool area. The colored boys were huddled near the restroom area, cowering, crying, cringing, and awaiting rescue or safe passage from their misadventure. There appeared to be no rage or rancor, none expressed, simply incomprehension, almost acceptance, as if the spilling of their blood, the discoloration from bruises, and the forever mending of broken bones was their due, their lot in life.

Then the cops entered the scene. There was no melee. Twelve Negroes sat, laid, and leaned against the walls for support. The white crowd twenty feet back looked on.

The police sergeant shouted, "OK, what the hell happened here?"

And a black answered, "We only wanna swim, cool our bodies."

"Come on, you guys, let's get on your feet and get the hell outta here." And to the standing blacks, another officer yelled, "Help those guys up, we can't stay here all day. Move it."

Slowly the group gathered itself, assisted the more seriously injured, and shuffled toward the exit. As they moved from the pool area, an officer was heard to say, "If any you got a complaint against anyone specific, you go to the precinct station and file a complaint." And almost as an afterthought, they could hear the sergeant ask, "Did you see any of the people who did this?" There was silence. Then, as they passed out of the gates, there was a cry from a bystander, "Don't you god-damned niggers know where you belong?"

The roar from the pool was chilling, like the cold rain of a fall thunderstorm. It rolled through the area like the cheer after a touchdown in a large stadium. Hundreds of bodies dove into the pool, shouting, splashing, hugging the celebration of a victory.

The crowd around Frankie and his pals was almost too great to penetrate. Much back slapping, loud talk, and merriment.

Danny sat at the foot of the diving board and watched. He didn't know how to feel. Sure, he was glad that Negroes were not swimming there, scratching you with their burr hair, and brushing up against the girls. But that blood! Danny had never seen so much in one place. And, it was red, too. He had never heard such smacks. It was a different sound than a bat hitting a ball. He could almost feel the blows and the pain. But, god-dammit, they oughta known better. Thank God for the boys from The Avenue, or they'd be here all summer, and more and more of them.

Walking home with his buddies, Danny wondered why he had not joined in the scrap. Had he been afraid, concerned about his face, or did the brutality turn him?

Aloud, he said to the others, "They had it coming to them, we could have all jumped in if there was any need. Hell, Frankie and his bashers could have taken on another ten of them. Maybe some other time," he uttered out loud, as if relieving himself of any fault or faithlessness in the cause.

Swinging his wet trunks, with the damp towel around his neck, he crossed the bridge into The Avenue district, safe and hungry, and yet not altogether happy. He was somewhat proud of the boys from The Avenue, but there remained that queasy feeling as he mentally regurgitated the blows, the bashing, and the red blood finding its way to the drains.

It was Summer, that was good. Maybe there had to be days like this.

He never could understand why, but he dreamed more in the heat of summer than in the winter. Maybe because the attic was the collector of all the accumulated heat and humidity of the day, like sleeping in a greenhouse, and ideas, like flowers, blossomed faster.

But it was always the same since Danny was about twelve years old, winter or summer he thought himself different. He liked his Mama. She was obese, short, round, always smiling, always working. She had black hair and dark skin. Papa was square, medium in height, aquiline profile, with light receding hair, who knew only how to work with his hands and back. There was no question these good, nice and caring people could not be his natural parents. Somehow there had to have been a mix-up. Some American girl in trouble had laid him on their doorstep. She had to have come from across the bridge, living in one of those brick houses with trees and flowers, and whose father drove to work each morning in a business suit, and whose mother planted roses and played bridge in the afternoon. He didn't think like Mama and Papa; working to eat and raise kids was not living. He was taller than most kids in the neighborhood, as well as his older brother and sister. He had a fairer complexion with a reddish tint to it. His big brother, Sal, was short and dark. He was different. He could not tell about Armando, yet. But Danny believed he was different. And what about his blue eyes! Perhaps some day they would tell him how he arrived at their house.

Awake, he called it a dream. He disavowed any personal will, any conscious reasoning power behind such an idea. It was stupid.

Chapter IV

School had started, the last year before going to high school. Summer was closing fast, and it had rained all day. The sun was setting and Danny and Ronnie, his closest buddy, decided to walk across the bridge, up the hill in the classy neighborhood, to pick some apples that should have ripened.

Ronnie had climbed the apple tree that spread over the circular drive. No one was home, there were no lights on, there was no car in the garage. Ronnie carefully dropped the largest and reddest apples to Danny, who had opened his jacket, storing them against his body. The shape of his front changed, he looked like the old guys from the mills standing in front of the beer joint on Saturday afternoon. Before Ronnie could get down, and before Danny became aware, a police cruiser had blocked the exit to the street. Two burly men in blue with stomachs larger than Danny's apple-filled belly alighted from the cruiser.

They were about the same size, stout, portly. They had the same demeanor, cruel, untamed. And they both spoke with the accent of the City splashed with some Irish syntaxes and inflections.

To Ronnie, the Sergeant yelled, "Get your Wop ass down the tree, and right now."

To Danny, the other cop said, "Come here, kiddo. Who's been fucking you? Your baby is ready to come out." He unzipped Danny's jacket and the apples poured out like coins out of a nickel slot machine. Such beautiful fruit — now bruised, dirty, and punctured by the gravel of the driveway.

As Ronnie climbed down, the Sergeant retrieved one of the fallen fruit, brushed it against his sleeve, and bit into it. With his mouth full, he gulped and garbled to his partner, "Let's take these bastards to the station and book 'em, open the back seat and stuff their asses in, Cooley."

The passenger side of the cruiser was parked adjacent to a four-foot privet hedge defining the circular drive. Cooley grabbed Ronnie and pushed him in first. To the surprise of the cops and Danny, Ronnie opened the passenger side door and leaped over the hedge. There was a splash, then the sound of running feet through the bushes. The cops roared with laughter, slapping their thighs, an extraordinary display of humanness uncharacteristic of the men in blue in Danny's neighborhood.

The crusty Sergeant, trying to recoup the aura of authority, stopped the patrolman from pursuing, yelling, "The little shit will get it from his old man and the old lady when he gets home full of mud and water."

The patrolman wanted to know what to do with Danny. The Sergeant grabbed him, headed him toward the street, and brought his size twelve shoe onto Danny's rear-end, propelling him almost into the street, shouting, "And keep your fucking Dago asses out of this neighborhood. You don't belong here."

Danny and Ronnie had joked about it, and reminisced about that street with the incline almost straight up and down. The winter had been exceptionally cold, with more snow and ice than usual. Ronnie, Danny and Mario had found an old sled, liberated from a backyard of one of the houses near the apple trees. When they started the quarter-mile ascent to the near summit, it was dark, about five o'clock. They started down, Mario on the bottom, Ronnie in the middle, and Danny on top. It was scary as the sled pushed off from the top, down the icy and slippery black top. The sled was moving at incredible speed, faster and faster, the wind tearing at Danny's blood red cheeks. Tears blinded his vision, and the noise tore at his exposed ears, he had forgotten to pull his hat down far enough. As the sled approached the bottom of the hill, automobile lights at the intersection showed no break in traffic. Mario steered toward the curb, hoping that steel blades would slow the sled on concrete, but a sheet of ice coated the pavement. The over-loaded sled was accelerating faster, and ahead was a parked Ford with Danny's head measured for the rear bumper. Mario couldn't change course; the steel blades on the ice committed the sled forward faster. Danny was frozen with fright. At the last moment, Ronnie rolled off to the pavement, pulling Danny free of the hurtling sled and into a snow pile on the sidewalk. Mario, head down, passed under the parked vehicle, with a piece of metal cutting down the center of his leather jacket. Some bruises and bumps, but no real hurt. Ronnie instinctively had moved at the right moment. Ronnie was a natural. What a buddy, what a guy to have with you in a jam — he had to have been a centurion in one of his former lives. He could not have learned it during his short lifetime.

Chapter V

Winter mornings were not only uncomfortably cold, they were cheerless. The dark smoke from the mills was heavier, blotting out even the most persistent rays of the early sun. The low fire in the coal furnace was only stoked once when Mama descended to the basement to commence another long day. Coffee and canned Carnation milk with a slice of hard bread with apple butter was breakfast. And it didn't take too much time, so one could stay under the blankets for several minutes longer after the first call to get up.

The guys all met at the Playground, the starting point, and as they moved toward high school, others joined the two-mile march.

The chatter began as soon as the gang started across The Avenue. He was expecting it since they had all seen him dance with the social worker at the settlement house. Jughead, in an aside to Apes DiNardo, which could be heard for a least a block, said, "Did you see Danny Boy whirl and twirl with that 'swell' yesterday at Cooper's Hall? He looked big-time, didn't he? He liked it."

The others looked at him. Danny kicked the ground with the toe of his shoe, and yelled, "Now I know why they call you Jughead, because you look like a milk bottle and that's filled with dirty water."

Apes spoke defensively, "Aren't The Avenue girls good enough for you, pal?"

He stopped and looked squarely at his buddy and shouted, "I know how you got your name, Apes, those arms of yours are too long to dance with anyone except another gorilla like you, and you act like one, too."

There was laughter and ridicule, and he forgot the cold and hunger. But he remembered her taking him out of The Avenue for a brief moment, and he liked it.

Somehow the freshman classes were not as boring that day; the English Literature class held his attention during the whole period. Even applying himself to the composition class was effortless. Danny even talked with some of the non-Avenue classmates. It was a beginning.

The long trek home after school always seemed the same monotonous movement, meeting the gang at the football field, and then deciding whether to take the long way home or the short cut over Beaver Lake. The penetrating chill of the sunless slate gray February skies decided the issue. It could snow at any time, and the lake must be covered by two feet of ice. They never knew why it was called Beaver Lake. No one had ever seen any beavers around there, it's waters didn't seem to move anywhere, and during hot weather it had a smell.

That afternoon the ice looked dingy. There were areas covered by soot balls that floated down from the smoking blast furnaces of the city. In spots, it seemed like a colony of ants had found an open can of chocolate syrup.

Maybe because it was colder than usual, or maybe because he wanted to avoid any talk such as the one that morning, Danny took the lead as they began to cross the lake. He picked up a fallen tree branch along the shore, and without thinking, he waved it in a forward direction. In the distance he could hear Apes, "Look, you guys, now he's a Boy Scout Leader. Them college broads at Cooper Hall musta really turned him on." Danny didn't look back, just plodded on with his head down, and every so often poked the ice with the stick to test its solidity.

About ten feet ahead he spotted a rather large area covered with those swirling oily balls of soot. He jabbed his stick into the ice, and nothing gave way. He slowed his pace and continued to thrust the branch more forcefully to the surface, like a blind man tapping the edge of the sidewalk before stepping into the street. Proceeding cautiously, he moved another pace forward. And in he went and down he went, abandoning the tree branch as he disappeared. The opening closed with a black mass of moving substances.

Apes moved the quickest, grasped the branch, lay down on the ice, and extended his long arms so that the branch reached the edge of the hole. Apes told the others later that he was praying that Danny would come straight up, otherwise, they'd never find him until spring. Apes could never recall how long it was before the sooty water became disturbed and parted. The balls of soot encrusted the top of Danny's head as the last light of day outlined a halo when his head broke the surface. Danny was gasping but not thrashing as he took hold of the limb. Apes slid backwards as Danny moved onto the ice. The edges held and he was pulled to the prone body of Apes. Apes raised himself on his elbows, looking down at the spitting face of Danny, and laughingly spoke, "You needed someone with arms like a gorilla today, old buddy. Now you better get your ass up and run like hell before you freeze your balls, you'll be the real iceman before you get home. Run before your fucking legs are frozen together. Tell your Mama you pissed in your pants when some American girl tried to fuck you. Run!"

He was dazed, but able to move. He knew that he had lost his woolen cap. He was not frightened. The water clinging to his clothes had not begun to freeze, so he nodded to the guys and ran. For the first time he could remember, the house appeared to radiate, some sun had appeared and it seemed a beacon of warmth and safety. He entered through the basement, always open, into the cellar where there was the only bathtub. His pants were as if glued to his skin, his hands were raw like the inside of a beet, and his shoes, sloshing in the lake water, had rubbed raw the heels of his feet. His mother came into the cellar as he was removing his semi-frozen long john underwear. "Donato, where you been? Che cosa fatta? You red like a tomato. I get towels." And she became excited, and her blood rushed to those oversized cheeks, and she slapped her forehead with her clenched thumb and forefinger. His Mama never screamed, she boiled, and moved into action. Soon there were at least four large drying cloths; former flour sacks which had been bleached almost clean of the advertisement.

The house was quiet, Armando had not returned from school, and Danny was at rest. The stillness and warmth of the water eased the muscles of his face and he seemed to drift into a state of almost sleep. But he could not blot out the cold dark water of the lake. Down and down his heavy shoes had weighed him almost into eternity. And it was timeless, a bottomless void. It was without life or death, without control, without direction, and without purpose — in hibernation.

Musing, suppose he had not risen straight up. Suppose he had missed the opening. It would have been all over, but would it? Is there an everlasting? And how long does it exist? What is forever? Maybe it would have been best to stay down, maybe another chance? There were people in the other countries who believed you would come back sometime, in another place, in another body, another family, and a different name. Like graduation, a step upward. Just suppose he would come back a pure blonde, named Alcott, and had a family who talked American all the time. That would be good. You'd never know, though, you could come back as black as an ace of spades and have to live like a rat. The chance would be worth it; it had to be better than what it was now.

Adding more warm water, he thought about the accident. It was miraculous, the intercession of a power that the priests talked about. By all the laws of nature, his life should have been over, but something intervened. Providence, or maybe just luck. Maybe there is something to the stories in the Bible — another Lazarus. Following this thread, he wondered, where he would go from there. A sign, a future, but in what? "How in the hell do I get out of this crummy place?" he spoke aloud in the miniature bathroom, a toilet and a bathtub, and the discolored linoleum curling at the edges. "I can't take it too much longer", he almost yelled, as he struck the surface of the water with the palm of his hand, splashing dirty water over the porous floor.

Two images appeared, two ways out. First, talk to Frankie. Frankie was quitting school in June when he turned sixteen. Frankie had plans. Some of the guys had been talking; Frankie had become a runner, a collector for the numbers guys. He had often been seen on the corner of The Avenue with the guys everyone said were part of the mob. They said he was beginning to dress like them, too, wearing a camel hair overcoat on Saturday nights and Sunday. No one reported that he had donned the snap brim felt hats seen slanted over the right eyes of the big guys. But Frankie always did like to show his short cut tightly curled red hair.

Maybe Frankie could find a place for him. "What the hell, going to school is only going to get me in the mills or on the railroad." He continued to ruminate about his future, visualizing life after ten years before the open hearth — a sloppy big belly, overweight, a fat and sassy wife, and four or five kids running all over the house, yelling and throwing shoes at each other, noses running snot. No sirree, that's not what he wanted.

The other alternative was to walk over to Cooper's Hall and talk to Mr. Appleton, one of the social workers. They were college graduates, and spoke gently, easily, and knowingly. They all seemed happy. They probably didn't make too much money. But who the hell was making it now, maybe the Rockefellers and people like that, or the biggies in the mobs. They had talked about going to college as a way out. Three more years of high school — then four years more. Where in the hell was he going to get the money? He was smart, but he didn't study too hard. How in the hell could he find a place to study in that house? It would be nice to talk as the social workers did; their English was like the teachers at school; educated talk, no slang and no "fucking" adjectives. It would be too slow; there was not enough time. There had to be a quicker way, through Frankie. That was the only answer. Like today. He could pop off any time, without having a dime in his pants, still cold and hungry. No, he had to talk to Frankie. Frankie would help — they were buddies. That's it!

It must have been the following Sunday, after Mass, when he saw Frankie on the corner with the boys, talking as if they were making the next moves for Hitler. Frankie spotted Danny as he came up the alley, stepped back from the circle of guys, and yelled, "Hey, Danny, did you get dry behind the ears yet? That was a hell of a place to take a bath, kid. Anyhow, I'm glad to see you on the upside."

Danny spoke quickly, before Frankie went back to the inner circle. "Frankie, I gotta ask you something. They tell me you're gonna quit school. So what are you gonna do?"

Frankie turned his head to the side as if not to be heard, and answered, "Danny, I ain't gonna do nothin, I'm gonna retire."

"Come on, Frankie. They tell me you will be working for the boys, full time. How about me, Frankie, can you cut me into the deal, too?" Danny was tense, and talking too loud.

Frankie took him by the arm, moved to the edge of the alley, and spoke softly, "Look, kid, I like you. You stay in school. You know me; I hate school, so I gotta find sumptin else. You're pretty smart. You'll do good. Me — I gotta find another way. Anyhow, things are slow everywhere. We'll get together and, don't sweat it — we'll talk later. OK?"

Frankie placed both hands on Danny's shoulders, shook him gently, then tightened his grip, and said, "Stay loose, Danny. Stick it out in school. No matter what, we're gonna stay buddies. Stay loose, kid".

Danny was not elated or disappointed. Still friends, he thought. He was sure that he could always count on Frankie; he thinks I'm smart, and OK, so maybe it's best this way. Anyhow, he wondered how long it would be before he would become bored loafing on the corner with the same guys talking about nothing important, telling the same old stories, or repeating gossip that reached all levels of the neighborhood in one form or another.

So for some time, Danny became outwardly more relaxed, yet more secluded and withdrawn. He spent more time at the library or at Cooper's Hall, but always alone. At the library, he spent many hours reading more than he ever had.

Spending more time at the Hall really involved listening and talking to the counselors. They seemed to say only things that mattered. For hours, he would sit on the floor in the gym, watching Miss Britten {everyone called her Miss B} directing a play. She was plain and about ten years older than Danny, solidly built, but she could move like a ballerina. She asked him many times to take a part, even a walk-on, or a non-speaking role. He always claimed he didn't have the time, or that he wasn't interested, both excuses which he and Miss B understood were not quite straightforward. He was afraid of failing, of being criticized, of being laughed at, of being evaluated. Walking to the library was ideal. Alone with his thoughts, anticipating the new characters he would meet in those books, and the far-away places he could visit. He could forget it all momentarily, The Avenue, the house, the family, and Frankie. The further he walked away from the neighborhood, the taller the people appeared, walking more upright, and dressed in more colorful clothes. The streets here seemed cleaner; there was no dirt in the gutters. But all that was a dream — unreal. Frankie had the answer. He would be better off spending more time with Frankie and his gang, than the fairylands created by the library or Cooper's Hall. Better stay home with people you know.

Chapter VI

Everyone knew everyone else in the neighborhood. It was like living in a large tenement house, there were no strangers. Danny knew every soul who walked the streets of the neighborhood, and everyone knew Danny, his family and where and how they lived. The neighborhood was more than frame houses fronting on sidewalks, and stone churches, and grocery stores displaying bushels of produce on the street. The Avenue extended eighteen blocks to the Carnegie Public Library. He had only recently learned that books were giving him an opportunity to meet different people and to vicariously share experiences in places beyond the world of The Avenue. It was also good because he could forget the cold of winter, the humidity, the sweat and dirt of summer. He had also learned that it was always nicer walking toward the library than from the library. Walking to the library was always like spring, the beginning of everything. It was anticipation, expectation. And so there was always a sprightly gait as he moved away from the center of the neighborhood.

It was early spring, and only weeks before Danny's sixteenth birthday, and he wanted to be in the library. The coming of the evening and the black smoke blowing in from the mills along the river enveloped the sky, slowly blowing the curtain down on another day. Although day was rapidly closing, there was light enough to see that the grass on the lawn of the Catholic Church on the opposite side of the street had lost some of its winter brownness. Sprouts of shining green broke through the uneven clusters of grass struggling through the cold clay soil of a fading winter. The shiny black painted wrought iron fence surrounding the church caught some of the rays of the fading sunlight and proclaimed its stateliness and durability. The entrance of the church was guarded by ornate massive spears of iron, tied in the center by a built- in bronze locking system. The entrance gates were closed on this day at this hour. The Church occupied a city block, granite, and limestone, impressively solid. It had been planned, constructed and erected before the Italians had moved to The Avenue and the surrounding eighteen-block area. Its communicants were not Italian; they were the shopkeepers, managers and professionals who did not now live in The Avenue neighborhood. Day laborers were not solicited to become members, nor were they indulged if they attended any of the services. It had nothing in common with Danny's Catholic Church. His church had no grass, trees or a fence of any kind. It was a sidewalk church, like the houses in which he and his neighbors lived.

Danny had always walked on the opposite side of the street from the church, walking along the sidewalk abutting the church property was almost like trespassing. He hardly ever saw Avenue people walking along the church property.

So, it was surprising to see people standing in front of the church gate as he hurried toward the library. Danny's first impression was that of two young men talking somewhat seriously. As he approached the point almost exactly across The Avenue from the gate, Danny thought he recognized Frankie, who seemed to be questioning the other man. Strange. Danny could not remember ever seeing the other person. He appeared small in stature, shorter than Frankie, and looked frail. And, as a hurrying cloud passed beyond the receding sun, he saw that Frankie was talking to a Negro, an unusual traveler in the neighborhood, especially as darkness descended. Frankie was not known to fraternize with colored people. The man appeared bewildered, and he seemed to be appealing to Frankie, more dazed than frightened as he looked up at his inquisitor.

When Danny was immediately opposite the gate, Frankie turned his head abruptly from his captive and shouted, "Danny, get your ass over here. Look what I found. A live crow. I may need some help. Move ass, buddy."

Danny wanted to be anywhere but there. The colored boy could not run. It was apparent that the Negro was being unwillingly supported, his knees were buckled and only the outside edges of his shoes grazed the pavement.

As Danny crossed The Avenue, he noticed that the ever-diminishing sunlight seemed to have centered on the cross rising from the apex of the roof of the church. And its shadow fell across the lawn between the brass — studded oak door of the church and the iron gate on the sidewalk. For a moment, Danny tried to imagine the countenance and demeanor of that captive some two thousand years ago, a non-resisting, yet understanding Christ being escorted to a cross by Roman centurions. But this man was black, he was confused and imploring his captor. Here, a son of a Neapolitan had a firm grasp of both arms of his captive. Midway across The Avenue, Danny could see that the hatless head of the dark man only nodded, he was not speaking. It was then that Danny saw fright had become frozen on the black face.

As Danny reached the curb, Frankie yelled, "Hold this buzzard, Danny; we can't let this bird fly away."

Danny, wanting to support the Negro, took hold of the man's belt in the middle of his back, and with his other hand held him somewhat upright by grasping his shirt collar at the nape of his neck. Danny was preparing to ask, "What the hell is going on, Frankie?" when he heard the blow that was viciously loud and unexpected, to Danny and the black man. The blow caught the victim in the mid-section, and he would have fallen forward to the pavement except that Danny was supporting him. Danny turned to speak to Frankie when the next blow from Frankie's fist went crashing to the right side of the Negro's face. A tortured look turned into a cry of pain. And then there came a crescendo of blows to his head, chest, and abdomen; rights and lefts to an immobile punching bag, and blood began pouring from the Negro's nose and ears. But the victim did not fall, being held upright by a stunned and dazed Danny, an unwilling accomplice frozen in position, and now voiceless.

The grinning assailant paused in his assault, looked knowingly at Danny, who opened his hands, releasing his grip on the battered form of a man whose ancestors may have been kings on the plains of Africa. The Negro fell face down on the sidewalk. His head, now bloodied, extended over the curb, his face coming to rest in the gutter. The lengthening shadow of the cross settled on the prone beaten body of the colored man, the upright resting from the top of his head to beyond his feet, and the transverse beam seemed to fit comfortably between his shoulders.

Danny did not move. Frankie tugged at his arm, pulling him back toward their neighborhood. Danny lowered his head and moved away. Frankie abruptly looked toward the downed Negro, shouting to the night that had descended, "Nigger, you're a sinner, you committed a mortal sin. You was on The Avenue after the Goddamned sun went down, and this is your penance. Bye-bye, Black Bird!"

Then Danny ran. Fast! No feeling, like he was intoxicated, drugged.

Maybe it had never happened. It could have been only a stirring of the imagination of a lonely youngster who was on his way to visit the repository of all kinds of tales. If only it were not true, if only it had not happened. Then he argued to himself, "I never struck a blow, I only held him. I thought he was only trying to scare the man."

That spring, Danny did not loaf on The Avenue; he did not want to be with Frankie or be seen with him. He hoped that he could forget.

Chapter VII

The summer played a healing role. Danny swam at the Park, played baseball in the Clubyard, and at night sat on the front porch listening to Glenn Miller and Jack Teagarden broadcast from the Glen Island Casino in New Rochelle, New York. He was doing time until he could find a way out. The Civilian Conservation Corps was an option, but, hell, it could make his body firmer, but it wouldn't prepare him for anything better. The Army would be available when he turned eighteen next year, but one generally came out the same as when one went in. There was no class there. All Danny's family lived in the Neighborhood. All he ever saw was the eighteen-block area. There were no uncles or grandparents who lived out of town, where he might lose or find himself. He had to stay put until he graduated, only one more year. But could he carry it that long?

The Church festivals helped. The Church had its patron saint, Santa Rocco. The parade came first. At the Church the statue of the saint was blessed, and the first dollar was pinned to a scapula across its chest. The band led the way. It all ended at the playground after dark with the bandstand, the band concert, lemon ice, cokes, and then the fireworks. And everyone was there, walking, talking, eating, joking, and listening to the music, which was neither modern nor classical, it was The Avenue Band music, loud, incisive, and unabashed.

He saw Frankie with his coterie. They now wore gold wrist-watches. They gathered around Frankie and occasionally looked toward the bandstand, often laughing. Frankie spotted Danny and broke loose from his circle and came over to where he was standing with Arty, the high school trombonist. Arty wanted to be a professional, and was talented enough, but he became a carpenter like his father, who insisted that the future was in building houses, if you wanted to earn a living.

Frankie took Danny by the arm and, without a word, moved toward an isolated spot in the field.

"Well, Danny Boy, how in the hell you doing?"

"OK, I guess," he answered, somewhat chagrined at abruptly being separated from his friend.

Frankie held each of his hands, and looked directly into his eyes. "Danny, you remember you asked me if I could find a place for you? Well, I think maybe I might be able to help, if you still wanna come along. You know, Danny, once you jump on the wagon, you can't ever get off. I've been watching you, and the others have too, you're OK, Danny, and maybe I owe you one, too. Whatta you say, buddy?"

"I don't know, Frankie. I'm kinda mixed up now. I don't know what I want to do. I still have another year of school, and I don't know whether I want to quit or finish. Maybe what I want more than anything is to get out of here, find some place different. I just don't know."

"Danny, I'm telling you, this is your world, everything is here. All you need is some gold, and I can help you find that. You won't be able to breathe out there; you'd be a fish out of water. It might be better with enough cash, but they ain't ever going to take you in like you are now. Wise up, pal, we're different only because they say we ain't like them. You'll never make it out there. Whatta you gonna do, work in the mills and live in the flats, or come with us and someday live in the country? We need guys like you who can talk good, who read and write. Use your noodle, Danny. Think about it, no hurry." And he walked away.

Arty wanted to know what the hell that was all about. "You're not going to get mixed up with that mug, are you?"

Danny only shook his head. "He only wanted to know how school was going and if I was going to finish."

"Bullshit, Danny boy, Frankie doesn't worry himself with anyone's well being, except the bosses. That's bullshit, and you know it," Arty scoffed.

"Forget it, Arty. It's like I said — he only wanted to know how I was doing," Danny answered too quickly and sharply. Changing his tone, Danny took Arty by the arm and laughingly said, "Let's get some lemon ice that should cool us off."

At the lemon ice stand, he saw her. Actually, they saw each other simultaneously. Amy spoke first, "Hi, Danny, you all right?" He didn't know what to say he hadn't been this close to her for some time. Amy came over to him, and, as if by pre-arrangement, Rita walked toward Arty, pushing him toward the bandstand. Amy moved toward the exit, and Danny followed, as if programmed.

They walked, neither saying a word, until they both sat down on the stoop of the first house after leaving the Club-yard. She said, "What did the big shot want with you, Danny? You'd better be careful."

Danny smiled, laughingly moving his head from side to side. "It seems like everyone in the playground was more interested in watching Frankie and me than the band playing Sousa. Weren't you watching the maestro?"

"Look, Danny, for your own good, stay away from that character; he's bad news. And some day he will end up like Jerry. You remember what happened to him, Danny."

Danny lowered his head, looked sideways up to her bright face, paused, then spoke softly and deliberately, "All he wanted was to know how I was doing; you know, school and everything." His words echoed hollowly, and he knew it as soon as he uttered the last word.

Amy had the good sense not to say anything for several moments.

"I don't know what to do. I'm not going to spend my life like my father. There has to be more. Frankie could show a way."

Amy said, "I guess it could be called a way out, the real exit — to the morgue or a paid vacation at the state penitentiary."

Danny didn't respond, so Amy continued: "I'll tell you something, Danny. I believe I'm goofier than you. I'm going to give you a third opportunity, with little or no risk, and absolutely no commitment. Let's go up to the elm grove in the Park, and this time let's make out. What do you say?"

Danny jumped to his feet, laughing. He pulled her to him and kissed her lightly on the lips. Stepping back and shaking his head, he would only say, "It's no-go, Amy; you're too good for me. I'm not much better than them. There ain't no safe place with me, on The Avenue or in the elm grove."

Chapter VIII

It was fall again, the year was 1939, the beginning of the end of school, high school. There were more job openings — the mills, mines and railroads were hiring. And people were spending. His brother, Sal, bought a new Ford, shiny black.

The rest of the world was in turmoil. The boiling cauldron of war had erupted in Europe. The Austrians and the Czechs were assimilated into the Greater Reich, and Poland had been ignobly destroyed. And in the Far East, the Japanese had concluded they, too, needed some living space, and had moved boldly and openly into China. The fire of that dragon was breathing hot flames and heavy metals into the bodies of their yellow brothers, the Chinese. And the Americans were choosing sides.

Danny now had the potential — hell, the probability — of a third alternative, being drafted into the military. He was now more relaxed, recognizing that perhaps it no longer was his decision. The determination of what course of action to pursue would be in the control of others. Certainly, it would get him out of the city, away from the area, new people, new sights, and new clues as to where he wanted to be.

There was new enthusiasm, excitement, and emotion. The sluggishness of the winters of the Depression seemed to be passing. They were manufacturing armor plating for battleships at the mills. The coal mines were working three shifts.

Danny was spending all of his free time at Cooper's Hall. He would be eighteen in June. He was five feet, eleven inches in height, and weighed one hundred sixty-five pounds. They said he was good looking. A calmness that came with relief of not having to make a decision brought about exuberance manifested for the first time. He was able to spend more time with Miss B, that is, more comfortable time. Time in which he was at ease, almost as if they were equals. It was apparent as they talked about what was happening beyond the oceans. She was a Quaker, and her father had been a conscientious objector during the war to end all wars some twenty years before. Her grandfather had been an abolitionist who refused to bear arms during the Civil War. And, as if reciting a theme at school, she argued the futility of war. Danny countered that without the Civil War, America could still be "enjoying" slavery. Miss B bristled and reddened to anger. "Emancipation would have evolved because slavery eventually would no longer be economically viable," she responded, adding, "Even the South wanted a solution, a way out."

"Look, Miss B, the Kaiser wanted to spread out, he wanted more territory, and now this bum, Hitler, wants the same, and the price of millions of lives is not too high. How do you stop the buggers? Sweet-talk 'em? Preach the Gospel? Brotherly love or even sisterly love would have no appeal to those gangsters."

"There never has been a war from the beginning of time," she almost shouted back, "which did not create more problems than were resolved. None!" Danny sensed he could only stay even if he rattled her, talk to her like the guys did on The Avenue.

"I guess you mean the Civil War, too. It created a hell of a problem, all the spooks now running loose over the Country," Danny pushed.

"Daniel, you are not to use that word 'spook' in my presence again, they are Negroes, they are human beings and must be treated as we expect to be treated." Miss B was now vividly angered. " This is so unlike you, you're mimicking those good-for-nothing loafers on The Avenue." Danny knew he was more than holding his ground because she was using the words of The Avenue, too.

But he realized he was off base and mumbled, "I'm sorry, Miss B." She smiled, changed the subject, and he knew he was forgiven. "Danny, have you read Tolstoy's *War and Peace*? I may have a copy upstairs, and if I find it I'll let you read it. Maybe," she smiled, "just maybe you will understand a little of what I have been trying to say to you."

Danny had to pass by the Frankie's corner on his way to Cooper's Hall, and he heard the stories about the "boys". The numbers racket was proliferating. Since jobs were more plentiful and wages were increasing, people were playing for dimes and quarters instead of pennies and nickels. All you had to do was guess the three digit number that resulted from the last three numbers of the volume of sales on the New York Stock Exchange and you "hit" — five hundred to one, fifty dollars cash on a ten-cent bet. Eureka! The "boys" were doing well. Their cars were larger and classier, and occupied the principal parking spots on The Avenue near the corner. Their clothing was more tailored, and even their fingernails were manicured. They were the upper echelon, the top guys, the movers and shakers, the bosses. "La Famiglia", the Family, was prospering.

One afternoon in the late fall, Danny was hurrying to Cooper's Hall when Frankie spotted him, waved, and charged across the Avenue, confronting him with, "Donato, where in the hell you been keeping yourself? How in the hell are you? What's up, Buddy?"

"I'm fine, Frankie. You look solid. I'm going to graduate, and then I guess the Army will draft me. So, I'm set for awhile anyhow."

"Fuck that Army crap, kid. Those bastards start wars to kill the suckers, and to make more dough. There ain't nothin in it for guys like us. Let the goddamn big shots fight it out. Not me, brother, I'm not going to play in their game. They'll have to find me, and when they do, I'll find a spot where I can't get hurt. I ain't chicken, there just ain't nothin in it for me or any of us on The Avenue."

"Frankie, you sound like a pacifist," Danny answered. "You know, settling all arguments by peaceful means, talking, and agreeing to work things out. Just like the Quakers at Cooper's Hall."

Laughing, Frankie said, "You may be right, Danny Boy, except when I'm involved for myself or the organization. If the other side don't want to see what is right, sometimes I just have to make things work out, maybe I'm one- half of a 'Patsy', or whatever you said I might be. Does that mushy broad at Cooper's fill you with all that shit, Danny? I hear you do a lot of listening to her. You getting any of that high-class stuff, Danny?"

Danny reddened, stiffened, and glared at Frankie.

Frankie sensed the change, retreated. "Hey, Danny, I was only kidding. Everybody sez she's a nice gal, and she's helping a lot of our people. Forget it, OK?"

Danny relaxed, his composure returned to normal, and he could say only, "Frankie, you've found your way out, I'm still searching. I envy you in a way. You understand yourself and you know what you want, and you've started the climb. Maybe I'm slower, Frankie, or I haven't found 'it' yet. I guess sometime you make your own path, or the current pushes you where you should go. Anyhow, I feel better now than I did three months — six months ago."

All Frankie said was "Hey, kid, I ain't sure what the fuck you're saying. Just take care of number one. Remember, I owe you, and I never forget. OK?"

"See you, Frankie," was Danny's only response.

The few blocks to Cooper's started it all again. Maybe Frankie had it pegged right, take care of Number One. The outsiders were not going to be of any assistance. And in this mood, he stopped by her office. She was talking to a girl who appeared to be leaving. Miss B indicated it would only be a moment, so he waited, looking at Life.

"Hello, Danny. How's it going?" she smiled at him. "Come on in. I haven't seen you for a week, where have you been?" she asked as they moved into her office cubicle. She closed the door.

Danny sat in front of her desk. She did not go behind the desk, but sat in the chair next to him. Danny was amazed at how much light could be found in her face, it sparkled, sprightly. It was as if each pore was a reflector. She was so alive.

His only response was a dull, "Not much, Miss B, school, mostly."

She rose put her right hand on his left shoulder, and as he looked up, she asked if he had been to the library for *War and Peace*. Danny admitted that he read several chapters at the library but had not borrowed a copy, and was thoroughly confused trying to keep track of the Russian names.

That broad smile shone again as she said, "Say, Danny, I've got a little over an hour before my next class. Let's go up to my quarters, we'll read together. And, oh, I just bought a new record. It's Russian, too, and you'll love it. Come on, before I get interrupted."

Danny had never been to the third floor. The counselors lived there, the women on one side and the men on the other. It was an attic room with a dormer window looking out onto The Avenue. There was a large bed, a desk covered with papers and books all over it, a clothes closet, and a table with a record player on it, and a rocking chair in which Danny sat.

After closing the door she went to the record player and held up a platter labeled, Tchaikovsky's Symphony No. 6 in B Minor. "I've wanted it for such a long time."

As the strains of the "Pathetique" filled the room, she sat on the edge of her bed and began leafing through a photo album. "Come on over here, Danny. I Just got these from home, pictures of the farm and all the clan during the 4th-of-July holiday."

As she turned each page, a new world was revealed. Row after row of apple trees with more fruit than he imagined ever existed, and everything was so green, so neat, so orderly. She had told him previously that her family owned a two-hundred sixty acre apple farm in upstate New York, and, of course, they also had cows, and gardens, and flowers, and trees of all varieties. As he turned the pages of the album, each scene was a revelation, the announcement of a world unknown to him. Even the people were unlike the people of The Avenue. As he continued to examine the contrast of their lives, Miss B laid on her side, knees tucked upward off the floor and stared at him. He was totally engrossed in the pictures, like a child in a candy store. Everything was in harmony, no discordant tones in all that was revealed. He was totally absorbed. He did not hear her arise and position herself behind him, nor did he see her as she loosened the two upper buttons of her blouse.

He sensed her presence only before she put her hands on his shoulders and nestled her breasts behind his head. And as he looked up, the top of his head rested firmly in her cleavage. Neither moved, except he could feel himself becoming hard. He slowly pivoted, adjusting his feet so that he was facing her. They looked at each other. He noticed the opening of the blouse, and her eyes, wide open, were directed to his mid-section. He blinked first, rose, and they fell backwards on the bed, pulling his legs with him so that his entire body was settled on the most comfortable mattress he had ever laid on. She put her body on top of his so that they could feel what each was offering. It was a good fit. She put her full lips to his, opened her mouth and pressed her tongue into the inner lining of the edges of his lips.

Then forces over which he had no control quickly took over, and he pushed his tongue into her mouth. He brought his hand to her breast, unbuttoned the last button, and lifted the blouse over her head. He unsnapped her brassiere and suckled the tips of her breast, so brown in contrast to the whiteness of her bosom, so hard in contrast to the softness of her breast. And his hardness was pushing further between her legs, and she started to lift her skirt, but Danny pulled it down and off, and onto the floor, never removing his mouth from her chest, exploring every cranny, salivating into each crevice. And they were breathing enthusiastically, but still hearing the music. As he put his hand to her face and held her, she struggled to remove those tight white panties that obscured his awaiting heaven. And they rolled over simultaneously, she now on her back and he touching the softness of the hair as he moved his fingers into the moist inner cavity of her womb and gently squeezed the small organ that had become slippery and swollen. She began a cry of joy, low, deep sounds of exultation. And then she reached for it, unzipping his pants, pushing aside the sticky shorts, and grasping it firmly with both hands, squeezing gently, moving her hands slowly upward and downward. He separated himself, removed all his clothing, looked intently at her from her eyes to the hair between her legs that was parted, revealing a deep, pulsating redness. He slowly moved her legs apart and placed his knees inside her hips and thrust, pushed, and forced himself into her. There was a groan, hurt and joy. And he moved inward and outward as he kissed her lips, her eyes, ears, and those brown tips on her bountiful breasts. And for many moments he neither knew nor cared where he was. A cry, not of her hurt, but a begging, pleading lament that it never cease, smothered his mouth. It was as if he had been born to such movement. Then he paused, held it so long it was painful, and then released it all in a burst that almost stopped her breathing. He waited, then came the hurried pushing for the final relief. And they kissed, stopping all other movement. And he moved his mouth from hers, moved his head on her shoulder, and she saw his first smile of gratification. Happiness was possible. He moved off of her, laid on his side, and looked at her face, unbelieving. She pushed herself up on her elbows, and lightly kissed him on the chin, then he believed.

And he wanted more. She put her hand to his lips and moved off the bed. "I have to clean up for my class, dear friend, lover boy," she spoke softly as she donned her robe.

As he finished dressing, he opened his mouth to speak. She looked at him, held up a hand, and turned him around to the door as she said, "It was good, Danny, everything's fine. We'll talk later."

And so it was. The first time. And she was right, it had been good.

Chapter IX

Danny went to the gymnasium. A shower and a swim were what he needed to bring him down off his high. He dove into the cold pool, swimming as if to escape from something that could hurt. Carl Gentile was sitting at the edge of the pool near the diving board. Danny stopped, grasped the ladder and spoke to him, surprising Carl. It had always been "Hi," moving away before any sustained conversation would ensue, but he stayed. Danny wanted to talk. He had scored in one league, why not another?

"Chip, I understand you spend a lot of time at the library. What kind of books are you reading?"

Now this was a surprise. Chip did not actually know if Danny would read. Chip had heard about the church incident with Frankie and that colored boy. He had seen Danny standing by at the "Pool Party" when the boys were playing baseball with the colored boys. Somebody had hinted that Danny was actually thinking of enrolling as a trainee with the Organization. It's funny — the newspaper called them the underworld, hell, they were on top of the world. You could see them anytime on the corner of The Avenue, suits, coats, neckties, hats, and shoes. They had the best cars and the classiest girls. They were more open and visible than the people who worked in the mills and on the railroad. You never saw them, they went to work when it was dark and came home in the dark.

Chip answered, "Oh, I read some history, political science and government, and some fiction. I guess I just like to read. There is so much that has happened in this world that I want to know about."

"What good is it going to do you, Chippy? It ain't going to help you in the mill, all you need there is muscles. That's where you're going after high school, right?"

"No! No, I am not! I'm going to college, that's for sure."

Danny shook his head, grinning, and when he started talking, his words were impregnated with laughter. "You going to college? Who the hell do you think you are the son of Rockefeller? Remember, your old man works in the stinking mill and your name is 'Gentile', all Italian, and from the wrong side of Italy. Forget it. Better look somewhere else. Anyhow, Chippy did you ever read *War and Peace*? It's what the world is all about — picking the winning side. And thinking about college isn't in the ballgame for us. We're going to be in this war before too long. They'll use us for cannon fodder and then let us go back to the fire of the mills — if we live."

Prolonging the conversation for no apparent reason, except perhaps that it was the first time one of the younger boys had taken the time to talk, Carl asked Danny what he was going to do when he graduated from high school.

"I don't know, kiddo, the Army probably has got first dibs on me. I'm not going into the mills, but I'm going to do something before they call me. I ain't volunteering for anything. Only suckers stick their necks out without getting something for it."

"Only think of Number One, heroes die young and poor, and there ain't no Italian heroes in this Country, only strong backs".

"You haven't been reading the papers lately. How about Joe DiMaggio, the great Yankee center fielder who hit safely in thirty-five consecutive games challenging George Sisler's record of 41 games. Hell, his father came from the Old Country, like ours, and he's making big money, and he's respected, and he's hitting baseballs instead of human heads. The whole Country is talking about one of us as a good guy."

"One in a million, Chippy. Where're the mind heroes?" Danny replied sarcastically.

"Yeah, how about that Mayor of New York City, LaGuardia."

"It's New York, Chip. More Italians there than in Rome, and besides that, he's half Jewish. His head is a Jew, only his ugly puss is Italian." Danny pulled up his trunks and headed to the locker room.

Chapter X

It had to have been a Sunday in the middle of that summer, when everything seemed to tighten. It was harder to take time to play, the papers said that the world was on fire. Miss B had gone home for two weeks, so he couldn't even look at her. The temperature and humidity were about ninety-five, the rocks in the Playground were hot enough to cook on. And in Cleveland, Ohio, some character no one knew before, named Ken Keltner, playing third base for the Indians, stopped DiMaggio's streak at fifty-six. It had to have been a damp field, lucky positioning, and two unerring throws that stopped what could have gone on forever. But the wind-up was the wind-down — the streak was over. So you start another.

And it could have been the Sunday after the streak ended. Sunday Mass had been warmed-over ritual on a hot, steamy day. What he could understand of the sermon was an impression that maybe the Italian government was justified in bringing the three C's — Civilization, Christianity, and Catholicism (Roman) — into the lands of barbarism and savagery. And the closing homily, "Faith provided the only answer; the Church pronounced the Faith". Maybe, because the priest's English was poor, he was talking about "fate". It could not be the doctrine of predestination that belonged to the Christians who had taken the wrong road. But he was talking about staying in line, playing a part, not forging anything, and everything would work out if not here, somewhere else. And Danny wondered about that connection. The pacifiers. The dispensers of sugar water and the wafered nipple. Don't worry too much about the comforts of life on earth. If you missed it now, and you were a part of the Church, it would not be lost forever. The conclusion had to be that the Catholic Church was going to be in supreme glory in the hereafter. Its constituents were not tasting any of the good things here. The Church's dominance was in the poorest countries of the world. The Catholics outnumbered their co-citizens in southeastern Europe, especially Italy, Poland, Spain and its former colonies in the Philippines and Latin America, where over-population, disease, malnutrition and illiteracy were tolerated, at least, not challenged, by the Church.

And it was no better on the corner after church. There were always two groups. Frankie and his bunch were matching dimes and quarters, and talking about broads and bread, and generally how they melded together. The younger guys, mostly still in school, talked about DiMaggio's streak, how it could have gone on forever, if. Nothing new in either camp; Danny just didn't seem to fit. The mood had returned. And he was lonely and alone again, so he withdrew down the alley, a short cut to home and Sunday dinner, and sameness. There would be pasta, rigatoni, meatballs, braciola, salad, bread and fruit. Papa had wine, too. And, as usual, no substantive talks. Surprisingly, Sis asked, "How was Church?" Assuming the query was addressed to him, Danny stopped eating, looked around as if to confirm that everyone was seated (because Mama was always jumping up to get something), he almost shouted, "the same old business." No one reacted, so he went on, "I don't think I'll go back there again. All I can get out of what they are saying is that if we do what they tell us, it'll solve our hurts, heal our cuts and bruises, and prepare us for everlasting life. Don't mind the pain. The good times are not in this life, but after death. As far as I'm concerned, they have it all wrong. It's here and now that counts. There surely is a God, the world just didn't happen. But not their god."

Like walking into church, there was silence. Not certain if he had been understood, he added, "They don't seem to know what's happening in the world, on the street, across this country, overseas, how people are living and dying. They don't seem to care about hunger, dirt, cold, sweating people."

Brother Sal could hardly empty his mouth of a spoonful of rigatoni before he started saying, "Now you wait one minute, smart guy. You ain't got it so bad — a roof over your head, good food, and clean clothes. We're a lot better off than a lot of others. I guess maybe God ain't so bad to those who believe."

"Sal, when's the last time you went to Mass? It had to have been Easter."

Sis, who hardly ever said anything, added, "You have to believe in the Church. It's the only way."

Her remarks were surprising because they came out spontaneously. Catholic teaching had obviously taken with her.

Mama was perplexed, disturbed, too, but not able to explain the help she had received from her beliefs. She only shook her head.

As it always was, Papa had to have the last say, which was preceded by, "now wait a minute", as he wiped the sauce from his mouth, pushed slightly away from the table, and looked to see if all eyes were focused on him.

"Don't forget, everybody's got a right to think for himself. Everybody's got to believe there is a God. So as long as you believe in God, you're on the right track, going in the right direction.

Like going from Pittsburgh to Washington — it don't make no difference if you go in a Pennsylvania Railroad coach or a Baltimore & Ohio train, as long as you get there. I guess there's different religion that can get you there, if you believe."

No one interrupted, so Papa continued, "Donato's OK, he's thinking, he just wants to find the best way, something he can understand. I don't blame him as long as he always remembers that there is God and there is the family, LaFamiglia. They is the only things that counts."

Danny started to interrupt, but Papa evidently had not finished, for he pushed out his hand like the traffic cop, silencing everyone. He took a sip of the wine, wiped his lips, and put the napkin down.

"I don't think the Church wanna us to be poor. Remember, the Church is the only one who'll take in the working man, you ever think of that? And if the Catholics don't take the little guy, we don't have a place to go. Maybe those Protestants leave the church because they don't wanna be too close to us. Maybe they don't like our rough hands, our baggy clothes, or our smells — but the Church said, 'We ain't gonna keep you from God just because you're poor or you get dirty when you work, or you don't speaka the good English.'"

With finality, Papa said, "It's all right to think, Donato, and it's OK to change, but don't rip out the insides of what you is made of and from. You can't keep warm if you tear out the lining of your jacket. If you get a hole in your shoe or lose the sole of a shoe, your feet are going to get wet and cold. OK? Capice?"

Danny was satisfied. He had a green light to make one change.

Chapter XI

Late that fall Danny saw Frankie on the corner of The Avenue surrounded as usual by three or four of his "boys". It was generally understood that he reported directly to Vento, The Avenue boss who reported to Pope, the tri-state Capo. And Frankie was the tough guy. They said he was the "big hitter", the clean-up man. When it had to be done finally, it was Frankie's baby. And thus they said he was respected. He was understood. He was believed. Frankie did something unusual — he didn't call out, he didn't motion that Danny should join him. He didn't send one of the boys to invite Danny over, he crossed The Avenue to meet Danny, and to walk along side of him as he headed west in the direction of Cooper's Hall and the library.

"Wait up, ole buddy," Frankie called as he dodged between two automobiles slowly moving down The Avenue. "Where you headed, Danny?" he asked as he fell in step with him.

"Going to stop at the Hall and then go on to the library," Danny responded.

Frankie seemed happy, and answered with that childish grin he had when Danny first met him. "They'll both make you feel good. The Hall is for real; the books are make-believe. How the hell is school going, Danny?"

"OK, Frankie. Another semester after this and it's finished here. Then I don't know. It depends on when I get caught up in the draft. I'll have to wait and see."

"Like I told you, Danny Boy, I ain't gonna wait and have those people ground me into a mud rat. If I'm going to die, it'll be clean. But I ain't gonna die in this thing. I'm gonna decide how to beat it."

"Don't kid me, Frankie; you'll never volunteer."

"Yes sirree, I'm going to the Coast Guard. It's all fixed up. I'm gonna be stationed on the Rivers protecting this gun-making town from spies, saboteurs, traitors, and all kinds of bad guys. I'm a volunteer." Frankie jubilantly announced.

"You have to be kidding, Frankie. What in the hell do you know about boats, and how can you know where you're going to be stationed?"

"Danny, I told you to stick with me. It's fixed, all the way to Washington, I tell you. I've been taking private lessons on the River. I can sure as hell operate one of those boats the Coast Guard uses on the Rivers. I've been practicing for six months now. I don't want to be no officer, I could if I wanted to, but I'll get some kind of enlisted rank and I'm set. I could almost drive to work every day, and, except when I got duty, they tell me I'll have my nights and weekends free. Whatta ya think, ole buddy?"

"It sounds great to me, Frankie, but how can you be sure?" was Danny's only response.

"It's all set. The local commander is a friend of Vento's, you know Vento. The Boss done the Commander some favors. And they built up the story to Washington that I know the Rivers like the palms of my hands. All set. Want me to see if I can find a spot for you, too, when you get finished at school? You got the brains;

I got the connections. We'll make one hell of a team. And when they all stop playing cowboys and Indians over there, we'll be in place to grow and grow. Stay close, buddy. Whatta ya say, Danny; you want me to start working out sumptin for you?"

"I don't know, Frankie. It sounds good for you, but I'm not so sure it's what I want or need. I think I want to get the hell out of here. Some place new, different faces, people, and way of living," Danny tried to explain.

"You're goofy, kid. What in the fuck do you want that we can't get you here? Money, clothes, girls, booze, and fun. And The Family. What in the hell else is there in this fucked-up world? Stay with your kind, Danny. There's sharks out there, they'll chew you up into little bits and spit you out between their teeth. America is for the Americans. Here, no matter what happens, you always got somebody who's gonna be with you all the way."

"Everything you say is down the middle, Frankie, but I guess I'll wait to see for myself. There has to be something out there, away from The Avenue, where I can fit. Maybe I'll have to adjust, and accept whatever I find out there. This I know — I cannot make it here, whether it's your way or my father's way. What happens when Papa can't work like a jackass anymore, or someone decides your group can't operate freely or openly as another economic system?"

"Frankie, I gotta go. I'll be in touch. And thanks; I appreciate your thinking about me. See you," and he turned and walked up The Avenue.

Danny tried to talk to Miss B, but she was busy. A group of girls were with her, planning a dance. She was nice enough, but unavailable. Sitting in the next office was Peter Appleton, the boys' leader, who appeared to be watching Danny's reaction to not being able to be with Miss B. When Peter attracted his attention, he motioned Danny to come in to his office.

"Hello, Danny, anything we can do for you," he asked.

"No, Peter, I just wanted to ask Miss B a question," Danny responded.

"Can I help?" Peter asked.

"Do you think we're going to get into the war?" Danny asked.

"I hope not, Danny, but based on our history, the answer is yes. The country will not permit Germany to conquer England, it would be the interring of Western Civilization for generations."

"How long before we get into it?" Danny asked impatiently.

"I don't know, but probably within the year," Peter answered.

"Will you go, Peter, if you're called?" Danny queried.

Peter's answer was clear and unequivocal. "No, I couldn't kill. I'd be a C.O., and perform whatever alternative service is available. No guns. No shooting. No killing."

"Suppose they put you in jail?" he asked.

"I guess I would go to jail. I wouldn't like it. I don't think they would do that," said Peter. And then asked, "What are you going to do, Danny?"

"It's a way out, Peter, and it may be the best thing for me. There's a world out there that I gotta see, no how."

"There are other ways to see the world, Danny," Peter responded. "What are the other fellows thinking about doing?"

"Hell, most of them are going to wait it out. Some will volunteer; some will even try to hide. Even Frankie's going to volunteer. What a patriot."

"Frankie, a liberator? What's his angle?"

Danny explained how Frankie intended to "volunteer," and prevent the incursion or invasion of the city through the Rivers.

There was subdued laughter. "I would suggest you don't 'volunteer' with him, Danny. You'll never see the world. You'll be locked into his world and you won't see much that will open your eyes."

Miss B had quietly posted herself inside the door, leaned against the wood frame, and ended the conversation by demanding to know what had generated such serious discussion.

"Danny is wondering about the war and what, if any, part he'll play in it," reported Peter. "He's in the right age group, and as soon as he finishes school, he'll be available. I guess it's a legitimate discussion."

"Danny, I have the Sunday New York Times upstairs, and there's some great reading on the subject. Come on up and I'll let you have it. I've got a break now."

Miss B closed the door after entering her room. Inviting Danny to sit down, she went to her desk and searched the newspaper for the articles that she wanted him to read. She dropped the pages into his lap, excused herself to "freshen up", and went into the bathroom.

Even a cursory examination of the Times' lead story showed concern over what was happening. "The maelstrom would inevitably suck the country into its vortex." Danny was so engrossed that he almost forgot where he was until a breath of air with an appealing fragrance caused him to look up. She was kneeling on the floor in front of him, and began removing the pages of the newspaper and tossing them on the floor, and then moving her hands from his knees along the outside thighs to his hips. As he looked down, her blouse was unbuttoned on top, and it was apparent she no longer wore a brassier. He could see her breasts firming and there was color creeping up into her cheeks.

As she rubbed her hands on top of his thighs, she smiled, and the aroma of her perfume engulfed him as she leaned forward, her breasts touching his knees. She looked up and softly whispered, "Relax, Danny Boy, you're too serious and tight for such a young man." As he leaned forward to nestle his face into the top of her head, the fragrance of her cleared the despair from his eyes, washing away any clouds of self-doubt. And he reacted, pushing his lips to the top of her eyes, nibbling at her ear lobes, and pushing his hands onto her breasts. And so it went, a blissful hour. And all the world had faded into soft colors, shades of pastels, with no grays. There was no Avenue, no Clubyard, and no "Eyetalians." There was a world beyond, and during those moments, it was reachable.

She didn't seem to be in a hurry to return to work. She laid on the bed covered by the sheet, and pushed her hands through her hair, shaking her head like a dog after a romp through a cloud burst.

"Danny, how would you like to visit at the folks' farm during the Labor Day week? I'm sure the family would be glad to have you, and maybe we'll go up to Vermont for a few days."

"I don't know. I guess my father would be able to get me a pass on the Pennsy. But I don't know. I've never been out of the city, never been too far off The Avenue.

"Danny, talk to your folks tonight. Let me know. It would be good for you, and we'll have some fun. I'm leaving on Sunday, and you can come up sometime at the end of the next week or the first of the following week. Now get dressed and move on, friend. I've got to meet with the Senior Girls' Club and plan the October dance."

"What will your Mom and Dad say," Danny asked, trying to postpone his departure.

"Look, I told them about a young man with a future — you, that you've never been out of the city. They're solid. They like people. They'll enjoy having you. So convince yourself, first, then your family. Bye Bye, Danny, I have to run."

Danny went down to the gym, swam for about half an hour, and took a shower, wondering how he was going to ask for a vacation. No one at home had ever been on vacation. And he would need a little money. And what in the hell would he wear? He wondered if the family had any luggage. Hell, it was only a pipe dream, forget it. You're stuck on The Avenue. No one would understand what it would mean.

It was remarkable. When he was with Miss B he could forget his surname, the house, the neighborhood, and the corner where the guys hung out. But he didn't understand her. Was she just getting her kicks out of a young stud? She couldn't be interested in him, otherwise. She was older by maybe eight or ten years, she wasn't Italian, she was a college grad and her folks obviously had money. They really had nothing in common. A girl of that class could never be serious about a guy like him, how could she ever talk to Mama? She could never take Papa — slurping his soup, or picking up a pork chop with his fingers and eating the meat away from the bone. And the toilet was in the basement. He could never take a girl like that home. He had to forget it. Stick with his kind, and never get hurt.

As he finished tying his shoes, Ronnie came in from the gym, sweating and red, breathing heavily.

"Where in hell you been? We were waiting for you to play some basketball. You know, we got a league game on Saturday," Ronnie stuttered.

Ronnie was a good friend. He was a natural athlete. He could play basketball, football, and baseball well. He was more a spectator than a participant, in the classroom. He attended and passed. His career seemed assured. His father was a tailor who had a shop outside the Avenue. Ronnie's father went to work in a suit, the only father in the neighborhood who did. Papa had one suit for funerals and weddings. Danny never was sure why they became close. Maybe Danny was impressed with his athletic prowess, and Ronnie was attracted to Danny's regard for school and books. They never talked about it, the basis of their friendship. They just were buddies.

Danny partially lied. "I forgot, Ron." He had gone to the Hall to play ball, but when he became involved with Miss B, he forgot all about basketball, Ron, The Avenue, and the family.

"Man, I don't know where your head is any more, up in some cloud, or I suspect in some gal's pants," Ronnie challenged.

"Nah, Ron. Maybe it's the war, or what happens when we finish school. Everything's all screwed up. I don't know where in the hell I'm headed. They stopped DiMaggio at 56; he could have gone on forever, except for that lucky Keltner, maybe the Yanks won't even be in the Series."

"What in the God-damned hell does the war, DiMaggio or the Series got to do with you reneging on a game, man? You're goofy. Anyhow, I had a good workout and we ought to win the tournament, unless you fuck up again. Hurry up, we'll walk home together."

As they were leaving, Danny saw Amy in the hallway with a group of her girlfriends. She smiled. She could smile so affably and invitingly that he wanted to stop and touch her.

"Danny, where have you been all summer? I never see you anymore. You don't ever come to the dances. Can't be school work, we're on vacation." Amy broke away and seemed to want to talk more than casually passing the time of day.

Ron waited at the door as Danny stopped, stammering something about not knowing what happened to all the time and maybe they could get together at the next dance. It was a put-off, they both understood, but neither knew why. Maybe he was "goofy," as Ron stated, whatever that entailed.

Ron giggled, wiped the smile off his face, and sternly said to Danny, "Now that should be the one for you. She's a looker, good family, plenty smart, and she's goofy enough to be crazy about you. Why don't you give her a tumble, Danny boy?"

"You're right, Ron, she's too good for me. But where in the

hell I'll be next year is the question. I gotta be free to move, with nothing to tie me down."

"Well, I'll be damned. I guess I know now what our friendship means. Once you take off, it's all over for us, too, eh, Danny?"

"Ah, come on, Ron, I'm talking about girls. We're buddies and we are going to be that way, always, no matter where we end up. You won't stop me or try to stop me from what I want to do. A girl might, or could. See the difference, Ron?"

"Nah, I think those counselors at Cooper's got you all screwed up. That Peter – he ain't for fighting, and your friend, Miss B; now she might screw someone like us, but she'd never take one of us home and say, 'Mother, Daddy, I want you to meet the man I'm going to marry, Donato Castel Forte'. Forget it. Hell, they're social workers; they're paid to make you feel good. They should be working with those on the outside, telling them we ain't so bad, we wash, don't steal too much, and we ain't dumb. We can work in banks and business offices, and can marry their daughters, too."

"You're too prejudiced, Ronnie. What if I told you she asked me to visit her family on their farm in upstate New York? Would that change your warped mind?"

"Not really, pal. She probably wants to show a native to the home folks, to prove that they're housebroken, and they won't steal the silverware. You know. Columbus brought some Indians back to Spain, Danny. Are you going?"

"I don't know. Would you go, Ronnie?"

"Hell no! I'd feel like one of those freaks in the circus. How do you think those Indians felt when introduced to that Queen in Spain? I don't want people looking me over, checking behind my ears to see if there are any bugs, like some monkey in the sideshow. Danny, when you go to the library, see if they got a book on manners, especially table manners. Maybe it'll tell you when you can or can't blow your nose, and whether you do it on your right cuff or the left," laughed Ronnie as he pushed him away and proceeded down the street to his home.

Papa was late getting home; there had been a derailment on the line home. The poor guy was tired. He was overly hungry and was rattling Mama, who had no way of knowing he was going to be late. The sauce with the pork and sausage may have been on the stove too long. Armando had been sick, stomach ache, and was in Mama's bed upstairs. Now she was hastening to prepare the salad and cook the spaghetti. And Papa was already at the table, he was ready, he had rolled up his long underwear sleeves to his elbows. Sis had finished tossing the salad and was serving it in separate dishes. Papa didn't wait for the pasta or anyone; he broke off a chunk of bread and started on the salad. Sal and I looked at each other, waited until we had been served some salad, and then started to chew and swallow. Not a word was spoken at the table. Mama was yelling that the pasta would be ready in a "momento". Papa only looked up to the stove once and then proceeded to push the crust of bread through the salad dish, sopping up the oil and vinegar juices, drank from his wine glass, and then he folded his arms across his chest and waited.

Papa was served the first bowl of pasta with a tomato sauce-saturated pork chop and sausage. He picked up the chop first, disposed of it, and then consumed the sausage, all without utensils. Then he began rolling the spaghetti with the fork in his spoon. He had almost finished his first serving before we could taste our portions. He must have been famished. The fried pepper sandwich for lunch had not been enough. Mama, in a hurry to serve Sal and me, spilled sauce on the stove; the hissing and smoke clouded most of the room. Papa never paused. Sis was helping to clean the stove and had not eaten. Of course, this would be another night when Mama would not sit down and eat with us. She was already clearing away the salad dishes and pouring more wine into Papa's glass. She was tired and hot and sweaty, but she smiled through it all, as if it were routine, and it was. Mama sat down when we were almost all finished, wiping her hands on the apron enveloping her ample waist, and proceeded to devour her pasta.

Danny had only picked at his salad, and had a few forks of pasta. He was trying to visualize the scene at Miss B's home at suppertime. He guessed that it had to be different, but he didn't know how.

Papa had evidently finished, for he spoke up, reversing the drift of Danny's thoughts from the farm to the reality of the table. "Whatsa matter, Donato, you no eat too much? You sick?"

"No, Papa, maybe I got too tired today, playing ball and swimming," he responded quickly.

But Sal could not remain silent now. He had to interfere with a caustic reference that perhaps the love bug had bitten little Danny.

Mama rose, put her hand on Danny's head, rolled his hair into a mass, and laughingly noted that Donato was too young for love.

Papa stood up, ceremoniously threw his napkin on the table, signaling the conclusion of the meal, and without a word marched out into the backyard to examine the twenty-foot by twenty-foot garden.

This was one night that Danny followed him. Papa had started to pull the weeds from around the six tomato plants, and he looked up as Danny spoke. "Papa, can you get me a pass to New York? One of the counselors at Cooper's Hall wants me to visit her family farm over the Labor Day week."

"You know you can only go during the week and only on certain coach trains. The passes ain't for Pullman cars, you know. You gonna go by yourself?"

"Papa, it would be good for me to see another place and other people. Have you ever been to New York?"

"Only when I came from the Old Country, and I don't remember too much. I don't stay there too long. Some paisans put me on a train to Pittsburgh. I remember there were lots of people, all kinds and all over all the streets. Sure, I'll put in for a pass tomorrow. Donato, will you need much money? The mortgage is due in the next paycheck."

"No money, Papa, I've got a few dollars, and there won't be any place to spend money there. There won't be any stores on the farm. No, money won't be a problem. But I have to borrow a suitcase somewhere, to put my things in. Maybe one of my friends has one. We won't have to buy one."

"You go, Donato. I wanna you to go. It be good to see something new. We'll make everything work OK."

"Thanks, Papa, I do wanna go."

Chapter XII

It had to have been the next day that Danny was approached by Frankie as he turned the corner as he started down The Avenue. Frankie was going down state for the weekend to a resort operated by his bosses.

"Come with me Danny, we'll have lots of fun."

"Look, Frankie, I appreciate your asking me, but you know I don't have any good clothes or money."

"Danny, all you need is some slacks, sport shirts, a coat and swim suit. We're about the same size and you can borrow a sport coat and slacks from me. I've got a closet full. I drive. And there we don't need no money. All recreation, all paid for, and the girls are great. Everyone there will want to make us happy. It's a coupla hours drive, so we'll leave about four o'clock, get there in time to clean up, eat some supper, and spend the night playing, doing whatever we want — gambling, dancing, screwing — anything — everything."

"Frankie, you know I'm only seventeen, going on eighteen. What about that?"

"No problem, old buddy. This is all private. Private ballroom, dining room, clubhouse, and bedrooms," responded Frankie.

"Well, what about your friends, Frankie? What are they going to say, bringing me, still in school and not tied in?"

"Danny, no problem. Everything has been approved. I only want you to relax and have fun for one time in your life. See how the other half lives."

Danny couldn't resist. He thought of Papa and Miss B, too. But, dammit, he owed it to himself. He had to know what it was like, if he was going to have to make a decision. Frankie had always been a friend, and maybe his buddies were good guys, too.

Danny met Frankie on the corner on The Avenue. Frankie had the car parked in front, shiny clean. A new Ford. Danny carried a pillowcase with his socks, underwear, tooth brush, slacks, and shirts.

"Dump them in the back, Danny, next to that brown suitcase, that's yours. First, try on the sports coat and see if it fits. Great, You look good. Perfect fit."

It was the first time he had driven out from The Avenue. It was the first time he had ridden in an automobile into the downtown area, the first time he had been outside the city. It was the first time he had driven so far. Frankie lit a large cigar, at ease behind the wheel, and Danny looked at sights never before seen the bridge over the river and the high buildings in the background.

Then Frankie talked. He had made his decision. He had committed himself to the organization, for now and forever. As Frankie had described the ceremony, it had all the sacredness of initiation into a religious order. It was all the sacraments combined baptism, confirmation, and marriage. There could be no divorcement; dissolution and death were simultaneous. There was security throughout life. "I never be alone. People gonna respect me and listen to me." There could be no discussion once a decision had been made. The discipline was more rigorous than the military or the church; the belief was as dogmatic and irrefutable as if proclaimed by the Pope. Rank had its privileges and responsibilities. A member of the organization could not marry without the prior approval of the Capo. The bride could not be an outsider, and preferably should be related to a member of the Family.

Darkness had come easily as the road led them through the mountains and then down into a lush valley. A mountain stream paralleled the asphalt ribbon of road lined with elm. Frankie tossed his cigar out the window and saluted as if to the world.

"There she is, Danny, a beauty eh?"

Then it came into view. A complex of buildings nestled against the side of the mountain. Lights outlined the buildings, approachable through an illuminated driveway passing under a stone portico.

The doors were opened as soon as the car came to rest. Three men were at their immediate service welcoming Frankie, as if he were royalty. And he evidently was royalty, there.

The suite contained as much space as Danny's house. Two huge bedrooms separated by a living room, with the largest radio set Danny had ever seen. It had a recessed bar stocked with more liquor bottles than any Avenue beer joint. Each bedroom had its separate bathroom, with tub and shower, and so many different sizes of white towels. Danny had to touch, to feel their thickness and softness on his face. He had to examine each bottle of shampoo, hair tonic, each colorful bar of soap, each facial lotion -all so orderly, everything so new, so clean, so orderly.

Frankie interrupted, "Take a shower, Danny. We'll clean up and go to the dining room. You wanna drink now?"

"No thanks, Frankie. I'm going to soak in that tub until all the dirt of the city bleeds out of my pores. I'll bet that tub will have the blackest ring ever."

"OK. I get you a shot of Strega, it'll clean the insides while the soap and water washes the outside. It'll relax you. I'll call you in half-an-hour, if you fall asleep."

Danny filled the tub, Frankie brought the Strega, and the warmth dissolved any lingering doubts as to whether he should be there. He had never envisaged such a set-up. And so he sat there, sipping on the Strega, occasionally rubbing the soft soap over his legs and stomach, adding more hot water, and watching the redness lighten his skin coloring. The body could remain there forever, but would the mind pay the price. He thought he was being given another opportunity, perhaps the last chance; the big sell had begun on the trip down. But, "why me?" would flash on and off in his head like a neon sign. Frankie wanted a second in his corner, someone reliable, someone who would not reach above, someone honest, someone who could talk "American", who could pass as an "American", someone who could take more education. He needed someone with class enough to talk to the judges and senators and councilmen whom Frankie needed and used. And on and on he thought, until Frankie yelled, "Get your can out of there. I'm hungry."

Danny pulled the plug and the dirty water flowed into the drain, but the thoughts about such a life stayed within him, unresolved.

He was too nervous to enjoy dinner; too many people came over to say hello to Frankie. Danny was always introduced as a friend, except to those customers in furs and evening clothes, when he introduced Danny as a "college" friend.

Danny was confused by all the dishes, glasses and silverware. Frankie wasn't much help. Danny devoted too much time to closely watching people at the other tables. And when the girls joined them, Danny would not chance another bite, not even dessert.

The girls were older, of course, twenty-two or so, well built, and American. They were not Italians. You called some people Polacks, Jews, or Colored, but all the rest were Americans.

Danny pretended to drink, and he danced with Susan, but it was all strained. He enjoyed the softness of her body, but it was mentally enervating and even painful trying to talk with her. He could talk with Amy and converse with ease with Miss B, but with Susan, he could not draw out those words whirling through his consciousness. She was a student at the State College ten miles away. Her father was an attorney and a senator in the state legislature. She said she loved to gamble. She and her girlfriend, Judith, had met Frankie at the crap tables and he had befriended them, showing them how to play and how to win, or not lose too much. Frankie supplemented their losses when the odds were working more positively for the house.

Frankie gave Susan and Danny chips and they gambled. Danny drank some whiskey and Susan jabbed him from time to time when she won, and the spirit changed in him, the strain eased, and he found he could smile. She responded, wrapping her arms around his shoulder, kissing his face, and tickling his ribs whenever there was a win or an almost win.

Soon after Frankie and Judith were no longer in the Casino; and Susan suggested that they might go to his room where she could freshen up before they started home.

Susan asked him where he was going to school. The evening had made him bold enough to answer, "The City University, Business School." He now talked now as if he had applied, had been accepted, and it was only a matter of reporting that Fall. They held hands as they walked back to the suite. When they arrived at the suite, he noticed that although the door to the sitting room was open, the door to Frankie's bedroom was closed.

She asked Danny to fix her a brandy as she headed toward the bathroom. He found the brandy decanter, but was puzzled as to the proper glass to serve it in, when his memory kicked in and he recalled a movie in which the star grasped the base of a rounded glass with a stem, and watched the liquor spinning nervously without spilling over. He was feeling more confident as he handed her the brandy glass and watched her twirl the liquid before bringing the glass to her lips. She smiled her thanks. He poured some into his glass, cradled the neck of the bottle in his left hand and nudged her into his bedroom and then locked the door.

It was all working, the best refined alcohol, the surroundings of affluence, the fragrance pouring from millions of pores built into a statuesque body, her cultivated mind and habits, and the apparent willingness to accept him almost as an equal, slowly eroded the facade of distrust, shyness, and timidity which he had arrived with. He now believed he was twenty-one, and he could perform. So for now he became a believer, and then a convincer when she responded.

And Susan gave no indication of slowing, pausing or stopping the frenzy that engulfed them. She bit and scratched and finally mounted him when he found he could push down no further. He could not come anymore; even her orgasms had ceased. He could not remember whether he had pushed her off or she had rolled off.

He must have slept. It was totally dark and he was alone, a sheet between his legs and a cold breeze blowing curtains over the headboard. His mouth was dry, musty, unclean, and his body was damp and dirty. His penis ached, it was semi-hard, and he needed to relieve his bladder. His head hurt, and his eyes refused to focus. In a moment he recognized the room, knew where he was, and wondered what had become of Susan. He rolled off the bed and staggered to the bathroom, turned on the light, looked back and saw Susan sitting up in the other bed reading, her head was wrapped in a towel. He weakly raised his hand acknowledging that he recognized her, and shut the door. It was almost an hour before he emerged, bathed, shaved, hair combed, and a clean towel wrapped around his middle. He was smiling as he re-entered the bedroom, still of the opinion that he had done well, that he had enjoyed himself, that it had not been a mistake to have made the trip. Cementing the belief, he walked over to Susan and gave her a wet kiss. She dropped the sheet covering her breast and moved his hand to replace the cover. Danny backed away. "Maybe we ought to get some breakfast, at least some juice and coffee."

She tossed aside the sheet covering the lower portion of her body, unraveled the towel holding her hair on top of her head, and laughingly said, "And there is breakfast and breakfast. I think I'd rather have what we can cook up here." And she beckoned. He dropped his towel and moved onto the bed.

It was daylight now and there was a banging on the door accompanied by raucous shouting, "Anyone alive in there? I'm going to call a doctor if I don't hear somebody god-damned soon." It had to be Frankie, and he stopped when Danny yelled they would meet him in the dining room in forty-five minutes.

They almost didn't make it when Susan decided to jump into the shower with him.

At breakfast, Danny was somber and distant, after the usual jovial greetings. Susan noticed and kicked him twice. But the mood settling in was like the heavy mist of late summer falling on motionless bogs, daylight fading into nightfall. Susan grabbed Danny's hand and exclaimed, "I promised to show him around the grounds." He followed her, commenting, "See you later, OK?"

"All right, little boy. Did someone hurt your feelings, or did you stub your toe getting out of bed, or is the way of sin weighing in on your Catholic consciousness? Let up, Danny. You can go to confession, the penance won't be too bad. Recitation of a few prayers, I'm told."

He continued to walk without talking, moving only his legs and arms, his lips closed, drawn tightly.

"Gotta problem, kid?" Susan said and reached for his swinging hand, grasped it and held on.

"I was happy, at least not unhappy, until this morning, and then I started to think, and problems began falling out like I'd hit a quarter jackpot on the slot machine."

"You have no problems, Danny. You're young, and you won't age too soon. You're good looking, you're an OK dancer, you're great in bed, and you'll get better. Oh yes, you have a start on becoming educated. So what is your hang up?"

"I don't like where I am, what I'm doing," pointing back to the complex. "I don't want to take that route. Frankie's a good friend, but I want something else."

"Do you think this is all I want or will be doing for the rest of my life? Hell, no. But I must admit, I'm enjoying this. It's fun. The serious time will come later. And there will be a husband and family. And then I will do all the things the Good Book tells us that we mortals must do to attain salvation. I'm enjoying this more than parking my ass in front of the life guard at the country club pool, hoping to see him get a hard on." Susan squeezed his hand and flashed all her white teeth.

"Would you take me to your country club, to swim, to dance?" Danny shot back as he stared into Susan's green eyes. "And if you did, how would you introduce me? A nice kid I found in the street, and his name is Danny 'something' which ends in an 'e' or 'i' or 'o'."

Susan was honest. "Maybe we could change the name — Americanize it. How about Daniel Smith or Danny Castle?"

They both laughed.

They didn't talk again on the return trip to the lodge until she stopped and, leaning back against a tree, said, "Maybe things will change. Maybe in ten years it won't make any difference. Nobody will care who your parents were or are. A lot of the so-called acceptable families had some free booters in their background. Money and education and the passage of time changed it all".

"I'm not going to live that long. You're one great gal, Susan. Thanks."

Danny didn't want to talk on the drive home. Frankie was expansive, shirt open almost to the navel, and a Havana cigar between his lips, he wanted to talk. Danny sensed that Frankie wanted an acknowledgment that this had been the weekend of his life. "You like, Danny, was it good?" Frankie probed.

"Frankie, it was a great couple of days. I enjoyed everything, the food was the best. And that Susan was a real lady. Thanks, Frankie."

It evidently was not enough for Frankie, he wanted more. Maybe he wanted a mental genuflection, or a kiss on both cheeks. Frankie demanded an admission, admit that having brought the cup of life to his lips, he would never toss it aside. You'll drink and drink.

"Whatta you think, kid, you wanna join up? You see how these guys treat me with respect — that means a lot, and I ain't even been involved that long. They have the right feeling of who should be honored, who's going to be up there some day."

Danny did not want to pursue the subject, he wanted a period of non-thinking, non-involvement, of non-confrontational somnolence. But Frankie would not let him rest. So Danny decided to break it off. "How do you earn their respect? Do you threaten to break a leg or shoot between their legs close enough to singe their balls, unless they kiss your ass? Now I don't mean you, Frankie, I mean the boys upstairs. How do you earn the honor, except maybe through fear?"

Frankie didn't say anything for about two miles. He took three long puffs on his stogie, blew out the smoke as if in exasperation, and then tossed the large butt out of the window before he spoke. His face tightened and became redder than usual.

"This ain't like the draft, Danny. As I told you, we have a volunteer army — no draftees. You join if you want to, nobody twists your arm. Only thing is, once you sign on you're a lifer. There ain't no dropouts. And everybody gets taken care of for life, or at least as long as he lives, and most times even his family is taken care of after he's gone. Better than Social Security, huh? So don't give me that scared shit. You see any unhappy faces there with my friends?" He paused.

"I ain't going to talk no more about it. We ain't supposed to go after people to come in, we don't recruit. You're special, so if you want in, OK; if not, forget it. Nobody owes nobody nothin. Maybe you're too fucked up with all that school shit." Frankie ended the conversation.

No more was said until they reached The Avenue. Frankie parked at his spot on the corner, and as Danny alighted, Frankie said, "Keep all these clothes and suitcase, Danny, you'll need them, no matter what".

Danny started to walk away, and turning, could only repeat, "Thanks, Frankie."

Chapter XIII

Danny's railroad pass came. They planned it so he could travel at night, arriving in New York City at about eight a.m., taking the Dayline up the Hudson, where Miss B would meet him. There was no reasonable or rational excuse now to prevent his going. And yet he was not eager, he was almost indifferent now that the time was approaching. Perhaps it was an act to show that it was not unusual to take a vacation in the summer. All the worldly, the indulgent exercised that rite of summer. Maybe it was apprehension, looking ahead to an unfamiliar experience. He felt exposed, almost as if he were walking naked down the Avenue. But evidently they didn't know, or did not care. No one but Ronnie, and now Amy, knew about his trip, and maybe he was disappointed. There were no hurrahs.

There was a dance at Cooper's Hall the night he was to leave. Amy was there and they danced. She was the same, wholesome and sweet. She asked him if he was excited. His response was bland, an unsuccessful pretentiousness of sophistication. And she smiled demurely, she knew. When he had to leave, about ten p.m., she walked to the outside with him and handed him one of the roses that had decorated the hall. They obviously wanted to kiss, but they touched hands only, and he ran home.

Papa walked him to the depot, gave him an extra five dollar bill, and would only say, "Watcha yourself, Donato, and be a good boy."

The coach cars were not crowded, most of the passengers were much older than Danny. He placed the rose in the metal ticket holder on the window and its reflection swayed with the rolling of the train over the breaks in the tracks. The clanking of the steel wheels meeting the divisions in the rails sang, incoherently at first, but paced itself into a steady harmony that eased him in and out of sleep.

He was awakened again as the sun broke through the lowered window shade. He could feel the movement of the swaying cars as they slowed into a large railroad yard. Raising the shade revealed a massive built-up area, a river and tall buildings, as the conductor announced their arrival at the Broad Street Station at Philadelphia. The sun was fighting to break through the smog-laden atmosphere, and the dirty windowpanes were streaked with paths of condensation. He supposed that all big cities were overcoated with soot, dirty clouds and dirt that had permeated into all man-made structures occupying space between ground level and the tops of the skyscrapers, now closing in. The night had hidden the mountains, the rivers and the trees between the two metropolitan areas, so he was still in the dark as to anything but land saturated with buildings, roads and people.

The last leg of the journey was the best. He had had coffee and juice. There were more passengers in the car. The newcomers were all men, most were dressed in suits and ties, carrying briefcases and reading newspapers. Danny had never seen so many clean-shaven, well-groomed men going to work. He had read about such people in newspapers and magazines, and had seen them in movies and newsreels. The clothes and the men wearing them seemed to fit. The guys on The Avenue who wore suits and ties often did not give the appearance of matching one to the other. Maybe it was the way they walked, leaned, sat or slumped. The clothes on the boys on The Avenue never seemed to fit easily and naturally. Everyone in the car was awake, the overnight passengers were walking up and down the aisle to and from the bathrooms. As the train neared New York City, Danny's sense of caution faded and the frenzy of the movements of man and machine was catching. His mind was opening to the new sounds and becoming attuned to the new pace.

The euphoria of motion of people and things peaked as the train moved into the 34th Street Station, New York City, and slowly the mystique of the unknown began to seep into Danny's consciousness. Would he find the right subway, could he find his way through the labyrinth of corridors of concrete and humanity, could he find his way in time to meet the boat at the pier for the trip upstate? So he moved out, gawking like a tourist, but the instructions were more than adequate and he made it to the dock with time to spare.

The trip up-river presented vistas, which he could never have imagined. Bear Mountain, West Point, the playing field of future greats — The Grants, Lees and Pershings of yester-years, the officers who led (and would lead) the ranks. Most of the time he spent on deck as the boat pushed up-river. He found he could say hello to some of his fellow passengers, but could not make sustainable conversation. Everyone seemed educated; that is, they spoke respectable English — good American. It was as if he were visiting a foreign nation now that he had left the Avenue.

Miss B and her sister, Matilda (Matty) were at the pier when the Dayline docked. They shook hands, and Matty, who must have been four or five years older than Miss B, smiled broadly and pumped his extended hand.

The view of the farm opened as they drove off the paved state highway onto a county road, more gravel than pavement. Hundreds of trees, all similarly topped and rounded, dominated the landscape as they moved to an unpaved lane into a cluster of buildings -the farmhouse in white surrounded by shade trees and flowers.

Miss B's mom and dad were there as they drove up to the house. They appeared warm and greeted him kindly. Father Britten had a sly grin, which would have been devilish at seventeen, but was now benign and friendly. It was not a full smile, only an abbreviated parting of the lips with the movement of the lower lip as if turning away. Danny liked him immediately, especially his informality, which was punctuated by the overalls he wore. Her mother was what a farm mother should be to a boy from the city; round body with a stack of white hair piled on top of an oval face, with cheeks brushed red by the outdoors. Her ample waist was embraced by a cotton apron over a gingham dress almost covering her ankles. She did the talking.

"So this is the lad," she said, after the introductions. The accent was, as he subsequently learned, pure New England, twangy, and correct. "Did you have a good trip, Daniel?"

Very deliberately and, in a subdued tone, Danny responded, "It was fine, Mrs. Britten."

"Speak up, lad, I can hear you, but Silas sometimes forgets to wash deeply in his ears and misses much of what is said around here." Mr. Britten, intoned facing Danny, that perhaps there was not very much worth listening to. Danny grinned, and he and Silas became pals. And Danny wondered where the leprechaun genes had come from. It was understood that the Brittens were English before there was an England. He was a sprite, no doubt.

Danny had his own room. It was unadorned, but very clean, and the bed was large and bounced nicely. The other furniture was plain, too, and probably had been there even before the birth of Mr. and Mrs. Britten.

That afternoon, Miss B. escorted Danny through the barns, the storage sheds and into the orchards. Acres upon acres of apple trees, all bearing fruit in various stages of maturity. He had never seen so many fruit trees, all neatly trimmed and orderly spaced, bursting with fruit. Like a woman in full pregnancy, apple trees prior to harvesting were in their full beauty; it was a period when even the unattractive woman became comely, and malformed trees appeared pleasingly symmetrical.

Supper was an experience. Everyone sat down together. The food was all on the table in serving dishes. When Mother Britten sat, it was a signal for all to grasp the hands of their neighbor, all bowed their heads, and silently spoke their prayers. Father Britten served the meat, slicing pieces of beef from a roast. Salad plates were already in place. The vegetables were passed around the table. And people talked to one another. Mr. Britten asked his son, David, about harvesting. Mother wanted to know from Matty how many eggs had been gathered. And about service last Sunday, who was absent, who looked well, any ill, and were there any visitors?

Danny ate slowly, watching the others, pausing before each mouthful to decide what utensil to use and never crowding the mouth too much so he could answer the random questions addressed to him. He was uneasy and anxious not to knock over his plate or spill his milk. It must have been apparent, for Miss B nudged his leg with her foot. And Matty put it simply, "Danny, relax and eat," then laughingly asked, "You have many girl friends?"

Danny reddened, lowered his head, and indicated by this act of shyness that there were none.

The trip to the cottage in Vermont, Christian Cove, was hilarious. Father Britten read aloud all the roadside signs. He burlesqued caricatures of places to see and food to eat. He was witty, lighting the journey with mocking ridicule at the art or science of marketing. Danny could only stuff his handkerchief in his mouth to keep from giggling, or laughing outright. And Mr. Britten, aware of this, exaggerated his mimicry, and Danny almost choked when Mrs. Britten laughingly addressed her husband, "Father, stop that tom-foolery this instant, and Danny, take the handkerchief out of your mouth. Laughing is permissible in this family." Beverly winked at Danny, and Matty patted his head as he removed the wet handkerchief from his mouth and hid it in his rear pocket.

The water was cold. It was difficult to imagine icy waters in the heat of summer. The forests never ended. Pine trees reaching into the heavens, their soft fallings cushioning the ground, soundproofing that spot of earth, until a chirping bird call reminded the sojourner that he had not flown off the planet. The metallic voice of The Avenue was no longer real. How soon one can forget. He wandered away from the cottage one afternoon, aimlessly moving through and amongst the pine trees. The sun danced off the tops of the trees, casting shadows in all directions, all of which were indistinguishable. The shadows lengthened without revealing any openings or familiar scenes, and triggered in him an alarm. He could find no familiar landmarks, no street signs. As panic set in, there was fear that he would wander forever in these woods, and if found, the embarrassment of having been lost probably within several hundred yards of the cottage. So he sat on the ground propped against one of the stalwart soldiers of the forest, with all the misgivings of being away from The Avenue where he belonged, musing not about finding his way back, but staying there forever.

Hearing noises moving in his direction, he rose, backed against the tree, and waited for the maker of the sounds, which stirred his reverie. It was Miss B, looking for him. Danny sat down again, relieved. Miss B sat beside him. Both knew he had wandered too far and had been lost. But that time he had been found.

Chapter XIV

The Avenue had not really changed during his absence, yet it appeared more unclean, more run down, and more remote. The family was more distant. Friends were not as tolerable.

He had not seen Ronnie for some time, but he was back in school. The doctors were saying he was ill. He didn't look sick nor did he act that way, walking, talking and joking enthusiastically. But he had been in bed for several weeks during the summer. Peps Costa made the football team. He was a junior, so he didn't walk home with them from school. Peps was more solidly built than Ronnie, who had no interest in varsity sports. Peps wanted college through a football scholarship and was not bothered about the war across the ocean.

Miss B decided not return to Cooper's Hall after her summer vacation. She had taken a position in a settlement house in Washington, D.C., near Capitol Hill. Some of the older guys on The Avenue were joining up, some after returning from the Civilian Conservation Corps, and others to beat the draft, which had passed the Congress in September, only reaching the President after the House of Representatives passed the legislation by one vote.

And Frankie's boys operated with impunity. The numbers books were never hidden, almost always carried in the hip pocket and whipped out to confirm in writing each transaction. The people bet, and some hit. And the odds were at 500 to one. There was only one "Book", and Frankie was the overseer of that operation. Frankie was moving up, he now had a driver — Eddie "Bombs" Fanelli. Eddie had a penchant for war and fighting. As a kid he enjoyed making mud balls from a sticky clay and throwing the missiles at the enemy (any passer-by) and yelling, "EH Bombs". Eddie taught himself how to operate a forty-five, a thirty-eight police special, and other articles of war. He was a warrior. He was a Praetorian Guard, the protector of the consul.

Frankie called Danny as he walked across from the corner of The Avenue, Danny crossed over and nodded. Bombs started with, "Kid, you still snowing those teachers at school? When you gonna grow up?"

Danny, not waiting for Frankie to intervene, which he anticipated, responded, "I guess you must have graduated into making the real things, eh, Bombs?"

"Go in and have a beer, Eddie," ordered Frankie. Eddie shrugged and walked into the Dutchman's pool hall.

"How's business, Frankie?" Danny prattled to cover his uneasiness about the brief conversation with Eddie.

"Danny, you'll never believe it. Business is terrific. They used to bet their pennies and nickels, all they had, hoping to pull themselves up and out of their holes. Now that they're working they're betting quarters, half- dollars, and some dollars. They want it big, a new car, radios, or 'frigerators. And the coons are coming in now. They love to bet, and now they getting some work, and being greedy bastards, want more. It's good for us."

"I'm glad to hear business is so good. What the hell's going to happen when you go off to serve God and Country on the River?"

"Danny, I'll be close by, but I could use you, especially when I gotta go some place East for sixty days for training before I can be on active duty. Whatta you say, pal, coming aboard? Hey, that's something a sailor would say, eh, Danny?"

"You're getting nautical, Frankie, but I don't want to be a sailor. I never liked their uniforms, bell-bottomed trousers would never look good on me. Anyhow, Frankie, you've got the Bomber."

"He's good for one thing, Danny, which you ain't, knocking heads together. We can find lots of that kind. We need some brains, don't you see, Danny?"

"You could go to the colleges and recruit. 'Wanted — bright young man, willing to work long hours, good pay, advancements depending on how many up the ladder fall off or are pushed off before you, everything bought and paid for'," Danny quipped.

"Cut the shit, Danny. What is it — you in or you out?" Frankie demanded.

"I guess I was never in, so I can't be out of something I was never in," Danny shot back.

"Don't be funny, kid, I only wanna pay back what I owe. Capice?"

Danny answered too quickly, "You don't owe me a damned thing, Frankie, so put that out of your mind, I have."

"You think about it, Danny. You're batting your fucking head against a stone wall. You'll die in the fucking war or you'll grow up with a big belly and die in the mills. Shit. You know what the Americans think about us. Seton High School is ten minutes away across The Bridge, but all the 'Eyetalians' gotta go to George High School two and one-half miles away. They don't want no mixing, they don't want you screwing around with their daughters. You ain't good enough. There are lines all over this city showing where they think we belong. They want us on The

Avenue at night. We only leave to work our asses off for them. Wise up, kiddo. I ain't gonna ask you no more, OK?"

When he stopped to think, though, there were a few guys who had wandered out. Purps Piacenti, playing the piano so well at sixteen that he was called away to New York, Chicago, and Los Angeles, to play with the big bands — Dorseys, Glenn Miller, and Tiny Thornhill. But he had come back home, dying at nineteen, — too much drinking, smoking and dope. He had become a vegetable. All he wanted was to drink Coca-Cola and smoke his Camels. His mama wouldn't let him have either. She could not imagine her Enrico, not yet twenty years old, was going to die. But die he did that Fall, and his mama walked the streets wailfully beating her breasts and pulling her hair for failing her son, not giving him his last request — a Coca-Cola and a Camel cigarette.

Everyone knew who everyone was on The Avenue. Danny played ball and walked to school with Nickie Gentile, whose brother, Carl, had been to a big university in Washington D.C. the past year, the only guy from The Avenue who was attending college. Danny saw Carl at Cooper's Hall talking to Peter Appleton before school started. Danny sat with them and listened.

Listening, Danny had the impression that the University was too big, or he didn't fit in, Carl had not been happy there. It was after Peter had been called away that Danny pursued the question unresolved in his mind of why Carl had decided not to return to the University. Danny had asked, "How was it, Carl?"

Carl did not answer immediately. Danny wondered whether he had heard the question or didn't want to discuss it. When Carl spoke it was almost reluctantly, not that he didn't want to share his experiences, but as if he were sorting it out, trying to decide what was important or significant. Danny waited.

"So much was good Danny. I wouldn't trade it for anything. But, frankly, I wasn't prepared for some of it. Most all of the students were Wasps. They had common and shared social and po-litical experiences, and most had access to money, too. And they had a common impression of Italians — not too clean, not too honest, and not too trustworthy — gangsters. So that even when they befriended me, they would disguise their acceptance by pro-nouncing my name as 'Gentle', and suggesting that it was French, anything other than Italian, hoping I would nod my head or an-swer affirmatively, or simply ignore the question. It was fun watching the reactions when I said, 'No, it's an Italian name'. Most of the time there was silence, sometimes there was the line about their 'Eyetalian' friend he or she had in high school."

Carl paused. Danny said nothing.

"I liked the school. I did well. I was learning in the classroom and in their streets. Really, I may have exaggerated our differ-ences. Most accepted me. I didn't believe them. I attributed a mo-tive to their friendship."

Carl became expansive, but moody, when he related his final consultation with his University advisor near the end of the school year. After Carl recited how quickly the year had passed, and generally what a great experience it had been, the counselor interrupted, asking Carl if he intended to pursue the emphasis on government, history and political science, and to what end. Carl nodded affirmatively, adding that those subjects would be supple-mented in the next school year with writing, economics, and French. Impatiently, the advisor wanted to know what Carl had in mind. What was to be his field? There was no immediate re-sponse when Carl stated that he was planning a career in the U.S. Foreign Service.

When his advisor spoke again, it was not even, but came in broken utterings. "Maybe you should look at something else, Carl."

Carl, stunned, could only remark, "What's the problem, Mr. White? My grades are excellent and I'm at home with the subjects."

"That's all well, Carl, but there is something else. I don't quite know how to say it. Maybe you would be better to be a social worker. But what you want may not be what is the best for you."

And all Carl could say was, "I don't understand."

So, Mr. White told him. "Carl, I must be candid. They do not accept first generation Americans in the Foreign Service of the United States. You would be wasting your time. I'm sorry, but that is the way it is."

"So what're you saying to me, Carl?" Danny wanted to know.

"Look, Danny, out there it is real and everyone is a grown-up. There are no Mamas out there to cuddle you, to pat you on the head and tell you that 'you is a good boy'. But the ladder to get out of this place is only out there; when you find it, get on the bottom rung, and start climbing. Those above you will, sometimes, intentionally step on your fingers as you reach up. Those below will grab at your ankles and try to pull you down. And it will probably become chilly and somewhat cold if you get to move very far up the ladder, and if you move up too fast, maybe there'll be a nosebleed."

Carl rose from his chair and walked across the room toward the door leading to the hallway and leaned against the doorjamb. Noticing that Danny was waiting to hear more, he added, "But if you stay here, you'll be secure and protected, like luxuriating in the warmth of your Mama's belly, but not free, without a view to the outside world, but relatively unassailable, tied to an umbilical cord."

Carl smiled and continued, "The opportunities are out there. You aim and reach, stretching, sometimes hurting, too; and sometimes picking a rose without being pricked by one of its thorns. Personally, Danny, I have decided I am not going to stay here. I'm going out there. I have to chance it. It's a hell of a thing to say, but mediocrity, or even failure, out there will be better than playing it safe in here."

Danny only shook his head, like an Italian could, in disbelief, muttering, "They knock you down and spit on you, and you go back."

"Not quite, Danny. Maybe it's only part of the indoctrination to get into the club. If I can help, my folks will know where I can be reached."

Chapter XV

Times were surely getting better. Papa bought a truckload of grapes, enough to make about six barrels of wine, two white and four red. And as the youngsters on the street carried the crates from the truck to the basement, they ate grapes until they made themselves sick. Papa was now playing bocce on some Sunday afternoons.

Old Man Costanzo, three doors down the street, did not yell as loud, although he still unbuckled his belt and smacked the side of the stone pillar holding up the front porch to get the attention of his kids playing in the street. His wife, Philomena, was not heard screaming in fright or in pain as often.

The streets seemed cleaner. The city had put some men back to work, and some of the neighbors were painting their houses. And now you could see an automobile passing almost once every half-hour.

The joints on The Avenue where you could talk baseball, argue politics and bet on the numbers or sports were open and undisturbed. The private clubs, which also provided alcoholic beverages and dancing and gambling, seemed to flourish. The police, even the Micks, smiled as they moved up and down The Avenue.

Piggy Sarno, who had worked for Frankie, had moved up fast, but he had fallen from the steel railing off the bridge, almost making a perfect imprint, face down, arms and legs spread out, on the asphalt pavement below. The police called it an accident. The word was that he was forgetting to report some of the take. When they stood him on his head, the loot dropped to the street. So someone gave him a push, and down he went. Danny never could explain why, but he called at the funeral home. Maybe it was because everybody from The Avenue was there. The flowers, they were too many. And there were plenty of black dresses, ties, and armbands. Piggy's Mama, who looked like a sow, was crying all evening. As if on a prearranged signal, she would wail and everyone turned to watch her drop her head and shake it violently from side to side and lurch backward and forward. Piggy's sister and brother, Angelo, only a runner in the organization, tried to cradle their mother in their arms. Frankie and a half dozen of his boys were in the back of the funeral home, against the wall, facing the casket in somber conversation. One of the boys, Baloney, had delivered an envelope stuffed with green currency to Piggy's Mom. She responded by a wristy wave toward Frankie. He smiled and nodded. Everyone understood. There was no blame, no recrimination, and no revenge. Life moved on for the survivors.

Danny was there with Ronnie and a couple of others from school. Everyone came, even the girls his age. It was not really a celebration, and certainly not a memorial. It was something to do rather than something one ought to do. The Avenue forgave all of its departed, all were treated with respect and dignity.

It was like a festival, except there was no band. It was the time to visit, to exchange happenings since the last gathering of the clan, and, of course, to gossip. Hardly anyone talked of the deceased. The dead had no problems, the Church said, maybe a little purgatory, the transitional plateau before ascending into heaven. And if the living lighted enough candles and paid for enough Masses, the climb would be relatively easy and of short duration.

The gathering in the Church basement after the burial was marked by the real trappings of life — good food and everything one could want to drink. It was the celebration for those who remained rather than a commemoration of those to be interred. Sports was the subject of discussion, yesterday's baseball scores and Joe DiMaggio's streak, a winner for their side. And boxing, the knockout in round 13 of Billy Conn, the "great white hope", by Joe Louis, the colored champ, who had blasted the other Irishman, Jim Braddock, four years before.

Fazoolie "Full-of-Beans" Balentio, was the sports statistician and authority on The Avenue. Joe DiMaggio's streak was his theme. "DiMag was the only 100 percent, all-around ball player. He could hit singles, extra bases, or homers; he could field; a real glove, and he threw a rope from center field. Sure, Ted Williams could hit, but that's all. Joe was the true baseball player. Keltner was lucky, the right place at the right time, and the playing field was wet, harder for the runner, and the fielder was set. Jolting Joe could have gone on forever; he did for at least another 16 games after that 56 game streak. The greatest thing to happen in baseball since Doubleday invented the game. Certainly the most exciting story this freaking year."

Fazoolie's antagonist, Kid Chompie, whose nostril flared to the right ear instead of his chin, had to re-live the Joe Louis-Billy Conn fight. The Kid explained it all. "That ignorant beer-swilling Irishman was only thinking about pussy, you know he got a marriage license just before the fight. I'll bet the punk was fucking her before he got that license; and that's where all his juices went. He got anxious, the dumb fuck, about getting into her pants, and he got anxious to end it in the 13th round. He couldn't wait to win it on points. All muscle and no brains in that Mick."

And so it went.

Although the world was in turmoil, there was little talk about the war. Chubbie {who actually was skinny} Gaggliano, one of the few high school graduates in the middle 1930's, tried to say something about the present world situation, the fight between the Germans and the Russians. The only related response came from the Needler, Patsy Nunzio, who loudly voiced his sentiments, "Fuck both of them, let them kill each other off, then we won't have so many to kill when Roosevelt pushes us into the ring with those bastards." There was no more discussion of current affairs.

The old ladies in black dresses were glad they were here in America. Their sons were not yet in the war, and dying in Africa, the Balkans, and Crete, like their sisters' and brothers' children.

This was home to Danny Castel Forte. The future had been eclipsed by the reunion of the day.

It was sameness throughout that fall, except in October, when brother, Sal, was married. The event materialized without too much preparation. The girl was Saundra Pitti, the most exquisite female Danny had seen, including the girls in the movies. There was perfection in her being: her body was as if chiseled by a Michaelangelo, her legs, hips and breasts were without fault, nothing needed to be changed. To add or subtract from this whole would be to mar perfection. There were no imperfections in the marble- colored face, whose head was draped with jet-black hair, clear and radiant.

Saundra was a neighborhood girl who had finished high school with excellent grades in typing and shorthand, but could not get a job in any downtown office until after the war started. And, because they had not been "going steady" too long, rumors abounded. Many thought marriage plus children could help one avoid the draft, some others thought he had been too successful sexually. Had he got into her panties before she got him to the altar? You could never tell at that time. She wore the white gown with train and trimmings. They were married in the Church, and she had no bulge in the middle. Mrs. Carbone, after the ceremony, admitted she could not detect any evidence of an unusual midriff, but voiced too many plaudits to the seamstress wizard of The Avenue, Maddalena Tamburri, who could hide anything with her stitching.

Most of the guests didn't care. There was so much food, and an open bar and a dance band. The parents collected the gifts and the envelopes with cash. It was good for Danny. Sal and the bride were going to move into her parents' home. Now he had his own room. He could throw out the cot, and Sal's double bed would be all his. More time for the bathroom, too. Mama was happy. Sal maybe could escape the war, and there would be lots of babies. Papa was happy, too, but he was also concerned. Sal would no longer bring home the ten dollars a week, which he contributed, to the room and board. But Sis was working full time now, and Donato would finish school in May. "Everything going to be okey-dokey," he concluded.

Even Frankie came to the reception, he was a second cousin to the bride. That was good for the newlyweds, he always gave a fat envelope of cash as a gift. His status in the organization surely must have been elevated, he now had two bodyguards. Baloney was the point man, clearing the way and watching the front. "Hoot Owl" Perilli covered the rear, walking backwards. They say he had the best eyes in the business, but he never made a sound, either like an owl or a human.

Frankie paid his respects to the bride and groom, and then the parents. Then he moved around the periphery of the circle that outlined the dance floor, extending his hand, touching and nodding, always smiling, and always moving. Frankie actually moved and acted like a politician running for office, he had to be visible every so often to his people, his constituency. He liked to touch. He was generous; and all he expected in return was loyalty and respect.

Danny looked on, yes, in admiration, but not in envy. He could have been Machiavelli reincarnated. Frankie certainly had not read "The Prince," but he knew instinctively, how to maintain his authority. He had the poise and refinement uncharacteristic of The Avenue: there was no rudeness or brutality in his demeanor. But his speech had all the tonal qualities of the inner City — coarseness and vulgarity. Frankie made no public speeches, his talks were all private.

Frankie, in making his rounds, stopped in front of Danny. "Hello, pal, nice wedding. Sal got a good wife. Doing anything exciting, Danny?"

"No, Frankie. But school is OK. The last year is moving well. After that, who knows?"

As he moved on, Frankie remarked, "You know you always have a job if you want it. See ya around."

Ronnie and all of Danny's buddies were there. Even Amy came. They danced. She was beautiful. Danny, however, would form no emotional attachment. He couldn't see her "putting out" any more than he could mentally picture Mama having sex, or Sis shacking up, before she was married. Other girls, outside of the neighborhood, would. There was no wrong, evil or sin to make out with a girl from the outside. To shack up with a girl from The Avenue was incestuous. Sex was not discussed at home, at school, or at the church. Sex, fucking and screwing was often the topic of discussion in the Clubyard or on the corner. But none ever admitted consummation of the act of intercourse. And Danny never bragged of his moments with Miss B. They all alluded or hinted.

Chapter XVI

Football — that was real sport. Danny loved to hit, the body contact. And he reveled playing in the Clubyard, and the big game, football in the playground on Thanksgiving. The next to last time he played, Danny's Clubyard Cubs were to battle the Alley Rats, a team from the lower end of The Avenue. It had rained a week before the game, and snowed the day before. The field was muddy, slippery and cold. The Cubs had driven the length of the field twice before scoring, then Danny hit the center, stumbled toward a hole and ran unmolested for four yards, the only score. The touchdown held, the Cubs won. Only one more team to beat, and the local deli would present The Avenue Trophy to the winner.

The Tigers came from the other end of The Avenue, in close proximity to Cooper's Hall. For some reason they were bigger. It was all set, noon on December 7th. This was it, the Championship of The Avenue. It was non- varsity sandlot ball without the gear and paraphernalia of high school. They had no shoulder pads or pads of any kind, or head gear. They played in old clothes, work shoes and woolen caps.

There was a crowd that Sunday. Someone had even lined the field, the goal lines were marked, even the ten-yard markers were outlined. Chubbie Gaggliano and another "old athlete" were officiating. Peps Costa, one of the boys who played varsity fullback at George High, was coaching the Cubs. Someone had even entwined red, white and blue bunting in the chain link fence fronting on The Avenue.

It was an unusual morning, not too cold, and dry. The sun would sneak out from behind the cumulus clouds colored with the chemicals from the mills along the river treating the steel being toughened for war. Most of the crowd had gone to early masses. The Cubs practiced about an hour. The team members did not go to church, too many disturbances in church — chimes, bells, the organ, kneeling, standing, rising, sitting. At home one could lie in bed until nine, eat some breakfast, and be at the playground by ten o'clock to warm up. They ran some straight plays, warming up mostly, and doing a great deal of talking and joking. It was remarkable. There was no tension, no stress. They wanted to win, no question about that, but it would not be the end of the world if.... About eleven thirty the boys in the topcoats and felt hats began arriving, and you could see the fingers flashing as bets were being made. There weren't too many old people, none of the parents. Mothers were preparing the Sunday dinners; the fathers would adjourn to the Club after dinner for bocce or cards. They did not understand football, anyhow.

And so the game began. Up and down the field each side marched. At half time neither team had scored. It was a slugfest, like two unsophisticated heavyweights standing in the ring, toe to toe, throwing blows at each other, waiting, and hoping for his opponent to fall.

Then the Clubyard Cubs pushed one over from the three-yard line with only about two minutes to play. They held and won. The players were pounding each other on the back, and even graciously waving to their opponents. Someone was blowing a trumpet in triumph, then a crazy began blowing Taps. The shouting stopped, the calling back and forth abated, and the players assumed that one of the Clubyard Cubs' ardent fans was signaling lights out for the Tigers. But the crowd had quieted, there was whispering, and the people were not leaving the playground. Chubbie jumped on a box, cupped his hands to his mouth, and yelled, "Listen up". People stopped milling, and he shouted, "The Japs bombed Pearl Harbor. It's been on the radio for the past ten minutes. Lots of casualties and damages. Nobody is sure, yet. It's for real! I'm going home and listen to the radio. Maybe we all should."

The crowd started to disintegrate, breaking up into smaller groups, but still milling around, when Chubbie yelled, "Oh, one more thing, good luck! A lot of you young guys are gonna need it."

Ronnie and Danny were standing in a group with four or five of the other guys, including Peps Costa, all in high school, all within a year and a half of finishing, if they stayed in school. Draft was eighteen. Goofy Gilardo wanted to know where in the hell Pearl Harbor was.

At first there wasn't much talking, everyone was trying to absorb the news, some still hoping that it wasn't for real. Then there was only disbelief. Maybe it was all a mistake. But people came out of the houses adjacent to the playground. They heard it, too. Someone, regaining his voice, piped up, "There's a lot of them slant-eyes over there in Hawaii, and California, too, do you suppose they'd try to take over?"

Carl DeLuca shouted, "Them yellow bastards could have them fifth columns like those Nazi in Europe. I'll bet they're gonna wanna take over."

Sourdo Mannelli tried to assure everyone that The Avenue was in no danger. "No Japs live around here."

Like clouds breaking up after a storm, it became ominously quiet, the groups began dispersing, and by two's and three's they began retreating toward their homes.

At home that night, Mama was worried about Sal, but more about Danny. Papa seemed relieved. He knew he would be having all the work he wanted. He left the old country before the first big war, he was too young to serve. Sal was concerned, and probably pushed the sex button every night thereafter, hoping for a "blessed deferment." Not much was spoken. Mama said, "the world is too crazy". Papa only shook his head as the radio commentators colored each pronouncement coming out of Washington.

Danny's emotional pulse was normal. It was like an engine geared in neutral. There was no castle building or romanticism exciting the brain. Nor was he afraid. Nor was there dismay, depression or apprehension. He seemed to enjoy a sense of deliverance. Relief. He could breathe more easily. He was going to leave The Avenue, of this there could be no doubt now. He was going to see the outside. Perhaps it would have to be a guided tour, restrictive, and under leash, but with a string as long as the ends of the earth. And he smiled. There could be some fun, too. And, above all, someone else was going to be making the decisions, at least the big ones. Now there was no fear of living, it was ordained until it expired. Danny slept well that night. And he could not understand it. There was nothing funereal about his mental ramblings that night.

Walking to school that Monday was different. No one talked about the game, only about the yellow bastards with slanted eyes and buckteeth. There was more jabbing, punching, and running back and forth among the walkers to school. The blood was boiling, and talk loose and rapid. There would not be too much serious studying at school today. Everyone was hoping that the homeroom teachers would bring in their radios.

The same excitation of feeling prevailed in the classroom. No one seemed to talk much about the dead, that was the past, and everyone was looking ahead. There was no sadness or despondency, there was relief and release.

Mr. Belton, Danny's homeroom teacher, was calm, and did not lower the blanket of his authority over the almost holiday mood. Maybe Americans just like to fight. And he had his radio, announcing that the President would speak to Congress at about 12:30 p.m., and they listened to that voice.

"Yesterday, December 7, 1941 — a date which will live in infamy — the United States of America was suddenly and deliberately attacked...."

America was at war. Germany and Italy had announced their declarations of war. Now it was the world at war. Everybody was doing it, like a popular song of the day. Every human now was going to have a chance to kill or be killed in war.

Walking home the long way, since the lake had not frozen deep enough, the talk shifted to the names of Avenue men who were in Hawaii. Nicky Perilli was stationed at Schofield Barracks. Ernie Sarno, Piggy's brother, was in the Navy on one of the battlewagons; someone thought it was the Arizona. There was no news about them. Everyone was more gentle with each other that day, more tolerant, less critical. And they did not play in the Clubyard after school. Everyone moved toward home. Danny changed his clothes and walked to the library, to read, and to wonder, and to dream. He was going to be out of there.

Christmas was not too different that year, except the Depression was over, the money worries were gone, there were going to be too many jobs and not enough people. Sis was applying for a job at a war plant, more money and maybe she believed she would be helping. With the draft and the surge of volunteers in the weeks after, the number of guys moving aimlessly on The Avenue had diminished, and some had quit school for the publicized excitement of war.

Danny stopped at Cooper's Hall a week or so before Christmas. Peter was sitting alone in his office. Danny sat, too, and for some time said nothing. Peter wanted to know how the war was affecting the kids at school. Danny's only remark was, "The seniors are bewildered, and the freshmen are anxious, thinking it will be all over before they get a crack at the enemy."

"And you, Danny, what are you going to do?" Peter asked.

"I'll graduate in June, I'll be eighteen in June. The war surely will not end before those dates. I don't know yet — try to get some college, or volunteer. And you, Peter?"

Peter grinned. "I've already declared to my Draft Board that I am a Conscientious Objector. If they believe me and assign to me that status, I'll probably work in some hospital for the insane. If not, I guess I'll go to jail."

Danny grinned, too. "I guess your experiences here at Cooper Hall will help you in either event — how to get along with the cons or the goofies."

"Before I forget, Danny, I had a letter from Miss B. Washington has become a scene, the streets are crowded with servicemen, and those looking for the right deals. The carpetbaggers have returned, she says. She, too, is unsure of what role she must play. She asked about you, and is disappointed that she hasn't heard from you. She's very sharp, Danny, and I know she's willing to help. She writes well, too. Try her, Danny."

"I'm not sweating it, Peter, not concerned at all. Now I know I'll be gone from here within a year, and that's a start. Have a happy holiday, Peter. See you after the first." They shook hands for the first time.

Amy was in the hall when Danny started for the door. Danny had not seen her since the seventh, just before the game in the Clubyard.

"Hello, Danny, great game, too bad the war had to spoil any celebration. Can I walk down The Avenue with you?"

He smiled, nodded, pushed open the door, bowed, and watched her move to the sidewalk. "Your swish is getting better," Danny voiced as they started down The Avenue.

"What are you talking about, silly boy? I don't understand. Explain."

"Your hips are moving more easily, your skirt swings more freely, and your legs keep the cadence, the rhythm is poetry."

And she laughed, "Danny, you've been reading too much, but I like it. Tell me more."

"Hell, it's all I memorized. There ain't no more," Danny quipped.

"Be serious, Danny. What about the war? You have any plans?"

"Like the unsophisticated suitor, I'll say 'yes' if I'm asked'" Danny answered.

"Silly, you know you'll be asked, but are you going to volunteer when school is out in June?"

"Don't know, don't think so now. I would like to start college, at least a semester, to see if I can take it, if I survive the war." Danny's comment seemed rehearsed.

It was comfortable walking and talking with Amy. It was pleasant and he was at ease. And yet, he always considered her part of The Avenue — cozy, warm, sheltered. And they looked good together.

Danny touched her swinging arm and asked, "And you, what are you going to do? More schooling, a defense factory, or marriage and babies?"

"Probably work in some office in town for awhile. Marriage would be the next best option. I'm too brittle for the mills. But I don't have any offers as yet. College out. Girls in our neighborhood don't go beyond high school, if that far."

"It's never been a reasonable choice for the guys, either, but we're gonna have to choose to go or rot in this stinking environment forever," Danny answered.

They neared her house, and all he could do was to take her hand in his and say, "See you around, pretty nose,"

"Sure, Danny, don't jump too quickly," she responded as she released their touching hands and turned in toward the front door.

The end was nearing, or was it the beginning? It was almost June and graduation, and a birthday. Yet, nothing had really changed. The routine was the same uncertainty prevailed. The draft was taking its toll; those who were fit and wanted to avoid the Army volunteered for the Navy, and a few to the Marines. Danny didn't want to attend his graduation ceremonies; he didn't have a new suit. He didn't own a matching suit. He had slacks and a sports jacket handed down from Sal. He made no plans for the prom, same reason, plus no auto. But Mama wanted him to go, she had never been and she wanted to see her boy graduate, the first.

It was decided. Sal, Sis and Mama, with Armando, would attend. Sal was involved because he could provide the transportation. Sis had to quit school to help Mama, and she wanted to see what she had missed, what she had been denied. Danny had to borrow a necktie from Sal. Danny was not happy with the plans; he would rather have taken the diploma in abstentia. The ceremony was boring to Danny. No awards for him, but he was in the upper ten percent of the class. Mama was delighted in the procession of the graduates. Her face was lit with awe and reverence. She didn't understand the speeches, but was impressed with the majesty of the movement of the lips and the flowing words, of which she only understood the words "future and hope".

Mama became a part of it, when Danny's name was called. She tensed and the lachrymal glands worked, secreting tears that could not blot out the joy in her eyes or the smile of her parting lips. She was proud, her head was raised higher. Uplifted, the sotto voce joy of the moment became a vocal affirmation reaching the stage, "Thatsa my boy'" as Danny shook hands with the principal, who smiled and acknowledged the accolade with a second and prolonged grip of Danny's hand. The half-restrained laughter subsided as the next graduate accepted his diploma. Danny did not think of embarrassment as he walked off the stage. But when he joined his classmates he wondered if they were still silently laughing. He placed his elbows on his thighs and glared at the floor, noting the scuff on his shoes which could not be completely hidden by excess shoe polish applied the previous evening.

Mama hugged him in the car, she was still sporting those huge tears and the beaming smile. He and Mama sat in the back, and she held his hand most of the way home. Danny could think of nothing. Papa was at home. Sal's wife and her mother and father were there, too, as were Mama's sister, Michalena, and her daughter, Anita. Tony Perola, Sis' boyfriend, who worked in the mill but whose draft number was almost up, was digging for Cokes in the tub of ice on the kitchen floor. Some of the neighbors were there, too.

Papa stuck out his hand and pumped Danny's hand for several seconds, and could only say, "Good boy," as he raised his half-filled glass of wine and drank.

The dining room table was covered with dishes of salami, cheeses, peppers, salads, celery bread, and ham, enough for fifty people. There was a cake, too, glossy, "Congratulations Dan", white and green frosting with chocolate inside. No one thought of inviting any of Danny's friends or schoolmates. Just family. All older. They enjoyed each other, and Danny sat on the steps to the upstairs, alone, watching the family celebrate. It was strange.

He did not want to be a stranger, but he did not seem to know those people, although he recognized their faces and knew their names. There were envelopes with five-dollar bills, and a necktie.

Chapter XVII

And his eighteenth birthday passed, too. Sis baked the cake, as usual, and the gifts of socks, shorts and shirts were as in previous years.

Danny still had not decided what he was going to do. Colleges began their terms in the fall. Money would be needed for tuition, even if he lived at home. So, the highest paying job, millwork, was the answer. And they were hiring. He had an old pair of pants, heavy socks, and a sweatshirt. He only had to buy some heavy shoes.

Riding the train out that first morning at 5 a.m., with the brown sack containing a pepper sandwich and a banana, was an experience similar to that first day of school. Uncertainty and apprehension, surely, but intermixed with indifference and apathy. Negative. His fellow passengers were older, more stout, generally more somber and tired. A majority had closed eyes. The scene was the same to them. The towns and built-up areas along the right of way were no different than what they had left behind. Dirt was the common denominator.

Danny was assigned to the heat treating area. Steel was armor-plated in undersized furnaces, the openings of which had to be enclosed with brick walls to entrap the hundreds of degrees of heat generated in the process. Danny was a runner, a shielder. Grasping three or four bricks, he would run to the entrance of the inferno, place the bricks in the opening, run back with reddened cheeks and singed eyebrows and hair. The slag and ashes from the furnaces, from recent cleanings, covered the concrete slab flooring from the furnace door to an area beyond the overpowering heat that reached the inner layers of the nostrils.

After several runs to the wall, Danny was indistinguishable from the others, except he was leaner, and the soot had not become permanently engraved under his eyes or mouth. Pausing after the most recent trip to the furnace, a heavy set, dark, dirty man, with a huge bulge in his right jaw, yelled, "Hey, kid, come over here." It was the first human sound Danny had heard since he started. Sitting on what appeared to be a keg, was a huge man who looked like a surfeited raccoon with an infected tooth.

Danny had moved to his command, and as he approached the caller, dust erupted on the floor. The man was spitting tobacco juice, displacing the cold gray dust with the brownish wetness that dried almost on impact. The discolored spit reflected like stars in the dark solar system.

"You the new kid?" and before there was an answer, "What's your name?"

Danny recited his full name. And the man retorted, "Well, don't feel too bad about it, my name is Leopold Jasinowski. There are a lot of 'e's', 'i's', and 'o's' in this plant. Good thing, too, or they couldn't operate this god-damned hothouse to make tools to tear out stomachs instead of growing food to fill them."

The man stopped, spat, and pointed to a pile of cement blocks arranged as a sitting stool. "Sit down a minute, Danny. I gotta make a speech. Since no one tells you a fucking thing around here, I gotta say something."

And he spat again, then continued.

"First, put a wet handkerchief or towel over your head when you make your run to brick up the furnace. If you'd read Dante's Inferno in school, you'd know that."

"Second, you gotta have something to suck on in your mouth or you're gonna eat two gallons of iron soot every day. Try some tobacco; it keeps your throat clear. Or try hard candy, but that makes you too thirsty. A wad of tobacco is best. Here, try it. Put it in the right side between your upper and lower teeth, and spit when it gets too juicy; otherwise, some is gonna slip down into your throat and then more than spit is gonna come up. OK?"

"Third, walk up to the opening, don't run. Run when the skin feels like it's gonna blister. Take these gloves and use them, and when they're used up, come back and I'll get ya another pair."

"Fourth, don't eat too much. Drink alotta water. And call me 'Leo'. Now, get your ass back to work."

It never got easier, but it grew more endurable. He learned to bear up under the routine, the dirt, the heat, and the calluses. And the days ran, too, summer faded, and nothing changed. Except it became apparent that he could never bear up under the strain of walking into that fiery abyss each working day for the next thirty years. It would not be purgatory, it would be everlasting hell. The overhanging gut inflated by Iron City Beer, and the brown spittle marking an area of work was too high a price for the security of job and home.

It must have been in the third week of his labors. He was hurrying down The Avenue from the train station, hot, sweaty, dirty, tired, dropping, and almost ready to give up (it had been in excess of 95 degrees Fahrenheit in the plant), when a figure pushed open the swinging doors at the Dutchman's and blocked his progress.

"Hold on, working man. It's too damned hot to move so fast. Come on inside and have a cold one." It was Frankie in canary yellow slacks, brown leather moccasins, and a light blue sports shirt; too clean on such a humid day of sunshine and soot.

"I'm too dirty, Frankie; some other time."

"That's why you need a cold brew, buddy," and grasping Danny's arm, moved him through the door. It took too much effort to resist. Danny found himself inside where it was dark, and a ceiling fan was furiously pushing the air around the room, both delivering illusions of coolness.

"Beer OK Danny?" Frankie asked, as they sat at the marble topped table, "You can have anything you want."

"Beer's fine, Frankie." Danny looked around. The barstools were nearly all occupied, some of the tables in the back had customers, too. It was rather quiet, maybe it was too hot to talk.

"What happened to that deal with the Coast Guard, Frankie? I thought you'd be on active duty by now," Danny started the conversation.

"Just some bureaucratic bullshit, Danny. I went through all the training crap in Maryland for the past two months, passed everything, papers are supposed to come through this week, Chief Petty Officer. I got all my uniforms tailor-made. Ready to serve my country. How about you, Danny Boy?"

"Still planning to start college in the Fall. Going to the University and see what happens. If I get bored, I join up, if not, I wait until they call my number. I'm not sure what I want to do. I should have enough money for the first semester tuition. I'll be living at home with the folks."

"Good, Danny, stay away from those gung-ho nuts. If you need dough, I can always help. No strings, a loan. You pay me back when you can."

"Thanks, Frankie. I can make it."

"Say, Danny, guess who I ran into. That Susan doll, and she asked about you. Wanted to know what you were doing and how come you never called her. That broad's got the hots for you. Want me to fix it up? We'll double date."

And it began all over, wanting to see both sides of the coin at the same time, dedication for the upward movement, interspersed with ways of The Avenue, work and play, crying, and laughing. He had done nothing but work, read, and sit since school was out. He needed a leave from his monastic-style summer. Maybe a break was what he needed. It could get him through the torture of the hot and steamy July and August.

"Yeah, maybe that would be a good idea," said Danny. "I don't work next Saturday and Sunday."

"If the girls can make it, it's a done deal, Danny. The pool will be available. Hell, there's a creek running into a swimming hole down there, too."

Walking home, Danny became more than displeased with himself. He was exasperated, if not angry that he had not refused the temptation, that he couldn't break the tie that bound him to The Avenue. Maybe he had to move away and stay away to cleanse that impurity from his system. Well, maybe the war would do it. Hell, for now he needed relief, some fun. Another compromise.

It was almost eight when they arrived in the valley. The girls were already there, spread out on lounges in the bar room of the suite, dressed in flimsy attire, and lapping at Manhattans. Susan was glowing, obviously anxious, and seemingly impatient. As they moved into their bedroom, Danny laughingly pushed her onto the bed and ran toward the bathroom, shouting, "I gotta go, first." It was a partial excuse. He wanted a good long hot, soapy shower. At home it had been a wash cloth under the arms, across the chest and between the legs. He didn't feel clean. He locked the door, stripped and had the shower steaming as he lathered his entire body, rinsed and scrubbed until the perspiration passing through the pores was white again. Oh, blessed water.

Susan was yelling, "Did you die? When the hell are you coming out? Come on, Danny, please don't do this to me."

With the largest and softest bath towel that he had ever seen, he emerged, red, almost like a boiled lobster, brushing his hair.

"I had to get all that dirt out of me before I touched you."

He took his drink, sipped, looked down at Susan, who had removed her robe, and stared at the glistening honey-colored pubic hairs as she invitingly spread her legs. Yes, it was going to be worthwhile. There was no talk to interrupt the music being made as lips touched flesh, as groans bespoke of pleasures anticipated and reached, as the two bodies producing their own lubricants seemed to slide together and become one. Their desire could not be satiated; it started anew after a long cool drink of vodka and tonic. Her nipples had hardened, her firm breast was warm, and her mouth opened to almost swallow his pulsating tongue. And they separated, and he fell asleep.

They had dinner about ten o'clock. And it was everything, salad, pasta, lobster and beef, and wine. Everything. And Susan gambled, and she was daring, reckless, but they were Frankie's chips, and she won. They danced, but with very little conversation. Talking would eventually bring on reality. She did comment that she was looking forward to her senior year at the State University when Danny asked her about school. There was no follow up. Just smiling, laughing, touching and kissing a cheek, a lip, an ear lobe, whatever was near when the impulse demanded a physical manifestation. It was strange, they were together, and they wanted to be together, yet each wanted to pursue their own mood. They wanted nothing from the outside to violate the sanctity of the cocoon that made them inseparable, one, at that moment. Frankie and his date were with them part of the time, at the dinner table and in the card room, but they played no part in the blissfulness, which crowded out the mundane cries of reason and reality. Danny had never been so at ease with himself.

They were exhausted when they returned to their suite, but they were young and touching caused the blood to move faster and they reached for each other, caressed, held, and almost fell asleep, he into her.

Breakfast in bed. Danny was hungry, and now talk poured out like a volcano finally overcoming the rock encrustation sealing the top. He wanted to know about college, she about his plans, the war, school. They dressed and decided to hike down toward the river and the swimming hole. They knew Frankie would not be interested, and the hot dry day could be theirs alone. They had the chef fix up a basket lunch and started down toward the creek that was dammed into a pond that ran into the river. The hotel blanket was spread under an elm tree whose branches extended over the bank of the creek as it emptied into the pond. They laid on their backs looking into the almost cloudless skies. The clouds passing were white and looked like enlarged cotton balls drawn into the winds.

Danny pointed into the heavens. "See those two figures of clouds moving together. See, now they're touching, they're melding into one. Watch now, they're strolling away, hand in hand. Now look, from that unity a new cloud formed and is slipping away."

Susan punched him in the chest. "Danny, you're either a poet or you're goofy, no, you're a goofy poet. Clouds making babies, that's too much."

Danny dozed under the warm blanket of July sun. Susan prodded, and he told her about the mill, about Leo and the dirt, but he never told her about his tobacco chewing. Susan surprisingly wanted to know each detail in the process of making steel. She was interested in the people there, how they looked, dressed, talked and thought. It was a new world opening to her.

They swam in the pond, helped to dry each other, ate lunch, and drank warm red wine. Could this ever happen again? She made it happen once again. She had to touch, to prod, to kiss, to run, to expose, and to laugh. The grassy knoll was soft and her rear had found the proper curvature in the earth. Her legs moved outward and he moved inward, and they moved together until they had to hold each other too tightly or they would fall out of each other's arms. Why couldn't life be like this always? Clean and sharing.

Frankie had reserved a table almost on the stage for dinner. The ten o'clock show was advertised in superlatives. The head-waiter was solicitous to the point of groveling. They had met for dinner at eight-thirty. Danny had never experienced such a scene; the formality was unlike any of his experience, except some movie he might have seen. Susan was at ease. Frankie was in formal attire; he had learned well, he was relaxed. Danny was still the youngster before the candy store window, left-handed in manners, nose against the windowpane; and all the time reflecting his gawkiness.

It must have been almost show time. The music was playing and Danny leaned over to Susan to pick up on a remark she was making, when she suddenly turned, brought her hand to her mouth, erasing that smile that illuminated her openness. She lowered her head almost to her lap. Danny brought his hand to her chin, wanting to raise it so that he could see into those green eyes moving in that sea of white. Now a barrier to his line of sight was a stranger, a tall man in formal dress, soft gray hair groomed professionally, and success stamped on a handsome face not weathered by the elements. A face now fuming, a volcano no longer dormant, infuriated but still not out of control. But his voice quivered as he spoke.

"Susan, what are you doing here? You told your mother and me that you girls were spending the weekend at your Aunt Charlotte's in Carmel, tennis, dinner and dancing at the Green Valley Country Club."

Danny slowly rose and stood behind his chair. Susan was looking up now, but remained seated.

Frankie was leaning back in his chair, the Havana between his teeth, his right hand fingering the stem of his glass of cognac. He was the only one who did not appear ill at ease. His demeanor was almost cocky at that moment.

Susan's friend, Judith, was shaking. And Susan's father continued, louder, "What are you doing here in this place with these — these greasy wops?"

Frankie moved up in his chair and placed his cigar in an ashtray, and put out his hand like a traffic cop. "Now, Senator, why don't we move into the private parlor, have a drink, and you and Susan can talk this out, civilized, you know."

The Senator was fuming. He had removed his glasses and the color in his face was red. The rage within now becoming ungovernable.

"Don't you patronize me, you — you gorilla."

Susan, awakening to the savage tone, anticipating the eruption soon, stood up, faced her father, and calmly stated, "Dad, you know Frankie. And this is his friend, and mine, too, Danny. Please sit down, everyone is looking at us".

"I am not sitting down at this table." He was trying to regain his composure. "Now, you girls get up out of these chairs."

The music had stopped, an inappropriate intermission, and the other guests were pretending not to be interested. Two of Frankie's boys had moved in behind his chair.

The father became more angry, Susan had not moved. She spoke softly, "Father, I don't intend to leave tonight. Judith and I are returning to school tomorrow. I'll join you and Mother after the show".

It was apparent in his face that he had passed beyond pique or indignation or irritation. He was consumed and he exploded. "I meant what I said, now get your tainted ass out of that chair and get out of here."

Frankie looked back over his shoulder, and his boys moved over to the Senator, who was in shock, realizing what he had shouted and noting the huge tears, tinged with mascara, moving slowly over Susan's cheek bones down to the edge of her painted lips. The boys didn't need to support him as he moved out, but he walked as if in a stupor, defeated.

Frankie rose, in charge, and walked toward the door where Susan's father had exited, motioning us to remain in place until he returned.

Danny, in a torpid condition, awakened when the disturbance faded, looked at Susan, whose face looked like a peony recovering from a heavy rainstorm, took her hands which were entwined in her lap. She looked up, drying the tears. Danny was not sure how to handle it, what to say. So he squeezed her fingers, and Susan tried to smile, her lips opening slightly.

It seemed to help. Susan looked at Judith's lowered face, wiped her eyes, and took her by the hand. "Let's go to the lounge and see if we can repair some of the damage, Judy. We could both use an aspirin, too."

Danny started to rise, but Susan touched him on the shoulder. "Sit and have a stiff one, we'll be back fresh and clean and bright, and maybe, just maybe, cheery."

Suddenly Danny was alone, not alarmed, but certainly not calm. Not knowing what to do, averting the eyes of the other patrons, he swished the contents of his glass with a stirrer.

Frankie returned. He was in control.

"I got the Senator and his wife in a suite, and have some waiters bringing in some drinks. I told them the girls just came down to eat and see a show, and we joined them for dinner. Where the hell did the girls go?"

Danny was about to respond when Susan and Judith reappeared. Susan was almost restored, but Judith still was not smiling.

Frankie lit his Havana, drank his cognac, and explained, "You girls look great. Susie, I told your folks you two came down to have dinner and see a show, we ran into you and agreed to pick up the check. Your old man is having a drink and has cooled down a little. I got them in the parlor suite. In about ten minutes you go on up and join them. And be sure you give them the same story. You'd been studying too hard and you wanted to relax, something different. You were busy on some project at school until noon today. Maybe if they wanna go home, you go with them. I'll get your clothes and stuff back to school."

Susan looked at Danny and winked. "Order me a coke, Danny, and then I'm going to walk over into the eye of the storm. No worry. Mother will have him ready to almost apologize. If they want, we'll see the rest of the show, or we'll drive my car home after them, spend the night there, and get back to school tomorrow. It'll work out fine. Frankie set it up good."

Susan and Judith came into the ballroom later with the Senator and his wife. They sat at a table at the opposite end of the stage. Danny wanted to leave. He was no longer interested in drinking, the chair was now uncomfortable, and he could feel his face redden. He wanted to disappear. Not Frankie. This was his place, and no two- bit lawyer-politician was going to make him run. And besides, this was where Frankie held court. People came by constantly to see and be seen by Frankie, paying their "respect". The traffic increased now that there were no women with them.

Susan and Judith walked toward their table. They rose, and the girls sat. Susan spoke, laughingly, "The storm seems over for now, just a thunderhead. We're going to spend the night with

Mom and Daddy, and return to school tomorrow. Danny, I've enjoyed it all, and was looking forward to another night together and a swim tomorrow. Maybe another time; give me a ring at school. I might even be able to come up to the city for a weekend. Daddy is sorry for the way he acted."

All Danny could say was, "Sure, sure, Susan. It was good."

Judith clumsily shook hands with Frankie, waved at Danny, and the girls, arm in arm, walked away.

Danny ordered a fresh drink. Then, looking beyond Frankie toward the band stand, musing, "Would her father have been so mad if we were college friends with Anglo-Saxon names? He would never have blown his stack that loud in public."

"Danny, I guess you never listened or heard what I've been telling you. They may need us, use us, but they ain't going to accept us as one of their own. The Senator takes my contributions, he wants the freebies and the perks, but he ain't going to say we're friends in public. I know that, and I face it. I need him and use him. We understand each other. I know he's not going to invite me to a party at his country club or his house; and I won't embarrass him by asking him to my house or for a drink on The Avenue. We swim in different streams. When I need his help, my lawyer calls him at his office. When he needs dough, his man calls my lawyer. Neat and clean".

Frankie paused, re-lit his stogie, and had another sip of cognac.

"Like I told you before, Danny, the girls are the same. They want grown-up fun, dinner, dancing, and a tumble in bed, nothing else. They can't and don't want anything serious. After college they'll marry a guy like Daddy, old family, lotsa old money, and with the same manners. So you don't get romantic about it. Have a good time and enjoy. You'll do the same. Marry a girl from The Avenue, someone who knows all the rules, who'll face you and your Mama and Papa, and you won't have to worry if they "speaka" the good English. Her folks won't either. It's easier to swim with the current, Danny Boy, pushing upstream against the current is too goddamned tough, and you probably wouldn't make it. See, I already talk like a swabbie."

Danny's mind was in turmoil and he had to speak. "I don't understand, Frankie. That guy thinks we're something that live under rocks, calls us names, and you calmly talk about how we're different. If some character from The Avenue talked that way to you, you'd have his arms and legs broken. But this guy, you accept it. I don't understand."

"Like I said — we need each other, but we stay out of each other's backyard. I don't go to his club or marry his daughter, and he stays off The Avenue and out of my business. Don't you think his 'good word' helped me get in the Coast Guard? And I see that he gets enough votes on election day. OK. And I'll lay you odds, he'll come over and make his peace. No apologies. He feels he's above that. But he'll want me to know that things are the same."

It couldn't have been more than fifteen minutes later when Danny saw the Senator approaching. He couldn't tell from his face what to expect. He sat more firmly in the chair and grasped the edge of the table with tightened fingers.

The Senator walked over to Frankie, stuck out his hand, and speaking regally, said, "Thank you, Francis, for being kind to my daughter and her girlfriend. It was so nice of you to rescue two wayward college girls and treat them to a fine dinner. I appreciate it very much."

Uncharacteristically, Frankie stood and spoke quite correctly to the Senator, "My pleasure, Senator. Lovely and charming young ladies, and I knew you would have wanted me to. You wouldn't have wanted them to be alone being away from school. Have a good time, Senator, and come again, anytime."

"I appreciate it," Susan's father responded as he walked away.

They stayed the night, and drove back to the city the next afternoon. Then back to work, to the mill.

Chapter XVIII

Danny had not made a decision, join up or get some college time. He read the papers and listened to the news every day. U.S. troops had surrendered on Bataan, in the Philippines. Corrigidor fell. But the Battle of the Coral Sea and the landing at Guadalcanal showed resistance and pushing back. Boots Spinoza was with Carlson's Raiders as they opened some of the doors in the Solomons. He was wounded, but nothing serious. His brother, Spooky, said he had some shrapnel in his head, forgot to put his helmet on, anyhow, not bad enough for a trip home. The Avenue had its first Gold Star Mother, the widow Praterno, whose son, Gigi, was killed on December 7th aboard the U.S.S. Pennsylvania at Pearl Harbor. She refused to display the embroidered gold star banner, the emblem of a life given in combat for our country. She didn't think it was an even trade. And uniforms appeared on The Avenue with some regularity. Otherwise, it was the same work and sleep. Maybe if he didn't get in soon, the war could end and he would have missed it all.

And the newspapers and radio headlined the war. Now it was not all bad, and this then became a concern to Danny.

Peter laid it out so that even Danny could recognize the answer. He argued that the war would last at least another four years. Danny would become involved, the war would end, and if he survived, he would have a head start on all the veterans returning and seeking an education. "Get what you can now, Danny, it will serve you well, both in the service and when you come back. The fire is still spreading, and you're going to be called to help put it out. Relax. Take your time."

The clincher was that Danny could work part time at Cooper's Hall. The attrition of male counselors was depleting the staff so that non- professionals or trainees were being accepted.

Danny delighted his mother when he announced at Sunday dinner that he was going to register at the University, and that he would only be working in the mill another week. Papa agreed, without any emotion. He was an advocate of patience, "pazienza". His father belonged to the school of passiveness — wait to see what happens.

Frankie had been called to active duty, and was serving his country by day and his organization by day and night. And so long as he was not assigned to another location, or he was not implicated in his vocation, he would serve and be served. Frankie congratulated Danny for resisting the hysteria of the guys who "didn't understand the fucking world we live in". Frankie suggested that the people running the show, the ones so involved in the big picture, were so "fucked up", that Danny's number could slip through a crack and they would never know he existed.

Amy said she was happy, but Danny wondered. Her brother had joined the Marines and had endured boot camp in Parris Island, South Carolina. Maybe she wanted that closer relationship that he struggled to avoid. Maybe she, too, could visualize life after the war. At least, she was positive in the continuance of his schooling.

It was strange, like traveling in a new country. Boarding a streetcar and riding out of The Avenue into wide thoroughfares with stately residences, trees in abundance, and lawns with neatly trimmed civilized grass. Immaculate. And the people boarding the cars after leaving The Avenue, mostly men, all dressed in business suits and polished shoes, and carrying leather briefcases. Work for them began at nine a.m.

And it was different, seemingly, everyone was indifferent to him. He found his own seat, attended the classes he wanted, studied each subject as much as he wanted, no one seemed to care, unharrassed, free, unmolested. And it was frightening. But people smiled and nodded and some, occasionally, would pass the time of day. No one made an effort to initiate any introductions. There were chatting groups in the classrooms, hallways, and in the cafeteria. Everyone seemed to know someone, except Danny. He recognized no familiar faces, no classmates, no one he had ever seen before. And he made no endeavor to introduce himself, he smiled forcibly, and put on his most studious demeanor, reading before the class began, and book open while sipping his soup in the cafeteria. None of which attracted anyone, as far as he could determine. It was a lonely week, yet surrounded by thousands of young people. He was not in any circle, and he didn't know how to break in.

During the second week, while looking for an empty seat in the cafeteria, he noticed a table with only one diner, a face that he recognized, a classmate, another English Lit student. Cautiously, as if preparing to enter a minefield, he circled the area at least twice, slowly moved toward the empty seat, and stupidly inquired if the seat was empty. The student looked up from the morning newspaper, smiled benevolently, looked at the unoccupied chair, and said quite simply, "have a seat". Realizing that Danny could never set the tray on the table without dropping the books stuck under his armpit, he added, "Here, let me take those books, the soup in your stomach will make you healthy, the soup on your books will make your lessons illegible and could create heartburn."

After the soup and salad had been removed from the tray and his books deposited on an unoccupied chair, the stranger stuck out his hand and smilingly said, "I'm Adam Gilmore, sit and enjoy the colored water they call soup. Everyone, including Mother, calls me Sonny."

The first half of the semester went well, the exams were not too difficult, and his preparation was good. The British were doing well in Egypt, General Rommel was withdrawing, and Americans saw some action in North Africa, and the Russians were counter-attacking at Stalingrad. How much longer could or should he wait? It was late November and, without any discussion, he stopped at the Army recruiter's office on campus and signed up, subject to call in January, after the holidays and at the end of the semester. The winds of the Draft were blowing stronger. Volunteering might distinguish him from the boys of The Avenue, maybe it would throw him in with a different group, would give him an edge, and maybe it would relieve the stress of the Castel Forte.

Sonny listened and argued that if Danny volunteered, he should choose some service other than the Army. It was too hard on the feet. The only advantage of offering one's service was to stay out of the infantry. One could be a hero in the Navy, too, was it not our first line of defense? Sonny could laugh so easily, so unexcitably, and so inoffensively. But Danny had to wonder whether Sonny knew him that deeply, and was the smile, the grin sardonic, was Sonny laughing in his sleeve?

Mama would never understand. All she could say was that she would pray to God that he would come back whole. Papa shrugged his heavy shoulders and considered it an unavoidable act, and he would only say, "Keep out of any trouble."

He saw Amy at Cooper's Hall, and she accepted the explanation without any discussion. Her only remark was, "It might have been better if you could have finished a full year."

And Danny quipped, "More education wouldn't stop a bullet aimed my way."

Amy answered quickly, "No, but maybe they would use you someplace where bullets are not likely to be fired." They decided to see each other before he departed, it was indefinite, but they both understood it was a "date".

Peter was leaving after the holidays to serve in a mental hospital in Philadelphia. He was going to deal with a different kind of crazies; they mostly wanted only to kill themselves, not others. Maybe he could help to bring some form of peace to some. Peter was right, but there were many more Dannys than Peters in the world. Peter wasn't disappointed because of Danny's new association; he was more disappointed with his disassociation with the University.

Frankie was more pointed. "You're a first-class jerk, you don't ever volunteer, dumb, dumb." Frankie was inwardly a believer in education, and he was a believer in the odds. "Look, kid, you fucked up, but maybe it'll work out. You got good schooling, a good head and, since you volunteered, three to one you'll end up in an office, a company clerk or something like that. You oughta learn how to type. You'll learn how to use all kinds of guns, but nobody is going to shoot at you. Not bad. It oughta work. But remember, Danny, no more volunteering. Be studious looking, like a bookworm. Buy a pair of glasses in the five and dime store to wear when you read. That'll make 'em think you're real smart. But don't offer yourself up to do nothin."

Danny's aunt, who lived in the middle of the block, cried when she heard about Danny. Danny's cousin, Dominick, was not going to fight any more wars. He had returned from Guadalcanal, a Marine Pfc., who had been hit with shrapnel. The scars had healed, but his brains had been scrambled by concussion. He was now at peace. There were no longer any patrols or missions, except someone had to keep track of them, and Dom had a plan. The Japs were like the dirty flies passing through the ward. So he would catch the flies, tie white sewing thread to their tails, and release them into the air.

Proudly, he would shout, "Now I know where they are at all times. I can see the bastards before they throw a grenade and slip into our holes."

Visitors coming into Dominick's ward only saw the white strings floating in the air. But Dom knew who the strings were attached to. They would never sneak up on him ever again. The doctors knew, but only because Dom warned them, telling them who they really were. Dominick returned to The Avenue, never to work again, but to serve as the corner philosopher. Now he had all the time and all the answers. Danny's aunt was happy, her boy had come home alive, and he would be with her until she died.

Danny loved visiting his brother, Sal, and sister-in-law, Didi. Their apartment was spacious and neat, and outside of The Avenue. Didi was a good cook, and she was a friend. Danny wanted to date Amy, and he wanted to borrow Sal's Ford, but he needed help. To go directly to Sal might not get the job done.

So he stopped after school one day, ostensibly to inform them of his decision to go into the Army. He planned his arrival before Sal came home from work. Didi was preparing dinner, her hair pulled back, freshly bathed, and wearing a recently pressed cotton dress. She was blooming. She seemed to accept what he had done, not necessarily approving, but understanding the rationale. And he told her about ending the semester and more or less putting things in order, like wanting to take Amy out dancing and dinner.

Didi immediately understood, "So why don't you ask Sal for his car?" And Danny walked backward, as if to say he had no stomach for that, and Didi said, "Why don't I suggest that you borrow the car when I ask about you and Amy?"

The plan worked. Sal fumed and fussed about the news — Danny's decision to volunteer. "Why couldn't you wait? Remember what Papa always said about 'pazienza'? And he's right. But you done it, and now you gotta make the best of it." Didi persuaded Danny to stay for dinner, when she asked about school and The Avenue, Cooper's Hall, and Amy, in that order. Danny acknowledged that he had not seen Amy very often since school started in the fall, but he wanted to take her out to dinner before leaving. And, bless that beautiful heart, Didi, on cue, suggested that Danny use Sal's car for such an important evening. Sal was surprised, but reacted as expected, "Yeah, let me know when, OK?" And that part was settled.

They went to a restaurant about five miles from The Avenue, on a highway heading south, a roadhouse, where there was food and dancing. He had stopped there with Frankie one time, one of Frankie's boys operated the place. Augie would remember him, he was confident. And it worked out. They had a table off the bandstand, and when Augie recognized Danny, he offered a bottle of champagne 'on the house'. He didn't seem concerned about their age, he was going to be hospitable, and Danny was known as a friend of Frankie.

Surprisingly, it all passed so easily. They talked, laughed, danced, and it was all good. They fit. They touched knowingly as they glided across the dance floor; neither felt intruded upon, both acted as if it had all happened many times before. He laughed more than he could ever recall, except sometimes when the guys would tell those dirty stories and jokes. She would be a good partner, like Didi, if he were going to stay around The

Avenue. Out there, he didn't know. He assumed the radiance would fade when subjected to the glare of the lights of the Susans and Judiths, and their Kappa Kappa Gamma sisters. Out there they would be two odd specimens together. One might be acceptable, but two? Much more difficult. She would be better off on The Avenue. But would she end up with a guy who would take care of her?

Amy was enjoying the champagne, she was talking more, and touching, and inviting him to dance. The kitten, having ventured into the backyard at night, now wanted to perch and meow on the fence. He could not resist kissing her on the neck or gently biting her ear lobe while they danced. She moved her body in acknowledgment. He moved away from her at times to shield his hardness, which was an embarrassment to him, but which she had not avoided or recoiled from. Holding her did not prevent the hands of the clock from approaching number twelve, and he did not know how to end it except to pay the bill, tip the hat check girl, and drive home with maybe a good night kiss. He assumed they both wanted a different scenario, but neither knew how. She was more of a novice than he.

While waiting for the check, Augie came over and asked if there was anything else they needed. Danny knew that there were cabins on the property, but he was ashamed to ask, to be turned down by Augie, or Amy. Despite Danny's protests, Augie insisted that it "was all on the house, a comp, Frankie would want it that way". Danny did not want a scene, yet he was shown that Frankie could reach out very far.

Amy reluctantly glided to the entrance when the valet had opened the car door, and she moved closer as Danny prepared to drive away. Their thighs touched and she moved her upper body so that her face could not be avoided and had to be kissed. And he did. Amy would only say, "Do we have to go home? Let's just keep driving forever." Danny smiled; puzzled that he didn't know how to fulfill their desires without a commitment that would last beyond the enjoyment of the moment. That act would constitute a promise, which Danny would not make. One should not defile the flower grown in his garden. The girls of the neighborhood who you did not marry were sisters, to be sheltered and protected. It was different with a Susan. Amy was bending, too easily, and he was unwilling to proceed further, reviewing all the consequences. So he hesitated. And the automobile moved in the direction of The Avenue.

Amy evidently let go of any thought that it would proceed any further, but she showed no resentment as she cuddled into the front seat and spread a pleased expression on her face. She almost lapsed into a sleep that was comforting. She was awake when they stopped in front of her house. And she was smiling, a forgiving expression if his decision was of respect or that the code was too ingrained to be ignored, but contemptuous if his concern was of commitment. They sat and looked at each other, saying nothing. They embraced, kissed passionately and touched tenderly without talking. The only sounds were of pleasure. They evidently were both wet between their legs. They became exhausted, stopped, broke apart, and smiled.

"Thanks, Danny. A great night! I worry about you, Danny; you're always too tight. You gotta ease up. Sometimes you'll have to make a mistake. Now kiss me one more time, and tell me you'll keep in touch."

Danny responded, kissing her strongly. He held her tightly, and uttered something inane about never ever forgetting her.

After parking the car in front of Sal's house, he walked home thinking, maybe she was right, and that his bravado displayed on The Avenue or on the Clubyard was a facade, a veil of false colors. Maybe he was only frightened about being different, and getting out was only an excuse. He did not sleep well.

Chapter XIX

It was by train that he first departed The Avenue. It was by the rails again that he went to basic training — to war. And by train, he moved to the south as a contingent of northern recruits. Most of them were from the cities, transported to a strange land where it was warm when it had been cold at home, where there was still greenness when all had become bare and brown on The Avenue, where the spoken language had a softness that probably could not have endured the harshness of life of the cities of the north. And the people were generally fairer in complexion, except the Negroes, who appeared blacker than their brothers in the north. The railroad cars must have been of the time when Sherman had moved his armies deep into the south, seeking the destruction of the defenders of the rebellion. The seats were hard woods, un-cushioned, the lighting fixtures were converted oil lamps, and the opened windows carried the soot and cinders of the coal-fired steam engines into the cars.

He remembered their arrival at camp, dirty, hungry, sore and stiff, cold, then hot, and then chilled, recalling the jumbo hot dogs floating in oily water in kettles two feet high, and the cold lemon-ade. Cabins on cement blocks housing about thirty new ones was to be home for the next six weeks. And that platoon leader, Sergeant Gibson, whose great-grandfather had ridden with Bedford Forrest, was learning about the Country he was serving, too. He acknowledged having a hard time with the "Eyetalian" names. So he substituted the words, "stupid", "greenhorn", and "dumb fuck" when he could not pronounce Castel Forte.

Physically, Danny knew he could make it. Walking had been a necessity, and the gym and pool at Cooper's Hall had refined the athleticism that was required. Plenty of starchy food had rounded out the sharp corners. The city boys, especially the guys with Italian background, stayed in touch, they were the outsiders. He established a talking relationship with Johnny Bancroft from Anniston, Alabama, tall and gawky, who used a lot of "yeahs", but was pleasant and willing to be an acquaintance. But there was also a Rick Calhoun, who was apparently still defending his beloved South from the aliens from the North. And to him, the non-Anglo-Saxons were almost on the same rung of the social ladder as the "niggers". But Calhoun liked to use other derogatory names; he used Wop and Dago too often.

About the fourth or fifth week, when they were wallowing in the mud at the infiltration course, crawling under barbed wire concertinas with machine guns fixed to fire live bullets immediately over their prone bodies, that hero of the South, Calhoun, panicked, froze, and would not move into the last trench.

Danny crawled beside him and yelled, "Grab my cartridge belt and I'll pull you in, we're only a few feet to the trench, but, dammit, stay down and relax." Shoving him to the edge and turning him parallel to the ditch, Danny moved perpendicularly to Johnny's body and pushed with his two feet, toppling Calhoun into the trench. Danny rolled in, hit him on the helmet, and showed him how to attach his bayonet for the charge at the straw dummies beyond the field of fire. "I'll go first and wait until you get out, and when I rise to charge, just follow me. OK? Good. Let's go." They never became friends, but they understood each other better. And Johnny always addressed him as Danny, and Danny felt better about himself.

Nothing changed after basic training — he was infantry, a rifleman. And Danny neither contested his assignment nor envied his fellow trainees who were destined for specialties beyond the foot soldier. It was as if it had all been ordained. Forging no close attachments, he remained aloof. He accompanied the guys on liberty, but avoided the brothels around the camps, fearing the sexual diseases so vividly portrayed in the training films. And yet, when he was home on leave, he found an excuse to see Frankie. And Frankie always had the means to find girls who were fun and not adverse to sex. Frankie was serving his organization and his country, in that order. And he was serving the population who could not go to war away from home. The girls rallied when he called, he was good looking, exciting, had plenty of money and was so willing to spend.

On leave at the end of July, Danny and Frankie spent a long weekend at the resort down state. There were no dates. Danny could decide on his own catch. It was the first night and they were having dinner alone, listening to the music of the dance band.

Frankie called Danny's attention to the piano player. "That kid is one of the best in the world, and he's only nineteen. You should know his family, they lived in that alley on the other side of the Clubyard. He's been playing with the big bands — Dorsey, Charley Barnett, and Shaw — since he was fifteen."

"What in the hell is he doing here?" Danny asked.

"Look, dog face, this band is as good as all those so-called big bands, anyhow, the dummy has a problem."

"You mean he likes boys?" Danny chirped.

"Not funny, Danny. No, he likes those pills that make him forget everything except the sweet music that is stored in that fucked-up head. Here I can watch him, and I would cut off the arm of any bastard I find feeding him the shit. He's been pretty good down here, good food and rest, and no dippy pills."

On the way back to camp, he realized that he had only one dinner with the family. Sal and Didi had been over, and she was lovely, as always. Sis and Mama provided the food he had not seen, nor would he likely eat, in the Army — rigatoni, meatballs, brasciola, salad, bread, fruit, and homemade wine, Papa's premium, served only on special occasions. Danny spent more time on the corner, more time than he had contemplated with Frankie and his boys. He hadn't tried to contact Amy.

Chapter XX

Advanced infantry training intensified and it was only a matter of time. The word was out, they needed more foot plodders over there. Move it, buddy all they wanted to see was heels and assholes.

Danny had never been on a boat, except the Dayline, so when he walked up that gangplank the iron mast looked taller than the buildings in New York City. He followed the guys ahead, gawking, then they started down, and so far, down that he wondered if he would ever see the sky again. What he saw was bunks slung from the deck to the ceiling, soldiers, and equipment. This boat would never make it out of port.

He met Emmett P. Healey on deck the third afternoon out, and they talked about how good it was to be out of the bowels of the steel hell hole that trapped them twenty-two and one-half hours a day. Em, that became the name of a friend, was from Andover, Massachusetts. He had had a year at Dartmouth. Emmett's dad was a stockbroker, and their family vacationed at Hyannisport. Danny listened, never volunteering any information about his family. He mentioned that he lived in the city, near a park, not describing the bridge, or the chasm that separated The Avenue from the park. Danny wanted to be befriended by someone other than another Italian, especially those guys from New York who used "fuck" every other word, and who were too loud and boisterous in their talk.

The rumor was that they were headed for Africa — no, England, to train for the invasion. To Italy, where the Americans had landed at a place called Salerno.

It was the first week in October when his troopship moved into the Bay of Naples. It would have been some fifty years ago that his father had departed from these shores. Ships and parts of boats of all descriptions clogged the harbor; smoldering oil fires drifted seaward to meet them. But burning oil scum flashing into the skies was unable to obscure the outline of Mount Vesuvius, which was brightened by the rising sun. They took to the nets and landing craft, and headed toward the beaches. Confusion reigned as they moved to an assembly area. Danny saw casualties for the first time as he passed an aid station, seeing white bandages and red blood, and hearing the sounds of the hurting. He saw the gray body bags, tagged and filled, without movement or sound, pure death.

As they assembled by the road, Danny could see some of the soldiers who had moved northward from the landings south of Salerno. They were dirty, looked tired, and had dropped by the side of the road. One of them rose and moved toward Danny. He did not speak. Only his eyes moved, circularly, as if activated by a coin as in a pinball machine. He appeared to be looking at Danny but the spinning, tumbling eyeballs could not have been focused on anything. And he stopped, stared, and stammered inarticulately, touching Danny's clean jacket, and shaking his head as if he was meeting bodies from outer space. Danny could only gulp a hello. The face of the soldier broke into a half smile, almost recognition, when an MP came over and, taking the soldier's arm led him across the road to the tent area marked for evacuation. He had no apparent physical wounds, but the guy was certainly hurting, a casualty, maybe fucked-up for the rest of his life. Danny became apprehensive. If you were killed, it was over, done. If you were wounded and survived, you could remember how and when it happened. The poor bastard; would he ever know where he was or where he had been? Would he always be an aimless cloud floating in space, without direction or destination? Dead, but not buried, breathing, but not conscious of his surroundings, awake, but unaware.

Trucks began arriving and names were called. Danny was assigned to the first platoon, Baker Company, 1st Battalion of the 141st Regiment, 36th Division, the Texas National Guard outfit. Texans — loud, who talked like Negroes. Emmett was assigned to the same platoon and they jumped into the same truck, all replacements, all-clean and unmarked, chattering like Boy Scouts on a summer outing. The weather was the warmth of fall.

The trucks moved, stopped, started, and renewed movement, seemingly for hours. And they had passed through an area of ruins to a clearing, surrounded by buildings that had been warehouses and factories, but now abandoned. The first platoon was housed in the skeletal structure away from the road, the roof and third story gone, the ground floor partially covered by the material of the upper floors which had broken through. He took off his pack and laid on the floor.

Danny knew that he had to be close. The town was Santa Nicola and it was near Caserta, about fifteen or twenty miles north and east of Naples — Santa Nicola, the town of his ancestors. His father's brothers had to be alive somewhere out there, but their sons, his cousins, had to be in the Italian Army somewhere. He wasn't going to go looking for them. Papa hadn't written to them in all those years. Papa's mother and father had died.

He had talked about the fields miles away from their home, and the back-breaking twelve-hour days, but Papa never showed any desire to return. It was another life, another world, yet only a generation had passed.

He remembered the Sergeant asking if anyone could talk "Eyetalian." Another replacement, who sounded as if he came from Brooklyn, volunteered. Emmett punched Danny. "You speak and understand Italian, don't you?" Danny moved closer to Emmett, and almost whispered, "No! We never talked it at home, only maybe sometimes by my mother, never by my father. I know a few words." And then he wondered why he denied it. His mother always spoke Italian, at least a form thereof, the dialect probably of the area. He remembered she had been born in a town near Salerno, but he could not remember the name. He understood most of what was spoken in his presence, and in all probability could make himself understood by a native.

Emmett broke in again, "Hell, you might have been moved to Headquarters as an interpreter or something."

Danny shrugged. "We never used it at home. I wouldn't be able to help any more than you could."

Emmett wouldn't let it go. "Hey, Danny, where your folks come from?"

"My dad came from somewhere around in this area, a small town, I'm not sure."

Continuing to probe, Em asked, "Are you going to try to locate your people, try to see them?"

Danny wanted to change the subject and suggested that there was a war going on, and "no one is going to give me leave to try to find people that I don't even know and wouldn't know what to say to them."

The truck came. And they boarded like cattle, unaware of their destination, but unlike cattle, aware that they were bound for an abattoir. The trucks moved out slowly, and Danny listened. He heard the rain falling on the canvas covering, and the wind seemed to have picked up. The sound of explosions, probably artillery, became louder, more distinct, and all talking ceased. Many had dropped their chins to their chests, either remembering a different time and place, or contemplating something never before experienced. Mama would have said, "they all look like babies and should be home with their mamas." Many would never grow up to be men, they would increase the number of mortality of minors. Others would mature into manhood after the first bullet buffeted the air around their ears, and others would be mentally scarred and remain "babies" ever after.

There were stops — to stretch, to piss, to eat their K-Rations, cheese and crackers, and to inhale cigarette smoke in the open, uncontaminated by the dense smog of tobacco smoke captured in the rolling canvas bag of the truck.

The next morning they caught up with the regiment and were moved to the Battalion area, where guides marched them to the Company area. They were the replacements to fill the gaps resulting from the engagements at Salerno, Alta Villa, and so many other towns with names too difficult to pronounce. The Sergeant was curt and called them men, but he knew that they were still boys. And the veterans, those who had been shot at, knew that the replacements were not yet men. They were still relatively clean, and their faces were not drawn or creased. Many had not needed to shave, and they hadn't been away from shower stalls for that long.

As they moved closer to the sound of battle, the weather had changed; it was cold and the rain was icy, as if collected from a mountain stream. They were housed in barracks on the outskirts of Caserta which were formerly occupied by the Italians, then the Germans, who most recently moved out to the high ground to the north and west.

Danny knew he was home. The barracks were immediately to the south of the Palace, the Summer Palace of the Bourbon kings, the Palazzo Reale. When his father had talked of the old country, his eyes only shone when he talked of the Palazzo. He knew he was home when he saw the signs — Marcanese, Maddaloni, and Santa Maria. Names heard falling from his father's lips when he wanted to remember, which was not often. The Bourbon Kings had lived well. The mountains to the north gathered its waters and forced them southward, cascading over a fall into pools and fountains, which were channeled into a watercourse, which flowed to the entrance of the Palace.

Papa had to have seen the outside walls at least, from a distance of a kilometer from the piazza at Santa Nicola. And Danny wondered whether any of his forefathers had moved or worked the stone, which evolved, into this monument, which was described by one of the princesses that lived there as the "Versailles of the Kings of Naples". And Danny fantasized that a comely Castel Forte of the middle eighteenth century may have become involved with a Bourbon, a Frenchman, or suave Spaniard, giving the line more than its apparent peasant heritage.

He knew that his father and grandfather had worked rented fields and subsisted marginally, but had any of their ancestors before them been artisans or masters at anything other than the hoe or the shovel? He had seen some old men with collars turned up and hats turned down trudging along the roads with hoes slung over their shoulders. Probably relatives. Nothing much had changed.

One of the Texans was yelling across the barracks to a buddy, "I told ya to stay afar from them Eyeties, they'd steal the buttons off'en your coat. Down the road a piece, Jonesy put his canteen down and a snot-nosed, black-haired woppy kid tried to steal it. And they're damned dumb, too. Can't understand a darn thing you tell em. And they don't like to fight. But they must like to fuck cause you see all their brats all over the place."

Emmett looked at Danny, smiled, and aloud said, "I wonder if Tex ever heard of Michaelangelo, DaVinci, Rafael, or Caesar and the Roman Empire?"

Danny didn't answer, continuing to clean his rifle, reflecting on the two sides of his heritage. Had the brains of those who lived in the south of Italy ever been a part of, contributor to, or inheritor of the civilization which was recognized by academia, by the educated, by the elitists of the world, as civilization at its highest.

The loud one moved over to Danny. "Say, boy, I didn't ketch your name when the squad leader called you. What was it?"

Ignoring the "boy," his response was "Danny. Dan Castel Forte." He phrased the surname a soft Castlefort, instead of The Avenue pronunciation of "Castel Forte".

"My name is Scott Harrison Smith, and I'm from Russell, Texas. At one time we had all Texans in this here outfit. Now, they bring in you all. I don't know what kind of outfit we gonna have now. We showed them Krauts and Eyeties, they knew they'd met the best. We lost some good men cause we had some officers who didn't all come from Texas, you see."

Danny nodded, continuing to polish the stock of his rifle.

"Say, boy, what in the hell kind of name is 'Cassel Fart', that mean you can stink up a whole building?"

Danny put his rifle down, rose from the edge of his bunk, looked at Smith, and quietly but sternly said, "My name is 'Dan', 'Danny', whatever you like, but it's definitely not 'boy'. I'll talk with you anytime, just use my name. Understand?"

"Yeh, I understand. You don't wanna talk about being a dago around your friends here. OK, sonny, but you'll learn. At least, I hope you got some of the American fighting blood in you."

Danny looked — no, stared — reached out and grabbed Smith by his T-shirt with his left hand, swung a vicious right to the side of his face, and followed that blow with a left to the chin and a short right to the stomach. Smith fell. Danny walked toward the toilet area, not saying a word. Emmett followed, without comment.

Scott Harrison Smith told the Sergeant he had fallen from the upper bunk while asleep.

No one spoke to Danny except Emmett, who asked if he was all right. Danny's response that he was "fine."

On Sunday, Danny took off alone walking toward the Palazzo. The huge rectangular structure occupied several city blocks. The MP's permitted him to wander through courtyards where he could view the grandeur of the gardens, the waters, and the hills in the distance.

He had never seen such a staircase, from the ground floor vestibule to the second floor vestibule, marble columns reached into ornate frescoed ceilings. Danny reflected in wonderment. This was all visualized, planned, and created by man — Italians. If he had thought of it, he would have asked Tex if they had created anything like this masterpiece in Texas. But, maybe not, for he surely would have answered with the "Alamo," and Danny would have popped him again.

They moved out on trucks, the next morning and disembarked two hours later on a road near the base of a hill. They could see a town, stone houses cemented into the hillsides. And from the rear, American artillery began landing among the single-storied concrete buildings at the end of the road.

The first platoon took the lead, with the first squad on the left and the second squad on the right side of the road.

The Sergeant yelled, "down," and Danny dove into a ditch partially filled with water. And the earth shook, and his helmet fell off, and he put his face into the cold mud and brought his arms over his head. He had forgotten his rifle, dropping it to cover his head as if his arms and hands could shut out the noise or ward off the steel falling after the explosion. And he wondered if he would ever look up into the sky again, if he would ever stand upright again, if he would ever move again. He was dazed, numb and unfeeling.

Simultaneously, he heard a scream, a yell "I'm hit," and the Sergeant shouted, "Get up, move out off the road before it shits again. UP. UP. Move, you fuck heads."

And Danny's squad, moving on the left side of the road with some cover, advanced toward the village. Maybe it was now un-inhabited, hopefully, the Krauts had moved out. The enemy artillery was coming from the distant hills. He saw a man fall, then he heard the bullets cutting through the scrub growth, rifle and machine gun fire descended as if an explosion had torn open a hornets' nest. And he fell to the ground. This time he lost neither his helmet nor rifle, and he crawled forward behind a sheltering boulder. He saw no one, but he fired his rifle, aiming in the general direction of the incoming fire. It was the first time he had fired his rifle with the purpose and intent to hit another human. He heard a scream but could not be sure if it was on his or the other side. And suddenly it became hot, perspiration rolled off his eyebrows down the cavity between his nose and eyes, and his eyes smarted. It could not affect his aim, he was shooting blind, wanting to hit but not wanting to see what was hit.

The Sergeant crawled over and touched Danny on the shoulder. "Keep moving left, toward the edge of the clearing, toward that stone house, we gotta clear it out. Now move!"

Danny moved slowly, cautiously, creeping, crawling to an outcropping of shale turned on his side and, looking back, he could see two other forms slithering forward. Danny saw a stone wall about twenty yards from the house. He crouched, dug in his heels, and ran; faster than he ever had before. He drew fire, but he made it. Now he felt wetness on his thigh. Could he have been so frightened, so terrified that he had pissed in his pants? He was not trembling, shaking, shivering. Perhaps the unclean hands of fear pressed the bladder too hard. Hope the hell it doesn't dry and stink so the guys will smell it when they get here, Danny thought.

Emmett, Smithy, and the Sarge dove into the hollow beside Danny.

"We're going to throw some artillery and mortars in there. As soon as the fire creeps to the far side of the village, at the base of the hill, move out and clear out those houses. We gotta take this place before it gets dark. Everyone OK? Any questions? And the Sarge crawled to the east where there was another group of soldiers.

"You OK, Dan?" Em inquired.

"It got warm all of a sudden," Danny responded.

Scott was quiet, digging into his pocket for a cigarette, sliding his arm from under his pack.

Mortar shells were dropping, slowly at first, and then intensifying, an oratorio without a religious theme, only death and destruction. And he thought there surely couldn't be anything alive out there after that. And he thought of The Avenue, the Clubyard, and Cooper's Hall, and for the first time he thought of his Church, the sidewalk Church, and then the Church with the iron fence, and that scene of a crucifixion of so long ago. He didn't pray, he had no background in such communion, although he had in the past mouthed the "Our Father", "Hail Mary", and the "Apostle's Creed". He wondered why he had never asked for divine grace or a special blessing. Was it that he didn't believe, or that he was not deserving? He was as unsure of his faith as he was of his worth.

He could still feel the wetness, and it seemed to continue to move down his thigh. He was not peeing now, that he knew. He saw the torn pocket on the right leg and he could see redness where the edges were seared. "God-damn, I've been hit and I didn't even know it," he exclaimed to himself. "Son of a bitch. Not much of a hit — only a scratch." And before he could dwell on his wound or do anything about it, the shelling of the enemy had stopped.

There was a lull. There was no response from the village. Silence. And then the word was passed, "Get ready to move out." Danny got on his knees, still crouching, looking out to where there was smoke and burning and the smell of fire. The word came and he started forward.

Now it was too quiet, as if someone were waiting, making preparations in expectation of their arrival. As he moved forward, all his senses were alerted. The air was strong with the smell of gunpowder, of burning wood and smoldering clothing, and perhaps hair and flesh. The breaking of a twig by footsteps behind and adjacent to him was rackety. He could see to the end of the row of houses, and he could see that nothing was moving.

And then it came — like a sudden summer thundershower. Pouring metal. Filling the air. And then the cries — agony.

He saw them coming, no trumpet blasts, only running gray uniforms, black boots, and rifles with bayonets attached. He was sure he yelled, but nothing came out. He tried to push himself into the soft soil and hide his head behind the stone wall. He waited, his finger frozen on the trigger. As the enemy became larger, he fired and fired, and as the empty clips flew out, he mechanically forced another into its place, firing methodically and, surprisingly, unhurriedly. Danny saw him first, he fired first and a helmet fell off, and the boyish blond hair was bloody, the polar blue eyes looked skyward. Danny stopped firing, the butt of the rifle on the ground, the end pointing upward, and his head bowed, not caring whether it was in respect or in thanksgiving.

There was movement around him and everyone began yelling and running forward. And then it was over. Marching prisoners to the rear, claiming the dead, and treating the injured and wounded.

Danny fell to the ground under an old gnarled apple tree, amid the sweet smell of the rotting apples, which had been felled by the forces of nature, the rain and winds of fall almost approaching winter. Would the fallen bodies of man be so scented if allowed to slowly rot in the sunshine and wetness of the season?

He had survived his first battle. Emmett had been hit in the shoulder and was evacuated to the battalion area. Smith had made it. Danny had his wound — the scratch. A piece of shrapnel had cut through cloth and some of his flesh, which now had been cleansed and bandaged and recorded. He would only answer direct questions — no general talk.

Chapter XXI

As they moved north, the rain was colder and more incessant. The mud stuck to his boots and camouflaged the rest of his uniform.

They were told the Germans had moved into their strongest defensive positions, anchored by mountain ranges on three sides, with the American access to the valley blocked by a river. All that the GI's had to do was cross the river, silence the guns on the high ground, push up the valley, and walk into Rome. They were told of their initial objective, Saint Angelo, across the river Rapido. The regiment was to hit to the north, his battalion was assigned to assaulting the enemy's left flank.

It was cold and rainy that January night. It was dark. As they moved forward toward the river, they could hear the water chasing downstream. They walked single file within the confines of taped areas, supposedly cleared of mines. Off to the right there were explosions, sounding like detonating mines. And then our artillery began its barrage, and they slashed forward, uncertain of where they were or where they were going. And then the shelling began coming from the other side, some eventually finding targets as the screaming around him increased.

Danny's squad reached the river and they were packed into a plywood boat and unceremoniously pushed into the stream. There were only two paddles, and the corporal and all the men furiously pushed the water aside, frantically trying to force the craft to the other shore. The skies were lit, first by flares, then by bursting artillery shells and the tracers from the machine-gun fire. Boats were hit and there were screams and cries for help, "I can't swim, help me." The river wasn't too wide, only about thirty feet at the point of crossing, but the flooded stream moved too swiftly for the untrained boatmen.

The water appeared calmer as his boat approached the bank on the enemy side, and Danny grabbed the trunk of a scrub tree growing almost near the water line, and held. Three of the men who jumped out were hit by a mortar shell, throwing two of the bodies into the river, and scattering blood and tissue over those huddled in the boat. No one would move. Then a craft approaching the bank downstream was obliterated when a shell landed directly on it. Danny and the people in his boat scampered up the bank into the foliage hiding the bank from the mountain ranges on all sides. They were as if in the bottom of a cup, and it was dark down there, but there was some cover.

There were five of them from the squad, Danny, Scott, and three other Texans. They dug holes and waited for someone to tell them what to do, where to go, and when. No one knew how many had made it across. The mist now hid the river from their view. There was no moon or stars shining that night. And the men squirmed in their holes, afraid.

The first light of dawn brought artificial light, too. The area on the north bank, their small beachhead, became the target for German artillery and mortar fire, which stripped most of the protective foliage, so they were naked. And they dug deeper into the soil, which was held together by the thousands of roots which had tied the lush vegetation to the earth.

Now they could see boats being pushed off from the American side. The incoming fire on Danny and his comrades abated as it moved to the unprotected men in the open, on the river. Only a few made it. Danny could hear the Germans moving down toward him, and his squad began firing in defense of a foothold that was neither deep nor wide. Now he caught glimpses of the enemy, sunlight reflecting off of metal. And he fired. He reloaded and fired until his cartridge belt was empty, his grenades all exploded. And he waited, wondering if he would recognize death when it struck, how much time between impact and finality. Would there be an anxious moment when life and death were distinguishable?

To his right, he could hear the cussing and swearing of Scott. Then, "Hey, Danny, you all right? Bo and me ain't been hit yet, but two others is dead. One shell, when it landed, it almost blew us out of our hole. You OK?"

Danny spoke only loud enough to be heard by his comrades, "Anybody else alive down your way?"

Scott called back, "I see some squirming about four holes down the way, facing the same way we is, but can't see their faces. Must be some of ours."

"Do you have any extra M-1 clips, I'm out of ammo, any grenades?" Danny asked.

"We ain't got but two more each, Danny, and only one grenade amongst us. What you want us to do?"

"Stay put. I'm going to work around back of you and see what's going on down the line. And don't shoot, god-dammit. Here I come," Danny said as he started to crawl behind them.

He found two bandoleers of cartridges and three grenades as he scavenged through the abandoned, man-made holes dotting the perimeter. The sergeant laid on his back as if sleeping, a red hole over his left eye. He still cradled his weapon in his right arm. Bits of flesh speckled the shrubbery, which had not been torn from its roots. The dead Sergeant's nose was almost up to the heel of a boot encasing a foot of a comrade without a leg. Danny found a Thompson sub-machine gun which appeared operable, and he slung it over his shoulder.

He crawled into a hole dug by a mortar shell and saw two bodies, still facing the north with their rifles on the embankment ready to fire. But neither moved. He called. There was no reaction, no movement. They seemed whole, but they were dead.

Then he heard talking. American. He whispered sternly, "You guys, what outfit? I'm with first platoon,"

A soft, strained, trembling voice, barely audible, said, "Don't shoot, we'se been hit, my buddy can't move, all broken up. My right leg is bent backwards. Got any morphine? We'se hurting mighty bad."

Danny crawled toward the hole, peered over its edge, and confirmed the immobility of the two wounded men. "Sorry, but I don't have my first aid kit, how about a candy bar and a canteen of water?"

"Can you help us out, buddy?" the least wounded asked.

"Hang in there. We should have more people coming over, and they'll use the boats to bring back the wounded. Keep quiet and hang on. OK?"

Danny started back, rolled into an excavation, closed his eyes, but could see it all. Nobody was coming in, and the Krauts would be sending in their clean-up parties. Fuck it all. The generals had screwed it up real good. No sense dying for nothing. Before it all started again he could crawl down to the river, dump his rifle and gear, and swim under water the thirty feet or more across that no-man's land. Those two poor bastards were almost gone, probably better off dead. And that fuck-head, Smith, wasn't worth the powder to blow him up. And no one would miss Bo, dirty of body, mind, and soul. "I don't owe them fuckers anything," he said aloud.

Danny took his helmet off, wiped his brow with the sleeve of his jacket, and then hung his head. Not because of the situation he found himself in, but what was happening to his mind. Not that he didn't want to escape, or that he had no concern for those guys still out there, but that he was talking as they would. The words he was pushing through his head he thought he had left on The Avenue ages ago. He had always wanted to show he was as good as the Dartmouth Healeys and better than the hillbilly Smiths. This war was damaging to his character too; he smiled. The smile directed his thoughts homeward and he could see her smile. The first time he had thought of Amy for months. And he felt warmer.

It started anew, bursts of rifle and machine gun fire, the thump of mortars being dropped in their tubes and the "whoosh" as they were propelled from above, all directed at their positions. They would be overcome shortly, and he neither saw nor heard any movement from the river. Then he thought about Amy again. It was like dreaming of clean white sheets drying in the open air on a warm July afternoon.

He dove out of the bunker and started crawling toward the river. Save yourself. Save yourself to fight another day, if anyone asked about your solitary departure. There must have been at least six GI's huddled in a covered cove as he rolled down from the last hole he had explored. They had one of those plywood boxes that he had come across in, and were preparing to shove off.

Danny yelled, "Hold on."

A weaponless corporal pushed out his hand as if he were a traffic cop on Main Street, and cried out, "We ain't got no more room. Find your own boat. I saw one of those rubber dinghies down the beach a piece, it oughta do you, soldier. Sorry, one more and this shit boat will sink."

"Look, buddy, all I want to know is if we're pulling back or if reinforcements are coming over," Danny gasped.

"It's all over, bud, we heard it's every man for his fucking self. We is leaving."

Danny cautiously moved downstream about fifty feet. Hidden behind some bushes was a two-man rubber raft, inflated and apparently intact.

It was then he heard the enemy fire again. The bullets skimmed the water as the craft commanded by the retreating Corporal moved toward the center of the river, then mortar shells churned the water. The men in the boat began to stand up. A shell hit too close and the boat flipped over. The water turned red and separated arms and legs floated with the current, pushing toward the sea.

Danny was about to launch his boat when he heard rifle fire in the vicinity of where he had left Smithy and Bo. He paused, looked toward the far side of the river, and heard the firing of M-1's, return fire. He threw the dinghy into the bushes, covered it with some loose branches, and ran up the hill toward the firing and rolled into Smithy's hole.

"I figured you gone south, Danny, wouldn't blame you too much. There ain't nothin here but me and them Krauts up there. Whatcha find?" Smithy asked as he put another clip into his rifle.

"Not much, buddy, lots of dead and no resistance. Some guys tried to take off in one of those coffins. They got clobbered. They claimed everyone was to beat it back any way possible. I found a small rubber raft down by the bank," Danny answered.

"So, why in the fuck didn't you get your ass out of this? You probably could've made it, dumb shit."

"Where's Bo?" Danny asked.

"He moved down that-away a piece when they started down that ravine, he killed a mess of them. He musta been hit by a direct mortar shell. I saw parts of him fly up into the sky, part of him is in those trees over yonder. See?"

Danny didn't look. Touching Smithy on his left shoulder, he said, "Crawl down the hill, straight down to those bushes near the bank, I'll cover, and we'll take a boat trip together. Now get the hell out."

"It ain't gonna work that way, partner. I got some shit in my right leg and I can't move it too good. You go. I'll cover you. Anyhow, they tell me you "Eyeties" are lovers, not fighters. Scoot."

Danny grabbed Scott's rifle, threw it into the next foxhole, pushed him over toward the rear of their haven, and shoved him downward. Smithy cried out softly, "You son of a bitch, I'll kill you for this." Danny rolled out of the hole and grabbed Smithy by the collar of his jacket and pulled him toward the river. He was moaning and groaning. But Smithy was using his left foot to push downward.

Danny could never remember how he rolled Smithy into the rubber raft; how he was able to launch it into the river running madly with all the rain that had fallen during the past two weeks. He paddled to midstream without much difficulty, but he was tired, and the current was too strong. Smithy was out cold, flat on his back, eyes closed and teeth chattering. Danny dug his oar deeper into the cold water. His back and arms ached. And as they were getting closer to the safe side, a firefight broke out. The Germans had reached the holes of the 1st Platoon, using that cover to fire on them. Some of the boys on their side of the River were returning the fire, and Danny and Smithy were in the middle. Only about fifteen feet — if he were alone, he could dive into the water and swim ashore. It would be faster and he would be less exposed. But there was Smithy. As soon as the raft first scraped the muddy shore, Danny jumped out and started pulling the dinghy onto the shore. Then the hailstorm came. The mortar hit first, almost in the boat. He saw Smithy pop into the air like a piece of bread out of the toaster. Then rifle fire. And then darkness.

The ceiling was high, and it was white, and the walls were white, too. He was in a white iron bed with white sheets. His legs were suspended about eighteen inches above the mattress. Danny knew he was in some kind of hospital. He could not move his head it hurt too much. Moving the lids over his eyes hurt. His lips were dry, parched, crusty, and not smooth as he moved his tongue over their surfaces. It was a large room, and when he raised his eyes he could see other beds. He closed his eyes. It was more comfortable. Hearing someone approach, he opened his eyes. A nurse? It was a woman in the uniform of a nurse.

"Well, soldier, good to see you awake. You should have had enough rest by now," were the first words he heard.

"Where am I? Can't be hell, you're too pretty and clean. Can't be heaven, they'd never let me in." Danny surprised himself with his agile answer.

"Part of each, soldier. You're in a hospital in Naples. As to the hell part, there are arguments both ways. How do you feel?" she responded.

"My head feels like a baseball hit too often. And my legs, what's wrong?"

"Your legs were broken. They're healing and you'll be almost as good as new, slightly bowed maybe. Your head is going to be fine. Once the dressings come off, you'll feel normal. Can I get you anything?"

"Some water please. How long have I been here?"

She helped him as he sucked cool water through his parched lips. "Not too long, we hardly noticed you. Only kidding. The doctor will be in to examine you later. Yell if you need anything."

Chapter XXII

About three weeks later he had healed enough to be lowered into a wheel chair for a ride to X-ray. And he was able to read again, part time, without headaches. He had written home, assuring Mama and Papa that the "scratches" were healing.

It was late February and the sun became brighter. He would read and fall asleep in the salon, the sunshine pouring in, the heat of the sun passing through glass was good, his legs didn't ache as much.

Nurse Waters, a first lieutenant, in charge of the ward, was a looker. But she had been only a nurse until a few days ago, now she had become a woman, a lady. It was only during the past days that he noticed her legs, shaped to fit her hips that joined her narrow waist. Her bosom was full, her stomach appeared hard and firm. Her face was classic English, all creamy white, a nose, almost perfect as if chiseled in stone. It was not a warm face. Not an Amy face. Yet it was not stern or aloof. There was light in that face, confidence, and certainty. No noticeable imperfection. It was so unimportant last week. Now he could feel the stirrings, the excitement of flowing blood, the consciousness of his maleness. He was warm all over. The luxury of unhurried sleep, peaceful sleep, voluntary sleeps. Sleep in the afternoon.

He awakened, sensing someone near, someone clean, freshness. At first he was not sure it was not part of the make-believe mind dulled by the warmth of the sun and the lassitude resulting from the peace and quietude of his new environment. Stupefaction, the state brought on by the pills he ingested daily. But she was real, and he could feel her touching him on the shoulder.

"You have a visitor, Castel Forte, are you up to seeing some relatives?" he could hear her saying.

He wanted to pass. His head was clearing. Nurse was smiling. Feigning pain or emotional unsteadiness would be a sham that he sensed would be unmasked by Nurse Waters. He stalled, rubbing his eyes. He looked up into those knowing eyes of the beautiful messenger.

"Who? Who is it, you said?" he asked.

"There are two elderly gentlemen and a teen-ager, Italians. The boy said that the men are your uncles, and he is a cousin. They live in Santa Nicola, near Caserta. They heard from home that you were here. They are waiting outside," Nurse Waters, in all her professionalism, recited unemotionally.

It had all been so good before she appeared. No pain, no regrets, no problems or anxieties. And he spoke up, "Is it OK for visitors, for me to have visitors?"

"I have no problems with you seeing relatives, if you all behave and they don't stay too long. They had to come a long way, and I'm not sure how they made the trip. You ought to see them, Danny."

He nodded, "Sure, have them come in." And now he was pleased. She had addressed him personally, "Danny". She turned his wheelchair away from the windows.

They came in, the boy first. He must have been fifteen or sixteen and he looked like a boy of similar age would have looked playing in the Clubyard at home, the face, the hair, there was little difference. He held his cap in his hand, smiled, and said, "Hello,

I am Nicola, named after you Papa. I work mechanic for GI's in Caserta. I talka some American. Him is my Papa, Georgio, and him," pointing to the other, "is Luigi, mio zio; your uncles. They fratelli with you Papa."

Nicola walked over slowly and stuck out his hand, and when they grasped, Nicola pumped it vigorously, and reddened as he recognized his over- enthusiasm, and backed off.

The uncles looked at Danny, felt hats in hand, each dressed in a suit coat with collars upturned, unmatching baggy trousers drooping over field shoes the color of the clay soil they surely had marched through. They were look alikes. They all seemed to have been cut out of the same bolt of cloth. He could see the resemblance, especially Uncle Georgio. He could see Papa, although Uncle Georgio was several years older. They both seemed smaller, older, sadder, and more withdrawn than Papa did. Hesitantly, they moved toward his chair, each sticking out his hand, shaking Danny's hand, but gently, leaning over to embrace, but obviously afraid to touch too hard. The gown and bandages must have been intimidating. They smelled of the soil, not offensive, but old. They smiled. Uncle Georgio wanted to know whether there was much pain, and Danny shook his head, and whether he would be well, walk again, and now Danny smiled and nodded affirmatively.

Uncle Luigi reached into his bulging pockets and dropped on Danny's lap three navel oranges, the cure-all. He remembered when he became ill as a child, Mama would find a way to purchase an orange, to cure all ills and to cover the evil-tasting castor oil — the cleanser of the system, the antidote, prophylactic and bactericide. He wondered where they could have found oranges at this time of the year.

Nicola wanted to know when Danny would be able to visit. The family and the entire village of Santa Nicola were waiting to welcome him to the land of his fathers.

Nurse Walters carried in two chairs for the uncles, who seemed uncomfortable standing. Danny learned that Papa's brother, Uncle Jim, who lived about ten miles from Danny's home in Pittsburgh, and who was in contact with his Italian brothers, had written about Danny's injuries and hospitalization. Danny could understand most of what they said, he did not try to respond. He talked to Nicola, who translated. But Danny was becoming uncomfortable. Some of the other patients seemed intent on directing their eyes toward the scene of the visitors in old clothes, seated in front of Danny. Some avoided that corner of the room, others lowered the tone of their conversation as if not to humiliate their fellow soldier. He was becoming embarrassed. Everyone had glanced over to that corner. And then there were the loud ones, wanting to be seen, to be recognized, and wanting to know who the "paisans" were. The uncles seemed uncomfortable too. They adjusted their mud-caked shoes behind the legs of the chairs as if to relieve a pinch from the tightness of leather shoes that had been rain wet and sun dried too often.

To make conversation, Danny asked if they were happier, better off, safer, now that the Germans were gone and the Americans were there.

Nicola became excited, he talked about the "Jip," great machina, and he learned to drive one, now he could fix them. But the uncles did not react so favorably. They more or less ignored the subject, perhaps not understanding. Uncle Georgio, speaking to Nicola rapidly, authoritatively, and with control, did not appear as appreciative as Nicola. Danny asked Nicola whether the uncles had had any problems with the Americans.

Nicola wet his lips, pressed his teeth into the flesh of his lower lip, looked at the uncles as if deciding what, if anything, he should say about the subject.

"Americans all right, OK, they give us stuff to eat, but they always want women, girls, and our people gotta hide 'em in cellar. They can't go outta la casa." And Uncle Georgio spat out, "Sone come tedeschi."

And that Danny understood, "The American soldiers were like the Germans." The GI's had hot cocks, too. Too much time on the lines, too long away from liberty, and too afraid to miss what could be a last chance. The Italians would pardon almost anything except the violation of their women, especially the young girls, the virgins.

Danny struggled to find words to keep the conversation flowing, but it was mostly a one-sided talk, and it was frustrating. The barrier of language and customs resisted the colloquy that should be flowing among relatives from afar who now had an opportunity to meet.

Uncle Georgio was entreating, by words and the movement of his hands, that Danny eat one of the oranges, the cure-all. It obviously could relieve the necessity of forcing a one-sided, stilted talk, at least until the orange was consumed.

Nurse Waters reappeared as Uncle Georgio rose from his chair and moved toward Danny, wanting to peel the orange. She evidently had been watching for some time. Moving in between them, she looked down at Danny. "You look exhausted, soldier. Want some bed rest?"

Danny lowered his head, forced it from side to side, looked up into her face and smiled weakly, unevenly, and almost apologetically, perhaps ashamedly. She moved behind the chair, unlocked its brake, and turned it in the direction of the hallway. The relatives must have understood, the uncles stood and pressed toward the moving wheelchair, touching Danny's hand. Danny turned toward Nicola, stuck out his hand and voiced, "I have to go now, some tests, I have to see the Doctor, Dottore."

Nicola seemed to understand. He explained it to the uncles. "You musta come and eat with us when you better, Donato." No one had called him Donato in years, and only his mother had when he was a boy. He looked up at Nurse Waters. She had heard. She pushed her lower lip upward and under her upper lip, a quizzical smile formed, then comprehension, and a broad open smile, acceptance. And she leaned over, close to his right ear and deferentially, phonically, repeated, "Donato, Beautiful."

He thanked Nicola and the uncles. He remembered "arriverderci" and "grazie" on The Avenue, and he used them now for the uncles. To Nicola, "Tell them I'm happy they came. I'll write home and tell Papa and Mama about meeting you. And as soon as I am able, I'll come and visit you. Tell them there is no need for them to make such a long trip again. Thank you for coming and for the oranges." Danny had spoken slowly, and from the nodding head, he garnered that Nicola had understood most of what he said.

Nurse Waters understood enough to push him out into the corridor toward his bay. She wasted no time and did not speak until they reached his bed. She summoned an orderly and they helped him into bed. Danny looked up at her as the orderly withdrew and said, "I could have made it into bed."

"Sure, I know, but you look drained. I love the sound of your name, 'Donato'. Then pausing, and with a lilt in her voice, she turned her body toward him and softly purred, "It's our secret, Danny."

It had been almost ten days since the visit from the relatives. Danny was reading in the salon, the sun was shining, and he had dropped his chin to his chest several times as the noon hour approached. The book dropped to the floor. Startled, he shook his head, trying to clear away the membranes of sleep that covered his sight. A young man in an Army robe had lowered the upper part of his body as he crouched to pick up the fallen book. He supported that awkward posture with his wooden cane in the grasp of his left hand, as he retrieved the book with his right. Pushing down on the cane, he hoisted himself into an upright position.

"Your place has been lost, but the book has been recovered, and that is most important. Thomas Wolfe's, Look Homeward, Angel. Have you read any of his others?"

Danny smiled, "Thanks for the book rescue, and I have read the others."

"Hi, I'm Dean Snow, formerly of Michigan, more recently of the 143rd Regiment of the gallant, swashbuckling 36th Division. Another Alamo, but this one on the Rapido. I don't like those battles where the good guys are wiped out. Mind if I sit down? My legs are tired."

"I'm Danny Castel Forte. And I know the Rapido. I'm still digging some of its mud out of my ears and ass."

Danny looked at this intriguing specimen. One could find rare gems in the most uncommon environment, he thought. This guy talks and acts like a teacher, but he looks like a street fighter. His nose had been flattened, if not broken, more than once. The cuts around his eyes had healed, the markings suggested the touching of an artist with too bold a stroke. His lips were tight and pulled together, showing the smallest of an opening. Probably good for a fighter. His ears were surprisingly small and flush to the sides of his head, which was covered by tight, more yellow than brown, curls that resembled thimbles with their openings on top.

Danny asked, "Now what can I do for you?" "

Do you mean it? There are only two things that I would give my soul for — one, a scotch and soda, and, two, a good fuck with some clean and young, but aggressive, Italian sister. Can you help, dear brother?"

This was the first time Danny laughed loud enough to be heard beyond his own hearing, and he spoke loudly, "Well buddy; what you ask for is beyond this life. An illusion. But maybe I can point you in the right direction, someone who can give you most of what you crave. Nurse Waters. She's female, undoubtedly has, or certainly can, offer you a piece, and being an officer, she would have access to scotch. She's not too young, and I don't believe she is Italian, but this is war, laddie, we can't have everything we want."

High mettled laughter burst forth, too volcanic for such a small mouth. And he stopped suddenly, as if someone had clapped a large hand over that small opening. Looking up, Danny saw the reason. Miss Waters, in her rubber soled shoes, was within hearing distance before they recognized her approach.

"So the characters have met. And what could have generated such boisterous laughter? No, don't tell me. A bawdy girly story, right?" she cracked.

"Wrong. We were discussing a lady — you, Lieutenant Waters." Dean giggled.

"Cut the crap, soldiers. What was so funny that I could hear you a block away? Tell me, Danny."

"Well, Miss Waters, we were talking about what would do the most to help Corporal Snow to recover more quickly so that he can rejoin his comrades at the front. A lady and scotch were suggested, and we both thought of you instantly," Danny covered his mouth with his hand.

She wasn't angry, but straight-faced, with hands on hips, she calmly said, "I suggest — no, I'm ordering you rover boys to retire to your quarters and take a cold shower before mess call." She turned and walked off.

Dean stood, positioned his cane, waved and walked off, saying over his shoulder, "See you tomorrow, same time, same place.

Hopefully, you'll have a better solution to my problem. Arriverderci."

Danny was better. He could walk throughout the hospital, over most of the grounds, with only the aid of a cane. And mostly he roamed alone. The letters from home always asked about the relatives — had they returned, had he been able to visit with his uncles and their families'? Danny understood that if he stressed his wounds, Mama would imagine the condition of his legs to be such that he could not stand on them, or that there were no legs. Sis hinted, "Are you wearing shoes, can you tie them on?" If he were doing well, why had he not been out to see the relatives?

There was not much more that they could do for him at the hospital, he was being told by an orderly, and he probably would be shipped stateside for some programmed exercises to eliminate the reliance on the cane. And the orders would be coming soon. Nurse Waters asked if he was going to Santa Nicola, she would recommend, and ensure, that he could get an overnight pass.

It was spring, and it was warm, and Danny walked to the motor pool where he found a truck going to Caserta. No plans. Maybe something would happen and there would be a forced decision, an uncle recognizing him as he sat at an outdoor cafe, maybe he could see their house without being seen. He found the town of Santa Nicola, edging the built-up northern boundary of Caserta. The city and the town shared a common thoroughfare. He walked toward the street that the carbineri had mapped, showing the location where the Castel Fortes had lived for centuries. The structures were backed against the side of the mountain, with a solid fence of heavy fieldstone sealing the inside from the road, with an entrance door fifteen feet high of solid oak. It reminded Danny of the gates of the forts in western movies.

The gate was open and he viewed a courtyard of red brick dominated by a white stone furnace, fireplace for cooking, and a water well with oaken bucket. It was afternoon, it was hot, but he saw no one. It surely had to be the siesta period he had heard about; surely, they must be asleep, or resting. It would not only be impolite and inconsiderate, but in bad taste to interrupt the serenity. He could not visit now. He knew where they lived, he would return at a more appropriate time. He could always say that he did try to see them, he had made the trip, but they were unavailable at the time. And it would satisfy everyone. He was told that the houses on that street had been there some six hundred years, when the people had moved into that valley from the old city several miles up into the mountain.

He had no problems with good-byes. Nurse Waters was staying, but had gone to Sicily for R & R when Danny got his orders to return to the States. Dean was going home, too. They would be shipboard companions with easy time during the days of crossing. And his buddies? Really, they were no more than the acquaintances that he had made in the outfit, names that would be erased by the movement of time over the years. The relatives. No need. There would be no return. Nothing there to hang onto. There would be no recurrence, no thoughts of him returning to Italy, or the possibility of their visiting America.

The only things he might not be able to get out of his head would be the River, the Crossing, and the Retreat. The flight of arms and legs, separated from humans, being propelled into the air by projectiles fired from the rain- soaked hills into that flooded, smashing maelstrom, the Rapido. Some had to die. Leaving the newfound relatives was washed from his mind with the flushing of the memories of the River that would not permit any trespassers from the South.

The second day out, he knew. He had run, chickened, split. Something he had not done in battle. He had seen his image in the faces of Nicola and his uncles. And he did not like the reflection mirrored in his shuttered eyes. He had denied himself to himself once again. Maybe the River washing over a body face down in the mud of its banks should have been his last remembrance. He had severed the root at its source. There should be no more growth. And he finally slept, troubled. He awakened, troubled. Dean was pulling at his arm. "Steady, Danny; it's ten bells and all is well, wake up. The war is over. But your personal war, I'm not too sure about."

Brought back to memory, he saw Nicola and the uncles, before he focused on Dean. "What in the hell are you stuttering, Dean, the ship is going to sink?" Danny played with words to hide from the intrusion into his head, stuck with a mirror of what he did not want reflected to outsiders.

"You were jabbering — river, cleansing, roots, and no more — is what I could distinguish from the groaning from down below." Dean continued, "You were arguing, trying to persuade someone, probably yourself, that you'd made the right decision, justifying something you'd done or not done or not concluded. You couldn't lose; you were the defendant and the jury."

"Look, Dean, you've lost me again. I would call you Dr. Sigmund Freud, except there was no sex in your analysis," Danny laughed, relieved.

"You didn't let me finish, old pal. You may have been yelling about the loss of your root, the organ of copulation. You know, no dick, no fuckee, and no fun and games. As far as I know, none of that metal even scratched your bat and balls, so relax," Dean retorted.

"How many more days are we going to be on this ship? Not too many, I hope. With you as my buddy and doctor, it would be a long voyage. Let's be nice, Dean."

"OK, friend. No more bad thoughts," Dean answered, and continuing, asked, "Say, Danny, did you ever get out to that town where your relatives lived; you know, the root cellar, where it all started for you?"

Danny closed his eyes, hung his head, and waited for a fresh onslaught of verbiage. When there was only the churning of the ship's engines, he looked at his friend and spoke softly and solemnly. "I did go to Santa Nicola. I found the house, but no one was around, probably out in the fields working. They'll make it. They have been survivors from the beginning of time."

"Danny, I was not concerned about them surviving, I was thinking about you. I hope that you left nothing behind in passing through." Dean appeared solemn as he touched his right forefinger over his right eyebrow in mock salute, and walked away.

Chapter XXIII

Walter Reed Hospital became his stateside home. And Washington — so clean, so alive, so bustling, the park of stone reminders of those who had paved the way. Were they that pure, that good, or was time a generous forgiver? Were the Washingtons, Jeffersons and Lincolns ever stalled on a Rapido, ever guilty of pushing bodies into a stream to stem the overflowing of its banks, to keep the water in its defined course, regardless of the cost? Perhaps. And had it been worthwhile? Evidently. There were monuments to confirm the correctness of their decisions or to absolve them of any fault. And Danny proved to be a worshiper. As he became more mobile, he visited all the shrines; but the only altar before which he was inclined to genuflect was the Lincoln Memorial. Lincoln looked as if he belonged up there, all wise, knowing, fair.

He was still walking with a cane, but he wasn't sure he needed it. The physical therapy was working; he was moving well. But he wasn't making things happen, not pushing for discharge, or another assignment. Drifting. And no pressure from the Army. Maybe he could be transferred to Fort Meyer and become a ceremonial warrior with Washington for a background. But he could no longer stall. He had to take a leave, he had to go home. He had been in Washington six weeks, and he had made but one social contact.

He took a ride to Capitol Hill, and he walked about six blocks to a neat group of buildings tucked behind Pennsylvania Avenue, and looking residential. Miss B had remained at Capitol Hill Settlement House during the war. They had corresponded more since he was hospitalized in Naples. He had his cane as he walked in the front door and saw her emerging from an office, and she almost said, "I don't believe it", but could only utter, "Welcome home, soldier, why didn't you tell me you were coming?" She moved up to him, looked him over, and kissed him on the right cheek, like a French politician. She showed him around. It was smaller, much smaller, than Cooper's Hall, but working mothers of the area had a place to store the kiddies until they finished at the office or in the factory. Miss B had been active in the downtown USO, too.

"I would ask you to have dinner here, but the noodles and meatloaf are ersatz, or at least they taste that way — papery, with cheese sauce. So we are going out on the town, my treat for our returning hero. I know a little restaurant off of Connecticut Avenue, good food, and not too expensive. Let's go up to my quarters and wash up."

Miss B had changed. Still solid, but she moved too quickly around her quarters — in the bathroom, changing a blouse, and asking about his legs — but never stopping to touch, to kiss like they had. She was more mature? No, she did not have the same interests. Was it because he had grown up, someone to play with when young, but hardly someone forever? The restaurant was out of the way, yet in town, not many service people for a town inundated with olive drab and navy blue.

Surprisingly, she wanted to know about the battle and men in action, men dying. They even had wine, and she drank it knowingly. The Quaker had come of age; she undoubtedly had met her hero.

"Danny, tell me how frightened were you. Did you want to run and hide? Did you enjoy killing, did you see people you killed, how did it make you feel, do you forget them?" She was too damned serious, so he laughed. But she didn't join in his jocularity. She wanted to know.

"Bev. Stop. You surprise me. You sound like the wife of a colonel, or an Army brat. Sure, I was damned scared, not of dying, but of being mangled, twisted like a pretzel, or without arms or legs or balls."

"Daniel, don't tell me you had no fear of dying, that's ridiculous," she retorted.

"Look, if I had been killed, it would have been all over and I wouldn't have known about it. If I got mauled, I would have had to live with it until I died. And if I believed in your God, or my Church, it would be better there than here on earth. No reason to worry about dying, was there?"

"Danny, Danny, you're being flippant," she shot back. And he quickly answered, "You're sounding like a Baptist Sunday School teacher," and he laughed. She smiled.

Danny continued, "There was too much killing on both sides. But seeing more of our guys being hit was the hardest, especially along that bloody river. Too many GI's dead and wounded. The cries, the screams, the shrieks that still waken me at night. Never calling for Father or Dad; always Mama. Why, Bev? Except one man from Texas, who only shouted, 'Shit, shit, I can't believe it.' But he was unusual. And none went quietly, except the one who got it between the eyes and never knew what had hit him. I saw too many killed, mostly ours, but we killed them, too."

She was more subdued, twirling the stem of the wineglass, and finally looking up ashamedly, and softly saying, "Sorry, Danny, I don't know what's come over me."

There was silence. And the waitress wanted to know if they wanted more coffee. More coffee, and more silence.

"Danny, I'm engaged, a Marine platoon leader. He's in the Pacific somewhere. And I think too much, especially at night. And it's all your fault. If I had not known you, I would never have even talked to him. I met him at the USO; he was stationed at Quantico. And I miss him, and I want him back in one piece, and it's all your fault, Danny."

"My fault? Good God, he's not Eyetalian, is he?"

"No, Danny, but I would not have become serious about someone in the military had we not been friends. I knew you, someone in the service, and you were good, you see," she hastened to add.

"How did your family take to the Gyrene? Almost like you had taken a colored guy home, I bet. No, the mixing with a Marine had to be more offensive than a black man, especially if the Negro had also been a pacifist," Danny retorted.

She was almost crying. It was difficult to imagine the lady he had known had become a girl.

"I'm sorry, Bev, that was not funny, and above all, it wasn't fair."

The waiter began clearing the table, and Danny shook his head, admitting his flippancy was not only irresponsible but inconsiderate. He moved his chair closer to her as they drank their coffee. They smiled, then touched hands.

Danny was the first to speak. "Even The Avenue is going to look good. Hope that it hasn't changed. There can be no more excuses or delays. Either I go home or the family will surely come to Washington. They're beginning to doubt, wondering whether their boy has any legs."

"Danny, you may not believe this, but I wish I were going back with you. I miss The Avenue. I was happy there. That community had class that I had never seen before or since. Most were good people, solid, giving humans. Parasites, too, but not too many." She squeezed Danny's hand.

They held hands in the cab ride home, but that was all the touching. When the cab stopped, she kissed him lightly on the lips and then the cheek. "Danny, don't get out. I'm tired and I want to write a letter to that P.O. Box in the Pacific. Go home, Danny, and keep in touch."

The next day he applied for leave. The soldier was going home. He called Mama and told her he would be home in a few days. "Mama, I'll let you know. It will be soon, within a week, maybe."

The train ride was uneventful. At the station, the cab driver took his bag, opened the door, looked at the cane and ribbons, and chokingly said, "Thank God." There was silence and then, as if the cabby had to know, "Were you in Europe or the Pacific, soldier?"

"Europe, Italy," was Danny's quiet response. But rather than fight the battle again, in words, Danny continued, "The town looks alive. The mills are throwing a lot of smoke, making plenty of steel. You must be awful busy."

The cabby wanted to talk. "I work eight hours at Westinghouse, making bombs, and drive this hack for four hours, mostly to see you guys, especially those coming home. It makes me feel a part of it."

As they approached the entrance to The Avenue, Danny, as if awakened by an alarm, almost yelled, "Stop! Please. I want to get off. I'll walk the rest of the way."

The brakes screeched as they were thrust to the floor. The cabby turned, "Sorry, but it's still a long walk, I can follow you if you wanna walk a little."

"Thanks, I can make it, slowly, to be sure," as he handed the driver a large bill. "The treat is on me, soldier. Please. And, good luck," and he waved, put the car in gear and drove off before Danny could push the money into the window of the cab.

With his light bag in his left hand, and the cane in his right, he started down The Avenue. He knew he was home. The spicy smell, the aroma of the hot sausages, peppers and onions, and the mammoth hot dogs on the grills in the front window of the Emporium, the home of the "original" hot dog. Gourmet feeding. He wanted to stop, but Mama would be disappointed. Food was her specialty, too.

Then he paused, looking across The Avenue toward the Carnegie Library, wondering how such a stately, grand, imposing structure of brick and limestone, the entrance of which was shielded by marble gothic columns, had found a site on The Avenue. Danny lowered his head as if in reverence, repentant for the times that it could have been used and was not. He wanted to walk up the stone steps and witness for a moment the quietness of its chamber. There was no time now.

Slowly he moved until he was opposite the gate of the Avenue Church, and he sensed the color moving into his cheeks. He dropped his bag and looked toward that curb where that Negro man's head had rested. His glazed eyes wondered if the blood was still there. He wiped his brow with his handkerchief, picked up the bag, and walked toward Cooper's Hall. He did not look back as he had done that day when they ran, and Frankie had shouted at the night.

But his face lost its somberness when he saw the screaming youngsters running out of the entrance to Cooper's Hall — the building was his start, his beginning, where there was that first quick view of a place beyond The Avenue. Danny knew he had to stop, if for only a moment. And he had to touch the hair of the young boy running, shouting and laughing after pulling at a pigtail of a little girl who was yelling, "Miss Paddock".

It had to have been Miss Paddock inquiring, "Can I help you, sir?"

"No. Nothing, thank you. I wanted to see it again. I spent so many good times here. Is Mrs. Kingsley in?" was Danny's hurried response, as some of the children stopped and began staring at him.

"No, I'm sorry, she is away in town for the day. Any message?"

"Tell her that Danny Castel Forte was in, maybe we can get together while I'm on leave."

The children appeared healthier, fleshier, and were dressed more fashionably. The war had done some good.

The next two blocks to the corner seemed a lifetime. So long, and yet the butcher, the baker, the grocers were still in business. Nothing much had changed. And The Dutchman's Grille, with its imposing wooden door and the windowed side door painted "Ladies' Entrance," was as it had been. He stopped. The door swung open, and someone called out, "It's Danny". From the darkness of the interior, three or four people appeared and then Petty Officer Frankie Collizio of the U.S. Coast Guard. He looked the role. He grabbed Danny, held him tight, and then pushed him away, shaking his head, and pulled him again toward his outstretched arms. "God dammit, Danny, you look good. I like the cane, too. The mark of a hero. Son-of-a-gun. Come on in, we gotta drink one."

Danny was directed toward the bar, and spaces were cleared where there had been no light between the bodies bellying up to the bar. And there was commotion, everyone shouting their wishes of continued good luck. The Dutchman poured the scotch. Frankie banged the bar, "To The Avenue's newest hero, Salute"; and they all drank. Frankie wanted to know when they were going to get together. Danny thought perhaps Saturday night. He would call, but now he had to get home. Mama was waiting. No more drinks.

As he pushed open the door, the corner came into view, and loafers were there, talking. Danny started down the street toward the bridge and he thought again of Amy, of the park, the elm grove, and the park lake.

He was walking slower as he turned away from the bridge toward the house. And then Danny saw Mama on the porch, watering the flower boxes along the walls separating the house from its neighbors. She was smiling and talking to Mrs. Russo, the next-door neighbor. He waited, watching. She was so much alive, heavy, beaming. He pushed open the gate with his cane and she turned.

"Donato, figlio mio," and she made the sign of the cross, bit her lips, and grabbed him, holding him against her, too close to even kiss. Danny was motionless, as if in a vise, and he did not want to be free. In a moment, he stepped back, took her chubby hands and pulled her toward him. He kissed the tears flowing from those black eyes; and she continued crying, although smiling, as he moved her toward the wicker couch. "Let's sit down, Mama. You look so good, younger than when I last saw you. Are you well?"

"Except maybe I too fat, I feel OK. Good, now my Donato is home. The leg is all right?"

"Everything is fine, Mama. I can dance, and soon I kick the football in the Clubyard."

And then she looked up and past Danny, yelling, "Armando, your brother, Donato, is home. And he is good."

Armand, returning home from school, leaned over the porch wall and wanted to touch. He jumped over the wall, and they held each other. They started to speak simultaneously, Armand saying, "Tell me what all the ribbons mean," and Danny inquiring, "How's school going? Playing football? And how is Coach?" They laughed. And Armand sat on the rocker, looking at Danny and Mama holding hands.

"You want something, Donato, something to drink?" Mama asked.

"No, Mama, nothing now."

Mama excused herself to fix dinner. "Armando, call Didi and tell her Donato home. We all eat here tonight. She and Salvatore and the kiddies come when he get home."

He sat on the porch, Mama was cooking, and Armand was in and out and mostly on the telephone. Danny was still sitting there when he saw Papa approaching from The Bridge. Maybe Danny heard him, his walk, before he saw him. Papa was looking down as he approached the gate. Danny stood and waited as Papa unlatched the gate and entered the porch. It was then that he saw Danny. He stopped, pushed his hat back on his head, put his hands on his hips, and with a rare smile, shook his head.

Danny moved toward his waiting father, stuck out his hand. Danny could never remember ever hugging his father. Papa took Danny's outstretched hand, grasped it, pumped it up and down several times, and then Danny moved toward his opened arms. The first time.

Papa spoke first. "Thanka God, you OK, Donato. Everything fine?"

"Just fine, Papa. I can out-walk even you." And they smiled.

"I go and clean up, Donato, and then we talk," was all Papa could say. His eyes were watery and his English became more difficult.

"Sure, Papa. We have plenty of time. I'll wait for Didi and Sal," was Danny's response.

The dinner table was as he remembered it, or thought he did — food for more than the family. Didi was most beautiful. She looked like a Madonna holding the child, her second, and a son named Daniel. Sal and Armando wanted to hear war stories. Papa asked about his brothers and Santa Nicola. Danny told them about the uncles, Georgio and Luigi, and Nicola coming to the hospital. Danny then related his vain efforts to locate them, and his shipment home without further contact.

Sal wanted to know why he did not call or write to them. Danny, wanting to turn the conversation, too sarcastically pointed out there was a war going on and no one, especially the Italians, had telephones.

So, Danny began asking questions about the neighborhood boys who were away. And his war and the Italian relatives were diverted to the recitation of the whereabouts of his old friends. Danny became uncomfortable. Too much food. And everyone looked to him to talk. And there was nothing more to talk about.

"Mama, you can't imagine how many times I dreamed of a meal like this. It was too good, too much. I cannot eat another bite. I gotta go for a walk. Is it all right, Papa? I have to move the leg or it gets stiff on me. I'm going to walk toward the Clubyard."

Papa answered, "Sure, Donato. We got lotsa time to talk."

The sun had not fully set. Mr. Ragullo was sitting on his porch, leaning forward on his cane and looking toward the sun. He put his hand over his eyebrows, shielding the sun from the face of the approaching soldier. "Donato, you home. Now you got a cane, too. Maybe you can throw yours away, they gonna put mine in the casket with me. You looka good. You OK?"

"Fine, Mr. Ragullo, how is the Mrs.?"

"She good, go to Mass, pray for the boy. He's a prisoner in Germany; they shoot his airplane down. Red Cross lady say he is all right. No letter yet. We pray."

"Give my regards to the Mrs. And when you hear from Tony, tell him we're going to have a big reunion party."

He moved toward the alley, it seemed narrower; an automobile could only just squeeze through. The Flats had not changed. He saw Amy before she noticed him. She was seated on the top step, her arms around her knees, her head in her lap. She obviously heard the footsteps on the sidewalk, maybe the cane striking the pavement. She looked up suddenly, and screamed, "Danny, I don't believe it," and bounded down the steps, putting her arms around him, knocking the cane to the ground and hugging him so firmly. She released him ever so slightly and then kissed him repeatedly.

She picked up his cane, took his arm, and they marched off toward the playground. They sat on the edge of the sandbox, holding hands, looking, and then touching lips. "Danny, you look so well. No real problems?"

"Amy, I'm healthy, the leg is almost completely healed. I'm enjoying the status the cane gives, but, quite frankly, I'll have to give it up soon. You, you grow prettier every time I see you. Wrong again — more beautiful. Not married, I hope."

"How could I be, I've been waiting for you." And she laughed.

They walked and then sat on the swings. And the talk was of yester- year. Then they sat on the stoop, they would have dinner Sunday night. Her brother, Arty, was in the Pacific, alive and uninjured as of the last letter. Amy was working in town, secretary to the CEO of a large defense contractor. She looked good. So they hugged and kissed, adolescents again, in remembrance of what should have been, maybe a prelude to what might be.

"You can't imagine how good it is to see you, Danny, so well, in one piece. Thank God," was her parting note.

"Amy, you can't believe how often your loving face appeared when everything about me was mean and dirty. You helped so much. See you on Sunday, Pretty Face." And he walked toward the alley and home.

Chapter XXIV

Dino's was inviting. There were people crowding the bar and the tables were almost full. And there were women with brightly colored dresses, none in black. And none were of Mama's generation, they were all younger. The mamas of The Avenue did not eat in restaurants.

Frankie was at the bar. He looked like the All-American boy in that Petty Officer's uniform. The red hair was shorter but curlier, and in that room it appeared redder. His face was peach red, clear. He was handsome, the profile was what was called 'good looking', and he was smiling broadly. "Let's have a drink at the bar, our table is back near the wall. Whatta you want, Danny?"

"Scotch and soda," Danny answered.

"You look first class, you talk that way, and you drink that way. Scotch, that's uptown, tastes like medicine to me."

Frankie introduced him to several of the men at the bar. Danny recognized most of them. They were older, but they were all Avenue guys, the names came back.

The table was set for four, only he and Frankie were there. "Who do we have joining us?" Danny inquired.

"Danny, you'll never believe it, but I'm going steady with one girl, I'm engaged, they say. You know her, Johnny Grassi's sister, the middle one, the brunette, Emma, you remember her. She's going to eat with us."

"Well, congratulations! I do remember her. Pretty and well built, too. So, you're going to settle down. When's the wedding?" Danny beamed as he reached out to grasp Frankie's hand.

"Sometime this fall, she's gonna set the date. Yeah, I gotta settle down, the job and everything. She comes from a good 'family'". Frankie talked on. Danny interrupted, "It's a safe link-up, too, Frankie."

"Tell me, Frankie, did you get the necessary approvals?" Danny asked.

"My Mom and Pop know her and her folks, and they like her," Frankie responded off-handedly.

"What I mean, Frankie, did the boys upstairs — Marconio Vento — give their blessings, say yes?"

"They don't pick a wife for you, Danny; but they got to know who she is and where she comes from. You can't bring in any girl, a broad outside of The Avenue, without explaining things. And that ain't good. But a neighborhood girl — you don't say nothin! She understands, but knows nothin. She can't talk about what she don't know, and she won't talk about what she knows."

Emma walked up to the table. Danny stood and stuck out his hand. "Hello, Emma, long time no see. You're looking beautiful. So why are you hanging about with this mug?" And he smiled and pushed Frankie away with his hand.

"Em," as Frankie addressed her, was conservatively groomed. The pattern of the dress was simple, unadorned, but she wore a strand of pearls. Fashionable, all in good taste.

It didn't seem staged at the time, but at about eleven, Johnny came by and joined them. He related how unfair it had been to be born with a punctured eardrum, "it kept me from serving my country, maybe I could be a hero like you Danny." Still joking, he cracked that "someone had to take care of all the gals on the home-front." His visit only lasted ten minutes, and as he stood, he said, "I gotta get my rest, no noises, so my ears rest, too. Whatta you say, Em, you going home or you going slumming with these guys till the wee hours?"

Emma looked at Frankie. Neither spoke. Em stood, picked up her purse, and walked over to Danny's chair. He rose and they shook hands. She leaned over and kissed him on the cheek. "Good to see you home, Danny, be careful." Then she stroked the cheek she had moistened with her kiss. Continuing to Frankie's chair, she said, "Walk me outside, Frankie, I'm going home with my old brother."

When Frankie returned he was not alone. Although Danny had never formally met Marconio Vento, he recognized him. Marconio knew him, had seen him on The Avenue, and had several times nodded in Danny's direction and spoke, "Hi 'ya, kid."

"Danny, you know Marconio, don't you?" was Frankie's introduction.

"Of course, hello," was Danny's response as he stuck out his right hand.

Marconio grasped Danny's proffered hand, the handshake was firm and steady, his hand was manicured, and smooth, without calluses, his voice was surprisingly soft and cultivated. "So good to have you safely home, Danny. I understand you did a fine job over there," as he pulled out a chair and sat.

Frankie called the waiter and they ordered, Danny a Scotch and soda, Frankie a glass of Anise, and Vento a brandy. Vento was fashionably dressed; the suit was tailor-made. The shoes looked soft as leather dress gloves. He was handsome. He had it all, thirty-five, married, and three children, good exemptions from the draft. He appeared as if he belonged on the outside, with a different name and at a different time, he would have made it beyond The Avenue.

"How long is this war going to last, Danny? We should be moving across the Channel soon," Marconio said.

Danny was surprised by the topic raised, and was not confident of its purpose. He joked, "Well, the War Department has not consulted me, but I would say another two years to clean out the Germans, and those Japs, I don't know what it's going to take to blast them out of those islands."

"How about you, Danny, coming home for good, or have you healed so well that they could send you back into combat?" Vento asked, pursuing the subject of the war.

"Don't know now. When I get back, there will be a medical evaluation.

"Anyhow, what are your plans after it's over? There are going to be plenty of opportunities for young men with your background and experience," Marconio probed.

"I don't know who will want or need an M-1 sharpshooter when it's over. I want to finish school, get a college degree. I'm not even sure what I want to major in. I want an education. Then — then — maybe I'll know then," Danny answered.

Danny watched Vento nodding his head slowly up and down. The most that Danny could garner was that Marconio understood him, but with no discernible signs of either agreeing or disagreeing.

Marconio rose, shook Danny's hand, and said, "Good to see you, Danny. If there is anything I can ever do for you, don't hesitate to contact me. Frankie can always find me. Good luck, and keep your head down. Now it's time for old men to retire. Show our soldier friend a good time, Frankie," and Marconio turned and walked to the door. And like a carrier moving out to sea, two escorts, with broad shoulders and ever searching eyes stationed themselves on either side and accompanied him through the doors. He had been gracious and unassuming. He had grown, and he had never left The Avenue.

And he had that night with Amy. And Sal provided the automobile. He had never known any woman like her. Her outward appearance cast a reflection of one that was modest, unassuming, and unpretentious, sensitive and warm, but realizing at the same time that underneath, inside, there were qualities that defied what appeared on the surface. She wanted to go downtown to the hotel, the oldest and most renowned, plush, where the establishment people enjoyed their cocktails and dining away from the country club.

Questioned about reservations by the hostess, and not having called, obviously necessitated a conference with the headwaiter. He was impressed with the cane and the campaign ribbons; probably he could not afford a scene or a turndown to a "war hero." The tables for two was along the outside wall, windowed for a view of the passing pedestrians. He ordered champagne cocktails (he had overheard a waiter confirm the order from a nearby table), and winked at Amy. Neither had ever tasted champagne before, and they were animated by the initiation into a new social environment. The bubbles made Amy's nose vibrate, rabbit-like, and they laughed. They ate slowly, dancing between courses, enjoying togetherness, not wanting to finish too fast. There were other service personnel, all officers, mostly Navy, and a Coast Guard Lieutenant Commander. He could be in charge or associated with Frankie's flotilla blocking an invasion from the River.

There were no apparent wartime shortages in this salon. The selections on the dessert tray were works of art, colorful, fragile, and visually stimulating to the palate. Danny encouraged Amy, and she chose. He ordered a Napoleon brandy. The Avenue and the back streets that fed into it were forgotten. They were comfortable. And he wondered anew, maybe there was a strain that was not pure peasant; or maybe there were genes from a different strain, or maybe assimilation would be possible.

The waiter was most deferential. He suggested that a tip was not necessary, his nephew was fighting in Europe, and was embarrassed when he determined that he was being given twenty percent of the bill, and politely pushed it toward Danny. They left, and waved, and the old man offered his civilian salute, a nod and the right hand to the top of the right eye.

Not wanting to drive, they took a cab up to the top of the mountain overlooking The Rivers, the bar overlooking the lighted city and the silvery ribbons of water flowing through its bowels, the source of all its economic stamina.

Amy had enjoyed her champagne cocktail, and ordered another, Danny ordered a Scotch and soda, the restful drink. It was fairyland, LaMancha and Don Quixote. And when the war was over, the status quo ante-bellum. It would all be the same, and he and the Amy's would be the waiters, the cooks, and salad makers, not the customers.

As they were leaving, the waiter advised that the drinks had been paid for by an elderly couple eating dinner. Danny slipped the waiter some bills, and nodding to the couple, spoke, "Thank you very much."

Driving home, they mostly looked at one another and smiled. He was driving slowly, deliberately, sensing that neither wanted to return from the city that they had not known. Neither knew where they wanted or should go. They had descended from the mountain, but were on the pinnacle of a high that started when they touched their champagne glasses at the beginning of dinner. Returning to their homes would burst the bubble, which had been enlarged beyond reality. Danny turned to her and said, "What would you like to do now?"

Amy's response was as if she had anticipated the question. "Keep riding like this until we can go no further, to where we run out of roads."

Danny laughed. "My leave will end before we reach the ocean, don't be silly."

"I know", she quickly answered, "the Reservoir; we can sit there for awhile, I'd like that."

There was an empty bench, although the Park was not deserted. It was a warm evening. Amy turned and kissed him, her lips moistened and opened. "I could sit here all night, Danny."

He took her face in his hands, kissing her closed eyes, the bridge of her nose, and her full lips. But he remained silent.

"When will I see you again?" she asked.

Then he spoke, slowly, as if unwilling to start. "Don't know, Amy; there's no way to know. And when someone else is calling the shots, forget about anything in the future. When the war is over, I have to finish school, someplace, probably not here."

She was sitting so close their lower limbs touched. And she took his arm into her lap, rubbing his arm from the elbow to the shoulder, and teasingly kissing the side of his face below the earlobe. Danny made no effort to disengage, but offered no encouragement. He remained taciturn, silent. She cuddled, physically and vocally. Finally, Danny cradled her in his arms and kissed her hard on the lips, stopping her dialogue and her movements. Still embraced, he arose, pulled away slightly, and smiling, said, "Better take the pretty one home, it's late."

With a disappointed shrug, Amy moved ahead, then, turning back, she also laughingly said, "I'm no Cinderella, Danny, nothing will change now that midnight has struck. And since these are my best shoes, I'm not going to leave one behind. Anyhow,

Prince, you know who I am and where I can be found, but I don't expect that you'll be riding up on your white charger searching The Avenue for this fair maiden."

Danny did not answer. And he drove directly to her home.

Chapter XXV

Bexley University was a liberal arts institution founded in 1847 by a group of Presbyterians moving westward from New England — New Hampshire, where the Anglicans dominated. It was almost in the geographic center of Ohio. It was situated in a narrow valley whose northern boundaries reached into hills and slight rises among which were nestled the dormitories, classroom, administration and chapel buildings, all brick and stone, a facsimile of a New England village. In winter, with a covering of snow, it would be a picture postcard of a New Hampshire landscape. Now, it was green, and the trees shaded and shadowed the grounds and the structures, some grown old and covered with ivy.

The Pennsylvania Railroad had transported Danny there; the coach pass was still available through Papa. The direction had come from another source. Miss B's roommate at the settlement house, Sheila Monks, not only suggested but also recommended Bexley. She was a graduate and had met her husband, now a lieutenant in the Navy serving in the Pacific, while he was enrolled there in an officer-training program. She had described it well. After his discharge from the Army, Danny applied and was accepted. It was easier than he anticipated. He had no roots there.

His roommate, Donnie Starling, a junior, was established in the school community, having been a student there before the draft, as was his father and grandfather before him. He had been discharged that summer, too. His father and grandfather were bankers, actually, the largest stockholders of the largest bank of a town of 25,000, near Peoria, Illinois. He was round, big cheeked, and generally always smiling or laughing.

There was this girl in English Literature class whom he noticed. She always sat a chair or two beside, behind or in front of him, and they smiled at each other when their eyes met. She either was accompanied by the same girlfriend, or she sat alone, a chair away from anyone. Her face was inviting, open, comely, but not a Venus Di Milo, not perfection, but as pretty as a girl can be in black and white saddle shoes and plaid pleated skirt.

The afternoon was warm and bright, the classroom was hot, and all the windows were open. The students found themselves dozing. The girl was sitting to his left, an empty chair in between them, when he noticed her closed right hand move toward the writing surface of the chair to his left, pause, open, and deposit a folded piece of paper. The note was printed and unsigned, "May I walk down the hill with you?" He read, pushed the paper between the pages of his book, turned, smiled and nodded. And so it started.

That day the Student Union was where the talking began. And Coca-Cola was their drink. It was almost like a prizefight, sparring, and light touching, getting to know each other's style. She did most of the talking. She was a senior, and sociology was her major. She wanted to help people. Her family was in the furniture business, retail, servicing four or five communities in the northeast part of the state. And her paternal grandfather had been the founder. Her mother's family was in manufacturing hand tools. The roots were deep in that county, pre-Civil War. And

Bexley University had nurtured the offspring of both families, if males, preparing them to succeed in the business of their fathers; and, if females, to prepare them for marriage to the right man so as to perpetuate those institutions which had sustained them for those many generations.

It was his down day; he was condescending, almost charitable to Lillian Foster. He wanted to appear older. She downplayed any sophistication, wanting to know about his wartime experiences, life in the big city. He would only answer by asking questions about Bexley, her sorority, and campus life during the war years.

Lillian looked at him, and with a broad grin, said, "You probably had more fun out there than we did here. Too many restrictions on the fellas, and a large number of the girls had made commitments with their men on active duty."

In the mood of indifference, "Some of the dedicated sisters probably found occasions to do their thing for the candidates preparing to lead men into battle," and he grinned broadly.

"Everyone needed some help during that time, Danny, those who were left behind as well as those who went away."

"Were you able to cope with it all, the shortages of hose and men?"

"The men around didn't seem to mind bare legs, Danny. Those of us on the home front had to make sacrifices, too."

They parted at the Kappa Kappa Gamma House, and all he would say as he backed down the concrete steps was, "See you around."

They talked when they were together walking down the hill from class, or when stopping for a Coke in the Union. And for weeks all he knew was the campus environment. His only correspondence was a short note home to Mama and Papa, telling them that he was well and enjoying his work. The letters from Sis were dictated by Mama, and always asked if he was "getting enough to eat," and was he "sleeping enough." Danny occasionally wrote to Miss B, but that letter exchange had become too perfunctory, they were becoming too formal with one another, hollow, and so they wrote to each other less often.

It had to have been some time that fall when Danny was conscious of the difficulty some people had in pronouncing his name. On The Avenue, everyone knew how to say it without making it sound alien. In the service, he was indifferent to those about him, it was only a temporary association. But here, it could make a difference, a more lasting association.. It was easier to remember and repeat the name "Castle," than "Castel Forte." No fraternity had seemed anxious to rush him, although he would not have considered such an association at that time. There were no buddy-buddies. He definitely was not one of the boys. And he thought the name could be a part of the problem. It was a heavy handle to carry, especially in this environment.

Danny waited until four one afternoon, and stopped in to see Professor Morrison. Prof. was a lawyer in town and taught Business Law. He was nonscholastical in dress, demeanor, and attitude. Danny had seen him in the Student Union and he came off as one of the boys. He was not an academician, nor scholar, but everyone said he was a good lawyer. He smoked a pipe, and Donnie said he had to have his martini before dinner.

He was all of those things when Danny talked to him that first time. Morrison advised Danny that a change of name was one of the least involved procedures in modern jurisprudence. A petition by a person who had attained his majority — twenty-first birthday — after proper notice to the world (an ad in an obscure newspaper which no one would ever read), the passage of a term of the court, and an executed order of the court, and abracadabra, forever thereafter or until you changed it again, the name spelled out in the order would be how he would be addressed in words and on paper.

"But, tell me, young man, why in the hell would you want to change your name? Isn't there an ancient town in Italy with such a name? Great persons and events surely must have occurred there during the centuries of its history," Professor Morrison commented.

"It's always mispronounced, and after apologizing, I get, 'and what kind of name is that?' which is followed by, 'Oh'; and it's too long. And, quite frankly, there seems to be a stereotype of Italian-Americans, Mafia, organ grinders, or day laborers. Since I'm not interested in any of those occupations, the better part of valor would suggest joining those swimming in the middle of the stream," was Danny's long-winded answer.

"I must say, you have obviously thought about it a great deal. Have you ever discussed it with your family, your parents?" was the Professor's quick retort.

"No. They might not like it, but I'm sure they would understand," was Danny's subdued response.

"Well, son, think about it, and if it is your wish, I shall be more than happy to initiate the process. It will not be like cosmetic surgery, it will not make you more manly, or less or more recognizable, but it will be a great deal cheaper. I never really contributed anything of substance to the war effort, only bought some bonds, so this should partially ease my conscience. By the way, Daniel, how shall you be called after the change?"

"Can I change the first name too," Danny spoke quickly, "or add a middle name? My birth certificate reads, 'Donato Castel Forte'. I guess I would like it to read, 'Daniel P. Castle'."

"It sounds strong, definitely Anglo, and impressive, too," the Professor, with closed lips, nodded.

It was only as he was departing, having shaken hands and profusely thanked him, did Danny suddenly start shaking. It was a warm evening, but he felt cold. And he remained unsettled as he walked down toward the dorm.

She almost toppled him. "Danny, you owe me a Coke," Lillian said as she grabbed his arm from behind.

"Sure, why not," and he took her by the arm and directed her toward the Union.

"Danny, we're having a Halloween party at the House next Saturday night, beer and dancing, some cheese and crackers and junk like that. Will you come as my guest?"

"It's been a long time since I danced; I don't know", was all he could say. And she pushed, "It's informal, it will be crowded, and there won't be that much dancing. Anyhow, I told some of my sisters you were coming."

And so, maybe it was a good day after all. His first real date and another door opening, the change of name. Maybe his meeting up with Lil and the party ratified his decision. He was going to do it. And he did it that next week. Morrison had prepared the affidavit, he signed it, and the papers were filed in court.

He met Lillian at the Kappa House, a large, colonial with a double porch. The upper porch, furnished in wicker ensembles, rockers, straight backed, and tables, opened from a grand carpeted staircase. He wanted to go upstairs first. Danny sat and looked down the hill into the valley, and drank his first beer. It was still warm that evening, and the grass, although fading, remained green. He wanted to sit, to look, and talk. She had learned how he wanted his name pronounced, "Castlefort", and it did not sound too unlike the names of her friends.

After a few dances, and still early in the evening, Danny suggested they leave. He was sober; she had had a glass of wine. They had both nibbled on cheese and crackers and potato chips. She could not determine whether he was uncomfortable or was striking a pose, but for whose benefit? She was getting to know him, and those at the party didn't care. She took his right hand, swinging it high, cavorting, dancing in back and in front, and laughing.

She chided, "Where are we going, Danny? Oh, I don't care, wherever thou leadest, I will follow," and she kissed him lightly on the cheek.

Danny put his index finger to his closed lips and pulled on her outstretched hands. They moved toward the football field, toward the field house. It was dark now and there were lights over the doors. It must have been the third one he tried, when it surprisingly opened. He pulled her in fast, backed her gently against the painted concrete block wall, lifted her hands above her head pinning them against the wall, and moved his whole body against hers and kissed her open mouth. He moved his tongue to where her lips closed at the right cheek, playfully forcing an opening. She permitted the slightest penetration and then closed down on his tongue, moving her lips backwards and forwards. He covered her neck from the earlobe to the top of her breast with small lip bites, ever so small but wet.

They dropped to their knees on the thick cushioned pad used for wrestling. He unbuttoned her blouse, and she withdrew it from her skirt. He fumbled for the clasp of her brassiere. Smiling, she pushed his hand away and unlocked the hold. And she lay back on the mat, waiting for him. He pushed the skirt above the knees as she arched her back and pulled her panties down her legs. He removed them and felt her wetness. He touched her wetness with his forefinger, and she moaned softly.

Neither was able to restrain themselves once he had entered into her. His face carried the mark of her fingernails. She was not a virgin. She closed her eyes. The fire and warmth and the glow faded. She now could feel the weight of his body. She looked up and saw the ceiling of the barren gymnasium, illuminated only by the exit lights. Then she experienced the sensation of cool dampness covering her body, especially between her thighs. She had a feeling of nakedness. They uncoupled. She sat up, crossing her arms over her chest. They looked at each other and smiled.

It was in early November, and Danny and Lil had taken the bus over to Columbus, spending the greater part of the weekend in a downtown hotel room. Danny had only awakened. Looking up, he saw her cuddled in an upholstered chair, covered by her terry cloth robe, backed up to a hissing steam radiator, reading.

"Sleepy head, did you dream of me?" she quipped.

"I didn't know where the hell I was. What time is it?" Danny asked.

"Time to go out and get something to eat, and then its back to bed, lover boy," she laughed as she slammed the book shut and jumped upon the bed, pulling away the covers and tickling his exposed body. He squirmed, grabbed the bedspread to cover him, and pleaded, "Five more minutes, Lil, please, I'm tired. No more now."

After her shower and while dressing, she asked Danny if he was going home for Thanksgiving. He had thought about it but dismissed the idea, not enough time, and after seeing the folks for a few hours, what was there to do there? But he answered, "I haven't thought about it. I have classes on Wednesday afternoon. Maybe I'll stick around and study, it would be quiet."

"Come home with me, Danny. I told my parents I was going to invite you. They want to meet you."

"I don't know, Lil. What have you told them about me?" beginning to feel uneasy with the whole topic.

"Why, of course, I told them you are my lover, we have sex every night and twice on Sunday, that I have lost ten pounds." Noticing his face tightening and reddening, she jumped on the bed, kissed him, and laughingly said, "Silly. I told them you were a dear, handsome, clean-cut student back from the war."

"Did you tell them my name?" was his rather searching response, which came out rather sternly.

"Of course, Danny, what's wrong with that?"

"And what was their reaction?" he inquired.

"I've told you. They want you to come. They want to meet you. Don't worry, there is no commitment involved. We're friends. My folks have met all my close friends."

"The fella on active duty in the Far East, too?" Danny wanted to know.

"Yes, him, too. So can I tell them you're coming, Danny?"

He didn't answer. He rolled off the bed, away from her outstretched hands, darted into the bathroom, and started the shower. As she dried his back, she asked again, "Shall I tell them you are coming, Danny? Please."

"Who else will be there, Lil, a house full?"

"About twelve or fifteen; grandmother, an uncle and some cousins. No colored, no Indians, no Japs. All white Christians, all Protestants. Some drink. Most all will sip wine. Anything else bothering you, Daniel?"

Nothing more was said until the following Tuesday as they were walking down the hill from class. "Danny, are you coming? I have to know I promised Mother I would call her tonight. I want you to come."

"How will we get there?" he parried.

She was encouraged. "Dad can come and pick us up, or we can take a bus." Still resisting, Danny wanted to know how long the bus ride was. "Three hours, Danny. You can read all the way. I promise I won't touch or bother you in any way. I'll sit in another row, if you want."

"Do we have to stay all weekend? Can we come back on Saturday?" Danny wanted to know.

"Yes, dear Danny, we can leave sooner if you so desire. Come in with me while I call."

Chapter XXVI

Danny wrote a short note to Mama and Papa that, with only one day off and so much work to do, he did not have enough time for Thanksgiving. He would expect to be home for some time at Christmas.

He enjoyed the bus trip. So much farm land, cleared by the fall harvest, barren, breathing, broken, recouping, resting, waiting for the warmth of spring, drying, fertilized and seeded for another season. The towns were clean, quiet, and peaceful. Lillian was becoming excited, she wiped the moisture from the windowpane as the bus pulled into the depot, like a little girl with her nose against the candy store window. She was looking to see if someone was there waiting. She expected to be met, she wanted them to be there. Someone.

"You'll like them, Danny, I know," she smiled, comforting to both of them.

"It's too late now, Lil, there's no turning back," and he patted her on the head.

Daddy met them. They shook hands. "Welcome, Dan; Lillian has told us so much about you."

"How do you do, sir, thank you for having me," Danny answered.

They drove about a mile out of the built-up area of the center of town, slowing as they drove into a complex of Tudor houses, six, or seven, terminating in a cul-de-sac. The home was two-storied, of brick veneer, prosperous in tone and outside fixtures.

Danny liked Lillian's mother, she was matronly, but attractive, the apron wrapped around a body that seemed to be firm. Her handshake was of a lady, well bred, and her face appeared younger than her age. She seemed so many years younger than Mama, and she probably weighed fifty pounds less. "Come in, Daniel, welcome. Lillian will show you to your room," as she moved them from the entrance hall toward the staircase leading to the second floor.

Lillian's older sister, Abigail (Abby), a graduate student at the University, married to a third-year law student, was descending as he and Lil moved up to their rooms. After introductions, Abby laughingly scolded them for being late and urged them to hurry so that they could all have a leisurely cocktail before dinner. "Don't change. You both look beautiful, just wash your hands. Josh and Betty should be in the parlor before you come down, hurry."

Josh was a thirty-year old image of Mr. Foster, not yet grayed, not yet broadened by the foods and liquors of good living. The smile was the same as his father. Betty, his wife, was soft and quiet, unremarkable. As he took Danny's extended hand, he asked what he was drinking, and Danny asked for a Scotch and soda. Lil had sometime mentioned that "Daddy always drank Scotch."

While Josh and Lil retired somewhere to fix the drinks, Betty inquired about school and how he liked their part of the country. Not being sure of the purpose of the question, Danny answered with a smile, "Maybe for the first time, one of my decisions was right, the school belongs in this environment, and I belong in the school."

After handing Danny his drink, Josh pointed to his sister. "Has the brat been any problem?" Before she could react, he put his arm over her shoulder and pulled her into his embrace.

Janice and her husband, Monty, evidently had stopped in the pantry before marching into the living room with glasses in their hands. Janice was the oldest Foster. Her husband was in the business with her daddy. They would all be there tomorrow, too. Thanksgiving dinner, together with Lil's grandparents — the Fosters and the Smiths.

Surprisingly, it was not a quiet table. Many were talking at the same time with their neighbors on either side and across the table. It was not loud, but lively, conversational in tone. And mostly about business with the end of the war, a non-war economy will fuel a boom in housing. And furniture would be needed to fill all those rooms. And Foster Furniture would share in the prosperity. The mood was good.

Danny didn't eat much. He listened. He said little and nodded often, and was relieved when dinner was over. The evening became bearable when Lil suggested a walk around the compound. And he relaxed, no need to be on guard, pretending to be attentive to be responsive. The fresh, brisk outdoors made him smile as Lil hooked her arm through his. He went to his room early.

The next morning, he and Lil walked the two blocks to the First Presbyterian Church for Thanksgiving services. During the service most eyes in the congregation focused on Lil's male guest. They walked back to the Foster home after being introduced to the minister.

It was a traditional dinner, turkey and all the trimmings. Grandfather Foster gave thanks. Again, Danny said little, ate sparingly, and again only sipped his wine. He had difficulty sitting in one position. He squirmed. Lil reached under the table to grasp his sweaty palm. She knew how to calm him. Grandfather Foster was overheard to say to his wife, "that is a 'thoughtful' young man."

Danny wanted to return to school Friday. Lil agreed that she would return with him on Saturday, a compromise. "The family expected us to stay until Sunday, they all like you, Danny," she argued. He shrugged his shoulders. She pinched his arm and whispered, "We could stop off in Columbus and spend the night there, rest up for school," she joked.

Mr. Foster drove him to the store on Friday. It was downtown, encompassing a whole city block, and the display rooms were surprisingly large. Mr. Foster proudly exhibited the lines of furniture and household accessories, all that a well-groomed house should be dressed in.

"We're servicing six counties with about three-quarters of a million people," Mr. Foster volunteered, in anticipation of Danny's questioning such a large operation in the medium-sized community. "We're the regional headquarters for all of the major name-brand merchandise, and we wholesale some to smaller outlets throughout the area, too. We handle office and school furniture for the area, too. A big business. We have seventy-five or eighty people working for us, about two-thirds in sales," the proud entrepreneur explained.

Danny had lunch with Josh and his dad at their club, where most of the talk centered on golf. Danny would only say that his experience in the sport had been limited. The truth was that he had never held a club in his hand. "You're going to have to spend more time at it, Danny, it's good for the health and not too bad for business," Mr. Foster chided.

"Next Spring, you'll have to come on down and play," Josh chimed in.

Danny liked what he saw; he was affected. Now he thought he understood the meaning of the word "solid". All was on a solid foundation — the family, the business, and their acceptability in the community. Maybe that's what is meant by "getting to the table first." Papa had come too late, certainly for himself, but how about him and Armando? Sal and Sis were committed for this life. Certainly, if there were a door opened here, it would be like skipping a generation or two; the future would be advanced.

The excitation of those feelings began slipping as he thought of The Avenue, his family, and his friend, Frankie. Too much impedimenta; too much baggage; too many barriers. How would Mama and Papa fit in, the country club wedding reception, dinner, two worlds, and never the twain shall meet? Papa with the linen napkin stuck in the collar of his shirt, slurping the soup. And dear Mama trying to converse with Mrs. Foster. No way! He could not tell the Fosters that his parents did not exist. And Frankie was his buddy, but he could not be his best man. Frankie had plenty of furniture, but not the kind sold at Fosters. Frankie would know how to wear a tuxedo, but he would never leave the big stogies at home. And being a businessman, Frankie conceivably could plan for an expansion of his territory. And they were all businessmen. Now how would Frankie explain his business to Mr. Foster?

"Yeah, well, we is a service organization, we do things for people," Frankie would explain.

"You're consultants, then, Mr. Collizio," Mr. Foster would try to help.

"Yeah, people come to us before they do anything. We work with unions and companies, too."

The polite gentlemanly Mr. Foster would nod, and conclude with, "Yes, yes, I understand, rather interesting concept."

"Younz have any trouble with the union, the Teamsters? If you do, call me. I know them people, I can help."

"No problems, sir, our employees are like family, they don't want unions", Josh would chime in.

"You guys is lucky. If any of those characters try to organize you, let me know," Frankie would answer.

What a scenario. The Fosters would either have Lil back out, have the marriage annulled, or disinherit the poor child.

His ruminations on the possibility of skipping several generations of growing pains by jumping into a Foster Furniture bed were almost completely shattered when Mr. Foster asked, "And what is your Dad's business, Daniel?"

"Well, Dad," (the first time he had ever used the word in referring to Papa) "works for the Pennsylvania Railroad, freight expediter at the company's largest transfer center." That was really bad, too much, thought Danny. Now I know they should never meet. Papa expedited freight all right; he pushed it from one boxcar to another on a four-wheeled pushcart. The pushers were more obedient, somewhat more intelligent, and did not require the personal care as the donkeys that formerly had been used.

Having to wait two and one-half hours for the bus from Columbus to the college was reason enough to stay the night at the hotel. Lil was more anxious than Danny was; there had been no touching from the time of their arrival at the Fosters until they climbed back on the bus. Lil had been a lady throughout, modesty, virtue, pure and platonic. But as soon as he bolted the door to their room, she undressed. Over her head went the dress and slip, stockings were rolled down to her ankles and kicked off. When he came out of the bathroom, Lil was clad only in her panties and bra. She had become a trampolinist, jumping higher and higher on the firm mattress, up to the ceiling. And she laughed, high-pitched noises that bounced off the walls. Released. She was free. He watched in amazement, and smiled. She tore off the bra and pulled off her panties, throwing them in Danny's face as he was taking off his trousers.

There was no talking. They did not seem to be able to break away from one another. They were wet, from the fluids of their sex organs, and from general perspiration. They melded together, holding on tighter, closer. It must have been three hours later when he awoke, thirsty. He was cold, wrapping himself in the bed cover. Lil was wrapped in the bed sheet, only her head and face showing, a beautiful mummy, sleeping, and she began to shiver as she awakened. Lil reached for his blanket; he pushed her away, holding on to the warmth he had captured.

"Danny, please, I'm cold — I'm hungry, too," she pleaded.

"You're dirty, too. Get up, go take a shower, little girl."

"Don't you 'little girl' me, Mr. Castel Forte, I proved to you I am a mature young lady, knowing all about birds and bees."

Christmas vacation, what in the hell was he going to do? Mama was expecting him. Frankie had talked to Sal, who informed Danny that Frankie was expecting to see him. Lil wanted to know his plans.

"What I'd like to do is go some place warm, Florida, and sit and read for a couple of weeks," was his non-committal answer to Lil. Pressured for an answer, he told her he would spend the first five days — Wednesday, day before Christmas, until the following Tuesday — with his family, and he could meet Lil at her home for New Year's activities until the following Sunday.

Christmas Eve and Christmas day, Danny was at home, only family.

Danny attended Christmas Mass with Sis and Armando, Mama and Papa stayed home. He was recognized and greeted by many that he had not seen for years. Amy appeared overjoyed to see him and wanted a firm commitment of when he was going to visit.

Friday, before noon, he walked the two blocks to the flats. It was good to see Amy. They walked over to the playground. The Clubyard landscape was not physically inviting, the frozen crust had captured the dirt and debris that had floated freely in the neighborhood before the temperature had fallen. Arm in arm it was warm, though; and remembering the hot summers, shirtless, running the bases, seemed to raise the temperature above the dampness and coldness of the sunless afternoon.

Wanting to see Frankie, but not wanting to be alone with him, he asked Amy if she would have dinner on Saturday. A night on The Avenue, dinner at Dino's, and then maybe some dancing at one of the after-hours clubs. She was a little surprised about the dinner plans, but posed no argument. Frankie was planning dinner, but wanted to know if they were eating alone and then doing the town. After Danny advised him that Amy would be his guest, Frankie decided to bring Emma. On reflection, Frankie said, "Good idea. I should take the old lady out once in awhile, she'd like that."

Danny had not been explicit about the dinner plans. Amy was surprised when they were escorted to the table where Frankie and his wife were seated. The ladies knew each other. Emma was older and now a mother of a six-month old boy.

There were too many conversational lulls during dinner. There was no talk about the future, nothing about Frankie's work. Emma would only remark how lovely Amy looked.

Frankie pressed Danny about his wounds and school. Danny would only say he was completely healed, and college was going well. Frankie told how he had applied for and received his honorable discharge from the Coast Guard immediately after victory in Europe. "I did my duty, it's in the record." Emma never stopped smiling, but said little. About ten o'clock, she suggested that Frankie take her home. The baby had a cold and slight fever, and she had been up half of the night. No one seemed to want to keep the talks going. Amy and Emma kissed, and Frankie drove Emma home.

Amy and Danny were having cognac when Amy remarked, "You didn't tell me we were dining with Frankie and Emma. She's nice. You're not getting mixed up with him, are you Danny?"

"Amy, I thought I told you we were dining with them. I was committed to meet with him. Frankly, I did not want to be alone with him. Does that answer all your questions, sweet one?" Danny answered.

"Are we to be stuck with him all night?" Amy asked. "I wanted some time with you, Danny."

Frankie returned sooner than they expected, and drove them to the Algonquin Club, about two miles from where The Avenue merged into the established business district.

Frankie was joined by a friend, introduced as Patti Turner; blonde, comely, shapely and tall, almost as tall as Frankie. And her legs came almost up to her armpits. Surprisingly, she was well spoken, and she appeared to have a genuine affection for Frankie. She touched his arm when she spoke; she rested her head on his shoulder as they danced.

Amy admitted that she liked Patti, but wanted to know if they could get off by themselves. She wanted to talk, she was anxious to discuss something important to her. Frankie evidently overheard a remark, or saw it in her eyes.

"You guys look pretty serious, like maybe you want to be alone and talk, or whatever. I know what. We got a private room down the hallway, with some comfortable chairs and lounges. And all you do is pull a chord and someone will come in and get you whatever you want."

Amy reddened. "Frankie, you don't miss anything, do you. I haven't seen Danny for such a long time, and I do want to chat with him. You're a dear." And she pulled on Danny's arm, as the waiter, in response to Frankie's call, escorted them to the private suite.

The room was gracious. There was a fireplace, unlighted. They sat on a couch, and Danny smiled, took her hands, squeezed, and said, "Talk."

"Kiss me first." she said, as she rested her head on the back of the soft lounge.

He did, strongly, and held on for what seemed many minutes. When he released her, she smiled, pleased.

"I like your way of talking, there would never be wars if people would all talk that way. Is it what you call 'sex talk'?" and he bit her right ear lobe.

"I only wanted to forewarn you. I'm serious."

Danny kissed her again, and holding her face between his hands, asked, "I wonder if this couch is wide enough so we can make out."

"I'm ready, Danny-boy, but first, we have to talk."

Danny laughed, "Hopefully, I'll have the correct answers. Shoot."

"I guess I've got a confession to make. I've been seeing a guy, rather steadily, you know, a couple or three times a week. He's nice, says he loves me, works at Westinghouse as a technician since he returned from the war. Wants to give me a ring and then marriage. He was in high school with us, a year ahead, Al Runco."

Danny looked down, then facing her he said he remembered Al. He understood now. She wanted to know his plans. But avoiding what seemed to be a pointed inquiry, Danny asked, "Dear one, how do you feel about this man, other than he's a nice guy? Do you want to marry him? Do you want him to father your children?"

Following his lead, Amy softly asked, "What are your plans, Danny? Are you coming back to the city after college? Is there anyone else in your life, someone you're committed to?"

Silence. Touching of hands. Awkwardness. As if in quick sand, he feared any movement. Any commitment in any direction could be disastrous. He had been caught, embarrassingly, with no answers. Much later, he recognized how adroitly she had handled the situation; she had landed him on the distant shore and rowed away with the only boat.

She pushed, "We're old friends, Danny, level with me."

Flushed into the open, he responded slowly, unevenly, humbly submitting. I don't know where I'm headed, except I won't return to live on The Avenue or anywhere in the city. I don't know where I want to live. And I don't know what I'll eventually do. I know I don't own a damned thing now," and he stopped suddenly. He could see her eyes clearly, they were moist, and the brightness had faded.

With a lugubrious sigh, she said, "I'm so happy you're not going to tie in with our host, that would hurt more than anything, Danny. Tell me, is there anyone you are serious with?"

"I know a girl, she seems interested, serious. My answer would be the same to her. There would be too many bridges to cross to reach her, just friends, nothing spelling 'commitment', purely platonic".

And now he was burdened and his whole demeanor changed. Not only had he been less than frank, but he was not being faithful to their friendship. He didn't tell her about the change of his name. He had boxed himself in, trapped in a corner. So he pushed her down so she was prone, looking up at him. He kissed her hungrily. Her disappointment was evident, her understanding of his response was patently clear. They would remain friends, acquaintances, without attachments.

"We had better go out front, Danny, we should dance, you know. Let me stop in the ladies' room and fix this face. Wait for me. We'll go out together."

And so it was. So it would be for them. A fixed face. The appearance of togetherness, a dance, separation. In retrospect, it could have been fulfilling, but maybe it would have been too comfortable, self-defeating, a violation of the Arab saying, "Never be too happy". The goodnight kiss was only that.

Frankie's driver delivered them to her door. He could see the liquid in the eyes swim down to the hinges of her eyelids, swell, and erupt on her cheeks, then slide inside her cheekbone to the extremes of her closed lips. He kissed her wetness and shadowed his face as in sorrow. Another link with The Avenue had been severed. Frankie's driver returned him to the club.

To Frankie, he continued his game, everything was well, the school and the people.

Frankie's response had not changed or matured since the advent of the war. "Yeah, yeah, it looks good in school, it's all make-believe there, fairyland. Believe me, Danny, nothin's changed. I was here all during the war. The slobs, that's us, was needed. But when the danger is over, everything goes back to where it was before."

"There have been some changes, Frankie, I've seen them."

"No, no, Danny. You remember the State Senator, Susan's old man? Well, he got caught with some of his friends chiseling Uncle Sam on some defense contracts during the war. We had to go to bat for them, talk to one of our judge friends. But, you think he'd let his daughter marry me, or even you? Fuck, No! They got it locked up, same as usual, and it's gonna stay that way. Stay home where you belong, Danny. Nobody'll hurt you here."

Frankie paused, sipped on his brandy, held up his hand, and continued, "And that Amy. She's one nice girl. Emma knows her good, and likes her. Finish school and come home. We need smart people. We is growing, too."

Danny listened, reflecting on Frankie's arguments. He thought of Mama and Papa, he could help them while they could still enjoy. But he had seen and smelled the air out there, it appeared cleaner, and it smelled so much better. Finishing his education, obtaining a college degree, and with the change of name, he might pass. The outsiders need not ever know about The Avenue. All other things being equal, he could compete. He did it in the Army.

Frankie was watching him intently, and thinking, too.

"One more thing, Danny. In the Army, the government says everyone is the same, is equal. And in college, everyone wants to seem educated, so they're nice. It makes them feel good to think everyone belongs to the same class. It ain't so. I know what you're thinking about those buddies during the war and your classmates now. Them are all masks they're wearing, and when the show is over, you see the real faces."

Danny could wait no longer. He had to interrupt.

"Frankie, old buddy, you're right. You make sense. But I have to chance it. I must go. I have to see if I can get into the main ballroom; and then I have to see if I can dance with them and keep in step. I want to compete and I want to know if I can effectively compete with them."

"Danny, Danny. Sure, you're as smart, if not smarter than many of them, and I know you're good, better than they are. But that don't matter. You gotta be a member of the club, or you don't get in. Hell, it's like our organization. We just don't let anybody come in. We wouldn't want any of them birds, too many squealers. We're choosy, too. We only want our kind. They are no different. Capice, Donato?"

"I'm going to try, Frankie. I just have to. If it doesn't work, I'll know soon after I get out of school. Then we'll see."

"Basta. Enough, Danny. We have one more drink. We go downstairs for steam bath and shower, then breakfast, if you want. And if you feel like it, a nice girl, too. Whatta ya say?"

"Frankie, you're beautiful, and I owe you. I have to think. So, I'm going to walk home, down The Avenue. I always remember walking away from The Avenue toward Cooper's Hall and the library, uptown. The sun is coming up. I want to see The Avenue with the first touch of light, people should be going to church, dressed up for Mass. Thanks, old buddy. I won't forget."

Frankie remained seated, and his only remark was, "You know where we are, we'll always be here, and if there is anything we can ever do, you call. OK."

Chapter XXVII

The second semester of the school year passed quickly, uneventfully, and almost happily. Lil was available and surprisingly compliant. She hinted at a fixed, persisting and permanent relationship. Danny coasted.

They spent the long July 4th weekend with her folks. They talked about the family business, but no pressures. Her folks seemed to understand. Danny wanted out of school as soon as possible, maybe he could go home for Labor Day.

It must have been sometime in August. Lil and Danny had gone to the hotel in the city for the weekend. They were in bed, naked under the sheet, after an afternoon of laziness and sex and drowsiness. He told Lil about his name change. Danny explained it would be easier for future employers to handle the surname.

She was playing with the hair on Danny's chest, turning it in her index finger, kissing him where she had made the curls. "Danny, what did your mother and dad say about the name change?"

Danny was surprised by the question, he half-way sat up, and riposted, "No problems, they understood." Danny had not told his family. The opportunity had not arisen for he had not been home since the court decree, and there was no way he could spell it out in a letter so that they would understand, would not be hurt.

Lil snuggled closer, laying her head on his lap, and innocently asked, "When are you going to take me home to visit your mom and dad?" There was no immediate response, so Lil flirtingly followed up with, "Don't you think they'll like me, Danny? I don't look too bad, and I promise I'll behave."

Danny had anticipated such a request but had never formulated an answer acceptable to him. So he lowered his head and kissed her, laid prone and took her in his arms. He said nothing. He touched and petted and kissed her face and body. Satisfied, they fell asleep.

Danny did not return home during the Labor Day weekend. He called Mama. The studies were overwhelming. He needed to finish in May; he had to devote the free time to preparing for exams. Danny was not uncomfortable with those untruths, he was becoming more forgiving to himself. He did not think about it too much. Of greater concern was what he was going to do after graduation. And Lil. Where did she fit? And he had other excuses, so he never made it home for Thanksgiving either. Lil now had her own automobile, and so they drove to the Fosters on Thanksgiving eve.

Driving back to Columbus Saturday night, Lillian talked about how good it had been to be with him and her family on the holiday.

"Danny, Father asked why we didn't go to your parents' home on some of the holidays."

"And what did you tell him?" was Danny's immediate response.

"Well, that you had limited free-time; you wanted to finish school as soon as possible, and you wanted to spend more time with me too."

"And what else did you tell him about us?"

"Well I did tell him that you had your name legally changed to 'Daniel P. Castle'. Wouldn't Lillian Eloise Castle sound grand daddy?"

"And what did your daddy have to say about that, Lil?"

"He only smiled Danny, then he said, 'how would you like it Lillian?'"

Danny did return home, to The Avenue, to visit his family for three days at Christmas. The headlines in the local papers were bold and appeared heavier than usual, they were black. "Cantangelo Dies, Local Hood Moves Up." It was not unusual to extra the death of a monarch in Europe or a President in the United States. But in such political jurisdictions there were established rules of succession. However, the mob had never published the names of its leaders nor proclaimed its line of succession. Evidently, those tapped were solemnly and secretly anointed. A position had opened up. The Boss had died, the under boss, second in command, was moving up, so said the press, and a lieutenant was to be promoted to under boss. And Frankie, the headlines shouted, the local hood, had been elevated to the rank of Lieutenant, with responsibilities that encompassed more than the city. Frankie in the big time. And his picture, a photo that obviously came from a police blotter, was dark and menacing. The true bright peach color of his cheeks and the redness in his hair did not penetrate the ink black of the newsprint. It was a picture of a hood, a modern mobster, and a transplant from the Southern Mediterranean, Italy, not the descendant from the likes of the merry band from Sherwood Forest. Unidentified, confidential sources were attributed as authority for the story. Danny believed the story, although he also knew that the press had no source; it was speculation. It had guessed correctly, however.

Danny had an inside source, Frankie. Danny had seen Frankie on The Avenue at Christmas. They had a few moments together for a drink at Dino's. Frankie would only say that everything was "going good". He would like to help Danny. He suggested that soon he would be in a position to not only recommend personnel, but to pick and choose people.

"Hell, Danny, maybe we'll be graduating from two different schools at the same time." He continued, "Maybe I ain't saying it right, but a promotion is like a graduation, you're moving up and ahead. Don't you think so, Danny?"

Danny nodded ever so slightly, but made no comment. Laughingly, Frankie spouted, "You gonna send me one of your resumes, Danny?" Danny only smiled.

The article confirmed that Frankie was climbing up the ladder. Some day, under-boss, and, if he should live so long without being jailed or killed, Capo.

Chapter XXVIII

Danny returned to school. The resume had been reviewed and approved by Professor Morrison, the emphasis on his military career, his grades in high school and college, his espousal of the republican representative system of government in his statement of principles. It made sense in those days. The "Iron Curtain" had descended, the world was divided, red or near red was bad in business, liberal thoughts and Democrats were aliens in the community of those who controlled the machines that produced the products that filled the shelves.

His first interview was with Amcan Corporation, a leading manufacturer, and marketer of high-quality, branded bakery and associated products. Flour for home baking and the commercial baking industry, quality-baked goods and vegetables, processed foods. It also was an industry leader in feed ingredients. It commanded a great deal of shelf space in the grocery markets of the country. Almost every bakery used its flour. It was "establishment". Its officers and members of the board of directors were of the mainstream. And this was where Danny wanted to swim.

And everything began to open. Spring began early. The crocuses and tulips bloomed early; the robins arrived before that.

There were no pressures from home, Lillian was easy, and school was no longer a chore. Learning was becoming enjoyable. He was confident of an offer from Amcan.

He was studying in the dorm before Easter break, before the exams, when he was summoned to the front desk, a long-distance call. He expected that it was Lillian, expecting an answer to her invitation for the long weekend at the Foster compound. He was bright and breezy and alive, and ready to confirm the arrangement. He heard the "hello". It was not Lillian. It was a voice he recognized, and his mood darkened. How in the hell did he get this number?

"Hello, is that you, Danny? It's me, Frankie," was all the caller said before Danny, cupping his right hand over the mouth piece, extra softly, said, "Give me your number, I'll have to call you back. Too many people around here." Danny pocketed the number and walked into town, got change from the laundromat moneychanger, and strolled toward the public phone. He did not call immediately. He sat, thinking that surely Frankie's phones were tapped. Should he return the call, confirming an association, a relationship? Would it really make any difference if the authorities had traced the original call? If he didn't call, Frankie could make other efforts to call. No, he had better call back, find out what in the hell he wanted, not say too much, and make no commitments to him.

He was able to get through, and Frankie answered. "Hey, kid, sorry to bother you, but wanted to know how you're doing. What's up? I might have to come to Columbus day after Easter, some business. Maybe we can meet. Your brother said you weren't coming home for Easter, so I asked him for your number."

"Gee, Frankie, I'm sorry but I won't be in town. I promised to visit at the home of a school friend. I wish I would have known sooner, I could have canceled. It's too late now. I'm hoping to come home later. Why don't I call you then?"

"Sure, sure, kid. Nothin' special. Just wanna see you, talk a little. No big deal."

"Frankie, I have to run, three people are waiting for the phone. Be in touch."

He hung up, and then called Lillian at work. "Lil, I've cleared my calendar and the weekend sounds good. When will you pick me up?"

And the weekend went well. Golf lessons and some playing time, food and rest, and nice talk. Mr. Foster wanted to know if he had been offered a position with Amcan. He inferred he had been contacted by one of the vice presidents, that he had recommended Danny, suggesting that Fosters would offer him a position in their sales and marketing department if Danny wanted to associate with a smaller concern, concluding with, "We would be glad to have you, Danny."

"Thank you so much, Mr. Foster, for the recommendation. It is kind and generous of you to ask me to work with your company. At this moment, I'm not sure what I should do. I know I want to be in sales. And so far, my interest has been to become involved with a company that has a large, inventory of products and services. A broad range of techniques not connected to one product or line. I want to learn to market and sell anything. I want to master the principles before I become engaged in promoting a specific. I hope you understand, sir."

"Your approach is understandable, Danny. You evidently have dwelled on it for some time, and that's good."

In May, Amcan offered Danny a management trainee job in marketing and sales. He accepted. Danny was to train and initially serve in the Columbus area. And that was good. Good starting salary and a company automobile. He called Mama, who was pleased, but who really was more interested in when he was coming home. "Donato, everybody wants to see you, everybody aska about you." Sis wanted to know about graduation. She and Mama would like to attend; Sal and Didi would drive them.

"Well, Sis, graduations aren't a big occasion here. I'm going to start work even before school ends, the job is more important than the ceremony." If he could do both, he'd let them know. "Please explain it to Mama. I'm sure you understand. I'll call as soon as the dates are definite."

It would have been nice, but it would never have worked. Lillian and her family would be in the audience. He was not prepared for such a meeting. So he called Mr. Piper at Amcan. "Yes sir, my exams end on Friday, May 7th. I can report, as you suggested, on Monday, the 10th. Yes sir, it's good that it works out for the company schedule and me. No sir, no inconvenience. Thank you, Mr. Piper."

"Danny, I'm disappointed. Graduation ceremonies are important. And I planned on attending. Mother and Dad were expecting an invitation, too. They certainly can excuse you for one day. The training schedule can't be so rigid or so punctual. I'll bet Daddy could get you the day off." was Lillian's response when Danny informed her that he was not participating in the graduation rites.

"Please, Lil. I don't want an out. I want no special treatment. I must make it on my own. You and I can go down for the weekend and meet with our friends. You understand, don't you?"

"I guess I do, Danny, but bend a little. How about your family, weren't they planning to see their Danny boy graduate?"

Danny's only response was, "They understood".

It was a short letter home, to Mama and Papa. "You cannot imagine how good a year it has been. School, now graduation, and a good job with a big company."

Danny wrote to his parents as he would have written to Miss B, Peter, or Mrs. Kingsley. Not that someone else might see the letter, but letter writing was the mark of the educated. And he wanted them to appreciate his status.

"I can't afford to miss the start of their Management Trainee Program. It could be several months before another session. Amcan is such an outstanding company, a huge conglomerate that includes food, household products, and pharmaceuticals. Thanks for all your encouragement and your help. We shall plan a celebration as soon as my training program is completed in the fall. I am not sure where I shall be assigned after completing my training, but it should be in this general section of the country for a period of time. Please give my love to the family. Tell Armando to keep up the good work in school. Maybe he can come out to visit me this summer."

Danny was excused Friday at noon so he could attend the ceremonies that afternoon. Lillian reported that she had arranged for a bed for him at the SAE's, she would be staying at the KKG house. The parties would be many during the weekend. She was happy to be with him, and he needed a cheerleader in the audience when he accepted the diploma. She pleaded that he participate, she arranged for the cap and gown, and he marched to the podium. Lillian took his photo shaking hands with President Lewis. Hopefully, a copy would never reach his family.

They dined, danced, and partied until late. They walked the campus, found the gymnasium door open and made love in remembrance of that first time. She was in love, Danny enjoyed making love, making her love him, making her enjoy loving him.

It was Sunday afternoon and hot outdoors. They had bid their good-byes and were driving back to the city.

"It was a beautiful weekend, Danny. Thank you. Can you spend the night at my place?" Lillian had a two-bedroom apartment, a large living room and complete kitchen. Danny had rented a one-bedroom efficiency.

"I'd better not, Lil, we have a big day tomorrow. And I do have a great deal of reading to do. I am so happy you twisted my arm and made me participate." He paused, looking at Lillian, he smiled, adding, "And more importantly I shall never forget you, without you being with me all the way, it would not have happened."

"Thanks. But, hell, it sounds almost like a farewell speech. What about us, Danny? We've finished school, I'm working, and your career has started. And we're paying rents on two apartments."

"I'm not going anywhere, Lillian dear, except back to the apartment. Say, are you suggesting that we move into your apartment and live in sin?" Danny laughed.

"Not a bad try, Danny, but neither the Foster clan nor the protector of the Protestant ministry, Mr. Mercer of the First Presbyterian Church, would permit such blasphemy. They both preach marriage. And I would wager that even Mr. Piper of Amcam would take exception. I dare say his disapproval could take the form of more than a reprimand."

"You're right, as usual. So we continue to pay rent on our respective places, and enjoy each other on weekends."

And she laughed. "Maybe you should become a lawyer, nay, a politician. What a way you have to avoid answering a simple and direct question. Shall we ever marry?" She was resolved to know. Serious and staid. She gave the impression he had been trifling, if not thoughtless. It had come out, unplanned, and she was prepared to see it through. And Danny, confronted, recognized that flippancy or pertness would not carry this day. She would no longer accept flirtatious colloquy.

"Lillian, I would certainly hope so." He truthfully added, "I have never thought of marriage except with you. But you should know by now that I can't bring myself to take such a step unless I can afford it."

Lillian smiled broadly. "That's a start, Danny boy, but not the response I had hoped for. What is there to afford? The father of the bride pays for the wedding, I have a great big apartment, and at least big enough for two and we are both employed. What's the problem?"

"Too many to enumerate, Lil. Let me start with the fact that I do not have enough money to buy you an engagement ring. In fact, tonight I could not buy you a box of Crackerjacks, and if I could, the odds would be that there would be no ring in there as a prize. I suppose by the date of the wedding, I shall have accumulated enough money to rent a tuxedo."

"You need not worry about the ring, Danny. Mother has promised me Grandmother's engagement ring. It's been properly sized, cleaned and mounted for another generation. And we'll save our money for your tux. Anything else?"

Danny turned on the radio. They drove in silence until they approached the diner where they could have a malt and hamburger and french fries. He tried to verbalize the anticipations of the coming week. Lil munched on the burger. She was smiling. The waitress, while removing the remnants of cold fries and edges of the hamburger rolls, casually remarked, "Anything else, sir?" Danny put on his serious face, looked at Lil, and politely said, "Yes, one box of Crackerjacks, please."

As he opened the door to the car for her, he heard her cuss, the first time. "You're a bastard, but I love you," and she kissed his surprised lips.

The three months of training were the best. He was more at ease during that period than any other comparable period of time during his life. For the first time he indulged himself into believing that he fit, he could compete. He was good in the classroom, active in discussion groups, and was making acquaintances. The management team appeared impressed. He and Lil double-dated with some of his fellow trainees, and thus he was talking with other women, friends and wives of his fellow employees. So he was examining Lil, critically comparing her with the others. Lil was mentally sharp, incisive, and knowledgeable. And the Foster family was too solid, too much to pass on, too much to pass over. As the training period came to an end, she wanted to talk more about marriage. Lillian pointed out that the family would expect a period of formal engagement, and she began pressing for a visit to Pittsburgh to meet Danny's family. The training schedule was his excuse.

"Danny, I'll come with you to Pittsburgh. I can invite them personally to the wedding. Can we do that?"

And Danny would excuse himself; he could always fashion a reason why he had to terminate the conversation. And he wondered. Did he really need Lil anymore? Did he really want her? And especially, did he want to tie himself into a knot that would become more restrictive with the passage of time? Lillian was the only woman he had known so intimately for such a long period. Amy was as a sister, with whom there could be no future. They had come from the same mold. Miss B had been an adolescent adventure, educationally, sexually and mentally. She had been good to him, but now they could only be friends. She knew from where he came. Susan had been enjoyable, recreational weekends. But he realized that he had not arrived, that the position was not a guarantee to any further upward movement. He would need extra assistance, more help to climb up the ladder now that he had moved on to the first rung. So he had to continue his courtship with Lillian. She was in love, so the affair would continue.

Danny had made a decision. He knew now what his approach would be to the ultimate question as to whether they would wed, rather than when. It was a gamble. He could be alone by evening, if he had misjudged her; he would have to live the beginning of his career alone, unsupported.

They were sitting on the carpeted floor, backs against the couch, looking through the plate glass window into the courtyard of the complex, as Danny started to speak, softly, solemnly, but not funereal.

"Lil, you have meant so much to me. You mean so much to me now, and I want it to go on, forever. I want to marry you. The only problem is I'm afraid of a formal ceremony; you know the church and country club scene with lots of people. I want you Lil, I need you, but going through such a trial would make me a coward. I'd run at the last moment."

Lillian rose, walked across the room, looked out the window, and fitted her bottom in the small rocker she had transported from home. She rocked, smiled benignly, clasped her hands.

"That's a hell of a proposal, Danny. I need you, I want you, and I'll marry you, but not at home before family and friends. Do you know a local Justice of the Peace, or do we drive over to Pennsylvania where there is no waiting period? We can drive over the state line and be back for dinner, and honeymoon in the apartment before nightfall. Not expensive. But what the hell, the result is the same. The knot would be tied, and we would be one."

"Strong, Lil, but not like you. Try to see it from my point of view. My career is only starting. I have no money. I don't know how to explain it, but I'd have a hard time living with myself."

Quickly Lillian responded, "And you might also find it difficult living with me after that. Is that what you're saying, Danny?"

"I want to marry you, Lil, but I can't do it your way. After the training program, and before I start working, let's drive down to Tennessee, or Maryland, marry, honeymoon in some mountain retreat for a few days, and then shout it to the whole world, 'we're married.' I can explain it to your mother and father. Please try to understand, Lil."

"And what about your family? Are they going to be happy? They enjoy big weddings, too."

His only comment was, "They'll understand."

"I'm going for another walk, Danny. Alone."

He did absolutely nothing while she was gone. No thoughts, no planning. His mind was on hold. There was nothing coming in, nothing going out. The brain was muted, not even registering the passage of time.

Then he heard the door slam, and "Did you sleep well, Danny?"

"No sleep, Lil. Did you have a good walk?"

"No, not really, but it served its purpose. I know what I want to do. I really love you, Danny, and I want to be your wife. That's my honest and selfish side. So I can resolve my disappointment about no church and reception. But the family is where I have a problem. However, here is a partial solution, a reception at the Club or at the compound after we announce it to the world."

Danny said nothing. She could not tell from looking at him what his reaction would be. So, after a few moments, Lil continued, "Don't worry, Danny, it will work out. Do I tell my parents before we go, or on our return. I would prefer telling Mother before, and why. Otherwise, she might think that I'm pregnant."

She walked behind him, put her arms around his neck, and whispered, "You won't be sorry, Danny. I'll make you happy, my sad little boy."

Chapter XXIX

They drove, but only to the mountains in western Pennsylvania to a cozy inn. The round Justice of the Peace, who looked more like a small-town undertaker, and the wife, thin and severely creased by time, performed the rites and executed the documents. Knowing their clientele, they did not prolong the ritual.

Lillian telephoned her mother. "Mother, I am so happy. Thank you for your understanding of why we did it this way. Yes, two weeks from last Saturday will be splendid for the party at the club. Of course, I'll discuss it with him. Of course, Mother. Danny, Mother wants to speak with you."

Danny took the phone, wondering only how he would address this new relative — Mother or Mrs. Foster. He could not recall her first name. "Is this the mother of my beautiful bride? Thank you so much. I'll make her happy. Thank you so much for everything."

It must have gone well. Lillian put her arms around his shoulder, kissing the side of his neck and biting an earlobe.

They remained at the inn longer than she expected. She wanted to leave on Saturday to stop in Pittsburgh to meet his family. Danny delayed, wanting to hike further into the mountains, spending all Saturday afternoon exploring a streamed rushing toward the river from the mountains. He showed interest in the trees, plants and flowers. It was a part of Danny she had not known, and she admired his interest. But a suspicion, like a storm behind a dark cloud, was beginning to move into the heavens, which she believed she had only recently ascended. When she again suggested stopping to see his family as they passed south of the city on Sunday afternoon, Danny said there was not time enough. They both had to work on Monday; he wanted to be ready. Besides, he wanted a leisurely evening with her. She touched his right hand, then squeezed it, and agreed, but repeated, "When are you going to call your folks? I want to talk to them, to invite them to our reception."

And Danny's only remark was, "Lil, I can't wait to start tomorrow."

She mentioned it again during the middle of the week while he was completing a daily report of his calls. He pleaded for time to complete the reports, which would be needed in the morning. She became pacified when he told her they would spend their first week-end as husband and wife with her parents.

It was festive, and her family was genuinely pleased, but disappointed in missing the wedding celebration, but looking forward to the reception at the club. It had been a first in the family, an elopement.

Mr. Foster was gracious, putting on the appearance of total acceptance, making the best of the situation. The toast, "to our loved ones", made Danny regret the decision to marry now, or, perhaps, the decision not to marry publicly. He maintained the air of the little boy who had been caught ransacking the candy jar, the crime forgiven, but not forgotten.

It must have been during coffee when Mr. Foster asked Danny, "And how did your parents react to the announcement, or had they been forewarned, also."

"They were disappointed, of course. They have known about Lil, but I must admit that I did not tell them about the marriage. They are Catholic, Mr. Foster, and marriage outside the church is not easily understood."

Mrs. Foster, obviously wanting to recast the mood and brighten the discussion, chirped in, "They'll change their minds when they meet Lillian at the reception. We shall make them happy with the union. We shall like each other, you two love each other so much. Danny, your parents can stay with us, or, if they would rather, we can arrange for a suite at the hotel."

No one spoke. All eyes were turned toward Danny. Center stage. The audience waited. Lillian was actually staring at him. He lowered his head, almost as if in prayer and spoke deliberately, "My family will be unable to attend. They are committed and expected at a church retreat in upstate New York that's been in the planning stage for almost a year. So the party will have to be a Foster party. We can make some other arrangements later. Frankly, the church bit is a problem, too."

Lillian whispered, "Danny, why didn't you tell me? I should have known".

And before he could answer, Mr. Foster spoke again. "We're truly sorry, Danny. I assure you we shall do it again, when they will be available. We cannot, without much discomfort, cancel or postpone the club date."

"Of course not, sir. I am not sure when a date can be arranged. Maybe a get-together with just the two families would be the best," Danny struggled to temporize.

The reception went well. Lillian was proud at Danny's side, arm through his arm, smiling and appropriately blushing. The Fosters appeared satisfied. Danny's explanation of why his family was not present became more plausible as he repeated the explanation he had offered to the Fosters. Lillian had rehearsed the reasons why the marriage had not been formal. With her contemporary female friends, she assured them she was not pregnant. Because of Danny's schedule, they were unable to honeymoon in the Islands.

It was late that night, or early that morning, having satisfied their sexual appetites, Lillian, with her head across his naked chest, asked again, "Danny, when am I to meet your parents? I should know who are going to be the paternal grandparents of our children."

And so now he understood why there had not been that forceful objection to the quick marriage. She thought she was with child, she had an appointment with a doctor the following week. Danny should not have been surprised. He had never used any protection, and when he thought about it, he had assumed she had. The word "diaphragm" had been spoken once, he thought. And now the only words that flashed on his screen were, "trapped", "locked in", and "permanently committed". Danny kissed her opened mouth, touched her flat stomach, and asked, "Any problems?"

"None, Danny, no aches or pains."

It had to have been almost six weeks later. He called from a roadside phone to the public telephone at the corner on The Avenue. It was monitored twenty-four hours a day by one of Frankie's boys. He mentioned his name and the call number, and hung up. Frankie called within three minutes. "Danny, my boy, how in the hell are you? Everything OK? Need anything?"

"Frankie, I'm working for Amcam, love it. And I was married a couple of months ago. Great girl I met in college, fine family."

Frankie interrupted, and Danny laughingly answered, "She is an American, Foster is the name, furniture business. No big wedding, old buddy, or you would have been invited. We decided to run off and do it alone, without fanfare, no fuss, and no bother.

And, of course, her family was disappointed. My folks, well, frankly, that is why I'm calling, old buddy."

There was a pause. And Frankie's only response was, "I never heard nothing on The Avenue. I see Sal walking by the Corner, but he never said nothin. So, anyhow, I owe you a wedding present. Whatta you want or need? Anything."

"Frankie, I would like to reserve some rooms at the Valley Club for my family — Mama and Papa, Sal and Didi, and Armand, and, of course, a suite for me and Lillian. A get-together; a place where Lillian can meet the family. You understand. There would be no room at home. We need room, and someplace nice. We have to get together, the family and my new family."

"Hey, hey, stop it a minute. You don't need to explain nothin. It's all set. The least I can do. Tell me when."

"Probably, the weekend after next. After checking with Sal, I'll let you know."

"Good. Maybe I can be there, too", was Frankie's response.

Lillian was excited, but puzzled why they were not meeting in the city, was satisfied with his explanation that it was equal distance for both, and the family needed a holiday. And then Lillian pressed, "Talk to me about them, Danny. Describe them. Will they like me? Am I too fat?"

"You're most beautiful, and they'll love you. It's a great spot, set in a valley, a clean river running through it. It's owned by a boyhood friend. You'll like Frankie. He'll be there if he doesn't have to be out of town."

Lillian loved the approach to the valley. Danny planned to arrive well before the meeting time at five p.m. He wanted her to see the grounds, familiarize herself with the layout, and become engrossed with the beauty of the complex. And the suite of two bedrooms, a living room almost as large as their three-room apartment, kitchenette and a complete bar caused her to shake her head, dance from room to room, take Danny by the hand and pull him toward the bed. "Easy, silly little girl. Let me get the luggage in from the car. Relax and prepare."

Sex was good. Lillian seemed to want to hold on forever. Danny mentally postponed the family meeting. And that was good. He had over-rehearsed the introductions he proposed. They had showered, dressed, and he was examining the contents of the bar when the chimes announced a caller.

Frankie and Danny shook hands and hugged. "Lillian, this is my best friend, Frankie Collizio. He owns it all. We started grade school together. Frankie, this is my wife, Lillian."

Lillian extended her right hand. Frankie seemed momentarily confused as to what to do. He kissed her hand, like in the movies. "Is everything all right?" was his first remark.

Lillian responded, "Everything! The grounds, the rooms, and the services are outstanding. And we do thank you".

And there was another ring. Frankie opened the door to a waiter with a cart with silver service, and a bucket with a champagne bottle. Frankie toasted the couple, and "the baby, too," then reddened, wondering if he should have disclosed what Danny might have told him in secrecy. They touched glasses. Frankie reported that the family was meeting at 6:30 p.m. in a special dining room, a room set-aside exclusively for the reunion.

Mama and Papa were seated on an amber-colored settee, Sal and Didi were having their drinks mixed, and Armand was drinking out of a Coca-Cola bottle when Danny and Lillian walked into the reserved dining room. Mama and Papa started to rise as they approached. Danny motioned them down, and they responded immediately.

"Mama, Papa, this is Lillian, my wife," Danny said. Lillian was great. She bent over, kissed Mama on the right cheek, smiled, and spoke a "Hello, Mama." She took Papa's right hand and started shaking it. Papa tried getting up, but stopped as she kissed his cheek, too, and said, "It's so nice to meet you, Mr. Castle," having forgotten Danny's former surname.

And before any further conversation, Armand came charging across the room and rushed into Danny's outstretched arms. They hugged, and Armand blushed and tried to hide behind Danny as Lillian, trying to kiss his cheek, missed and lightly brushed her lips across his neck.

Didi was most beautiful as she said hello. Sal shook her hand with a "Glad to meet you."

Dinner went surprisingly well. Mama smiled constantly, ate sparingly, and nodded in response to questions proposed by Lillian. Her longest oral statement was, "Donato, you wife is so pretty." Lillian blushed.

Papa ate slowly, perhaps for the first time in his life. There was no hurry here. The slower, the less mistakes. But Papa could not refrain from being the gentleman. To Lillian he asked, "Donato, he treat you right?"

"You have a very talented, handsome and gentlemanly son, Mr. Castle. I love him very much. My family does, too, and we shall all have to meet very soon."

And so it went through to the lunch period the next day. The family was returning after lunch. Danny and Lillian promised to have dinner with Frankie. Mama never stopped smiling, her stamp of approval. "Donato find a nice woman." Lillian responded with an embrace, a kiss, and promises to visit.

Frankie ordered dinner. It was too elaborate. Lillian was awed. Frankie was affected. He was quiet most of the time, about when they were "kids," enduring, making it. Lillian never pursued any leads. It wasn't that she didn't hear the openings. She was content to be there. Her husband was being revealed to her. But in a manner, Frankie was also trying to distance himself from

Danny. Danny was the scholar, the war hero, and the reader of books, ever emphasizing the infrequency of their meetings and association during the past decade. At the same time, Frankie seemed to revel in his own unsophistication. But he could not disguise his brightness or success, or power. It was demonstrated by the people who served them.

Turning toward Danny, Frankie unexpectedly said, "You did, OK, kid. I must admit, I mighta been wrong about you leaving The Avenue. You're going to make it fine, especially now you have such a beautiful bride. You come here anytime you want, whenever you want to get away." And he was more than pleased when Lillian kissed him on the cheek at the parking lot before they drove away.

Lillian wanted to talk as they drove home, and she did, exploring the depth of his silence. "Danny, your family, I loved them. Your mother is so sweet, so innocent. What a smile. Armand is almost as handsome as you. We must have them meet my family. Didi is a beauty, as you told me she would be."

There was no comment from Danny. He seemed to be totally focused on the road ahead, and reacted abruptly when Lillian wanted to know about Frankie's business. "He owns the complex we stayed in this weekend," was his curt reply.

Lillian remained silent for several miles. Touching Danny on the arm, she asked, "Are you ever going to take me to see The Avenue, the Clubyard, Cooper's Hall? I would like to see that part of your life, too, Danny. Please."

"There will be a time. When you know me better, then you will better appreciate The Avenue."

Chapter XXX

Their first son was born in June 1949. The child seemed happy to be in the world; sleeping and eating with a regularity that appeared to have been pre- set. He weighed more than eight pounds at birth, twenty-two inches in length, and a voice more baritone than tenor. Danny suggested to Lillian that she name the child. She wanted him named Daniel, Jr., he vetoed that. She then tried "Donato", and he walked out of the hospital room. When he returned that evening, she told him the story of her great uncle on her Mother's side — Chumley Powers, a frontier lawyer, educated in England. "How about 'Chumley Powers Castle', is that too much for the little guy?" she asked him. Continuing, she said, "At least he shall have the same middle initial as you".

"Fine with me, if you think he can handle it when he goes to school, 'Chum' will be his nickname, for sure."

"Say, Danny, your middle initial — what does it stand for, what is your middle name?"

"No name, just an initial."

And the next two came regularly, twelve and sixteen months apart, and were named Emily and Bradford. Anthony arrived three years after Brad. At thirty, Lillian's trust kicked in, so they were able to purchase a five-bedroom house in the suburbs. Danny was promoted to the position of Area Sales Manager; Lillian finished her master's requirements, but continued her schooling for a Ph.D. The Foster family had a large cottage on Lake Erie, and August was vacation month. Danny had not been to Pittsburgh in two years. Lillian had never visited The Avenue, and his family had never been to the near Midwest.

Chumley was now almost six, and Danny was spending some time with his salesmen in the eastern part of the state, when he detoured and stopped for lunch at Frankie's place. He was not recognized, but when he inquired about Frankie, the waiter walked away and a well-dressed man in a tailored business suit approached. Danny recognized the face, but could not find the name to match; he was an Avenue boy grown up and dressed up like in the real world.

"May I help you, sir," he said as he approached the table.

"I'm a friend of Frankie's, we went to school together, grew up on The Avenue. My name is Danny Castle. And you — the face is familiar, but the name escapes me."

"Nils DeLuca, I lived in the Flats."

"Of course, I know your brother, Joe. How is he? We went to high school together," Danny followed up.

"Joe's married, works on the railroad like my father, lives in the Flats, and has a nice boy. I'll tell Frankie you're here."

Frankie was broader, heavier and his smile was wider. His arms were spread as he advanced across the floor toward Danny's table. He was redder, too. And his embrace was stronger and more positive.

After talking family and kids, Frankie wanted to know about Danny's job, and his comments were, "Not too bad, buddy, but you never gonna get rich that way, but I guess your old lady's family got lots of that old loot. No kidding, Danny, why don't you start your own company, food wholesaler. I'll help. You know the route now. You could make a hundred G's a year. I can help you get started if you need a loan. Think about it. We got contacts where you can get stuff, and people who'll want to buy from you."

Danny made no comment, except, "I love your food." He was enjoying his lunch — minestrone, pasta cooked in tomato sauce with squid, and a salad like Mama used to make. Danny asked no questions of Frankie. It was obvious he was still in command there, how far from the top was only speculation. The newspapers say he was No. 3 in the area.

"Stay the weekend, Danny. I won't go to the city. We can relax and tell lies about the good old days. And maybe we can find some bunnies, whatta you say? Tell the old lady you gotta big deal down this way on Monday, no use going home and having to drive back Sunday night. Anyhow, your customer wants you for dinner Saturday night."

Danny rationalized, he could use a free weekend. It had been almost six years since he had been away from his family for any period. A long weekend would be good for him, and Lillian, too. He had been taking himself too seriously, and it would provide him an opportunity to think anew about starting his own business.

He called Lillian. "Lil, there is an opportunity to meet with a big client on Monday, and maybe play golf with him on Saturday. It would not make sense to come back tonight and return next week. Can you do without me, handle that gang of ours? How are they?"

"If it's important, Danny, it makes sense. Where are you staying, if I have to reach you?" It was unemotional and almost unconcerned.

Danny interrupted, "Are you alright, Lil?"

"I'm fine, maybe a little tired. Chumley was in a fight at school and I had to pick him up. He claimed it was the other boy who started it. He's not hurt, except maybe his ego. He may be a bully, and he met a kid who was not scared off. I'll be glad when I can get back to school full time. Where can I reach you, Danny?"

"Oh, I stopped at Frankie's place for lunch. The client is down the road and we met for lunch. He wanted to know if I could visit his stores in the valley on Monday. He wants to play golf on Saturday with a couple of his managers." He read off the phone number.

"Is Frankie there? Have you seen him?" Lillian asked, after recording the number.

"He came by as we were having lunch. I haven't had an opportunity to talk to him, other than to say hello. I'll call you tomorrow. Give the kids hugs and kisses from me. Be home on Monday night."

He asked Frankie if he could have a room, he wanted to talk to Herb Williams, his client, who owned about seven stores in the valley. Frankie raised his hand and a well-dressed man approached. "John Ricardi, this is a close friend, a real buddy, Daniel Castle. Get him a suite. He'll be our guest for the weekend. Have one of the boys take his bags up. Give him your keys Danny."

Danny excused himself to change. But he only sat in the overstuffed lounge chair. He could not explain to himself what he was doing in this room. He should be in his car on the way home. What the hell was he thinking? Maybe he should call for his car, make an excuse that one of the children had become ill or fallen. Another lie. And the weekend had not started. He had to make a call to Mr. Williams and make an appointment for Monday, and maybe golf tomorrow, or call for his car. Indifferently, he tossed a coin. Mr. Williams was in the office and suggested a game in the morning. So he was committed. Danny changed, took a golf cart, and went out to the practice area. He hit balls and perspired and forgot about his telephone call to Lillian. Frankie drove out in his cart and challenged him to play nine. It was easy. And he welcomed the gin and vodka, and the second one, too. He agreed to have Frankie's masseur work on him before dinner. It was while on the table and almost asleep that he heard Frankie say, "You wanna have some company for dinner, Danny?"

"What? Who?" Danny said as he turned on his side.

"I gotta surprise, Danny. She was playing golf this morning. I told her you were here for the weekend. She wants to see you. She'll come for dinner."

"Who in the hell are you talking about, Frankie? You're goofy."

"Oh, hell, I forgot to tell you. It's Susan. She's now living with her family down the road. She's got two kids, three and seven, divorced about a year. Her blueblood ex liked the juice too much, and young gals, too. I had to stop his line of credit here. The Senator suggested it. I don't know where the hell he is now."

"Susan. You have to be kidding. What does she look like?" was Danny's answer.

"Danny, she is a beaut, prettier, more classy, really. Let me call her. We're only talking dinner and maybe a little casino playing afterwards. Whatever you wanna do."

She did look good. Beautiful, in fact. Her gown was almost white; her skin was brown, tanned evenly. The make-up accentuated the brown of her skin and the white of her dress. She looked like a lady should. She looked like she belonged. The girlishness was gone. Danny almost forgot to rise, he looked too long, too intently.

Her hands were extended; he took them, squeezed gently, moved back, smiled fully, and put his arms around her and kissed her cheek. "You are so beautiful. The time in between has been so good to you. Thanks for coming," were the only remarks Danny could express as they continued to hold hands.

"You guys going to stand all night looking at each other? Sit down so we can have a drink," called out Frankie. They laughed. Danny moved her chair out and they sat and took each other's hand, not moving their eyes from one another. The champagne cocktail glasses were touched, the contents sipped, their eyes riveted on the face of the other, looking for blemishes justifying the passage of time. He could find none.

Again, it was Frankie who broke the reverie. "You guys gonna ignore me all night? If you do, I ain't gonna spring for dinner."

Dancing closely, Danny whispered, "Can you stay the evening? I can't permit you to leave. Please."

"I don't know, Danny. I would love to, but the sitter is a teenager and her Daddy is going to pick her up at eleven. Mother and Dad were going out to the club. I'll try to make some arrangements for tomorrow night. I could never walk into the house tomorrow morning in this evening gown. Maybe we can examine your suite before I leave. Let's dance now. It feels so good you holding me, Danny."

After dinner, they excused themselves "to take a walk around the grounds." The walk was of short duration and was directly toward Danny's suite off the swimming pool.

"Please, Susan, let me undress you. I want to touch every part of you. I want to untie, unzip, loosen and kiss. I want to do it slowly."

The unraveling ended and she lay back on the bed and watched as he undressed. No hurry. He laid beside her, touching the hinges of her mouth with the tip of his tongue. He kissed her closed eyelids, the tip of her nose, and the bottom of her earlobes. Then the breast and the valley between those hardening mounds. Her stomach was still firm and the loins were inviting as he trespassed with touching. Time was eternity. There was no conversation, no noises. And he was in her for such a long time, prolonging it to the abyss, then the explosion and implosion that rocketed them beyond their experiences. The throbbing continued after they had ceased movement. Their lips met softly and Danny rolled off and they turned to each other.

Susan was the first to speak. "I never wanted anyone else."

Danny had lunch and played golf with Herb Williams and two of his managers. It went well, and the meeting was confirmed for Monday. In the nineteenth hole, he called Lillian, related the outcome of the golf game, and remarked that he missed her, and asked that she kiss the kids for him.

Susan had left a message; she could not meet him for dinner. She was eating with the children and her folks, but could meet him at the club at about nine, and could spend the night. She was going to be out with one of her "girlfriends".

Herb and the boys didn't leave until seven thirty; too many post-mortems, too many martinis. Danny had played better than usual, below his handicap, but not well enough to beat Williams. Danny lost thirty-six dollars.

Danny and Susan gambled and danced until about one a.m. before they retired. Not to sleep, but to live the night in knowing more about each other. They explored, and found pleasures they had never experienced before. And they slept deeply and into the morning after the sun arose, and they had to try again, never wanting to forget the pleasures of their being together, being one.

The conference with Herb went well. Danny was surprised, alarmed, and then pleased when Williams talked about Frankie. Herb acknowledged him as a golfing buddy, a friend. "I understand you and Frankie grew up in the same neighborhood in the city. Fun guy. Competitive bastard, though."

It was almost a formality. Twenty-six stores which now would be served exclusively by Amcam, through Danny. He enjoyed the drive home. It was good to keep within the speed limit. He was enjoying being alone, relishing the weekend. Satisfied with the business he acquired. And Susan was everything one could want in a woman friend. The office would surely congratulate him for the new business, the Williams empire had always been out of the company's reach.

And then he thought about Lillian. This was his first transgression since their marriage. He did not feel evil. He almost concluded it was his right, he had earned the interlude. So he prepared himself for the meeting. It had to be just right. Not too condescending, not too compensating, not overly 'hubby'. Do it as being away on an overnight business trip. He smiled. Tired, but glad to be home. A kiss to the lips and maybe a pat on the bum. Then a roll on the carpeted floor with the kids. How was he going to handle the bedroom scene after the children were bedded down? Maybe she could not, that sickness which could be a blessing. He certainly could not plead he was too tired. He was not in a mood to foment a confrontation.

He and Lil decided to have a drink after the children had quieted. They were sitting on the couch and she moved closer, snuggling, as he related his winning the Williams account. She was warm and wanted him to touch her. He talked on. Lillian finally put her arms around him. "Let's bathe and go to the bedroom, the children are sound asleep. I missed you so much, Danny."

She insisted on showering with him. She soaped his body, all of it. She handed him another bar of soap, and so he washed her breasts, the back of her rump. Danny slid his soapy fingers between her legs and she kissed his neck.

She was over-anxious in bed. He played with her, faking enthusiasm. And she made love. Danny rolled off and was almost asleep as he turned his head away from her.

Danny made four trips to the valley in the succeeding five weeks, to solidify his relationship with the new account, the

Williams stores. The golf and dinners provided the personal cement, which locked in his largest single account. But he was spending more time with Frankie; golfing and gambling. And he was meeting Susan almost every evening he was at the valley.

Frankie continued talking about Danny going it alone. "You got Williams, Danny, and I betcha you could keep most of your other accounts, too. And I can help. You'd make more dough and be your own boss. You gotta make a decision. I kinda spoke to Herb Williams. He likes you, and if you got an organization, he'd go along. You'll need an office, sure, and some start-up dough. We know a good management consultant in Pittsburgh. Go for it, kid, you only live once. Go for the brass ring."

"Frankie, it sounds great, but I'm satisfied. Everything is going so good. The house mortgage is shrinking. And the bank account creeps upward. The kids are growing up, Lillian is finishing her education and should end up with a Ph.D. Lil's family is helping with the extras for schooling for the kids, and their clothing."

"Get real, kiddo. Nothing stays the same forever, and with all that security what the fuck you got to worry about. If it don't work, you can always go to work for her family. You could even work for me, for the organization. I always told you that. Did you ever talk to Lillian about it — about starting your own business?"

"Hell, no, why the hell should I? I've never even thought about it myself. Forget it now, Frankie, let me think about it some more. Let's go out and play nine holes."

That night he had dinner with Susan. And he talked about the concept. Her reactions were neutral. But in bed that night, after they had satisfied each other, she appeared more positive with the query, "Why not try it, Danny. Thinking about it, I like the idea. Being your own boss, maybe I could see you more often. That I would like," and she laughed and tickled him and rubbed the sensitive areas.

Lillian was unimpressed, not in opposition, but inclined to favor stability. And Danny jumped on her opting for the safety umbrella of Amcam. "Don't you believe I can do it? Don't you have faith in your husband? Are the Fosters the only entrepreneurs?"

"Danny, you're being unfair, you know I'll go along with whatever makes you happy. I would rather have you home more often. We should be spending more time with the kids, and I believe Amcam will give us more leisure time. But, darling, the decision is yours."

Chapter XXXI

Castle Enterprises, Inc., came into being six months later. Two salesmen from Amcam joined the firm. The office manager was a bright young lady out of business school at State. And all of Danny's accounts stayed. New ones inquired and came aboard, maybe pushed aboard, as he later discovered, when referred by Frankie. And Castle Enterprises had the exclusive distribution rights of pure Italian olive oils and imported pastas in the area between Pittsburgh and Chicago on the north, and the Ohio River on the south. Danny traveled throughout the area. He was gone most of the week, and several weekends a month, spending more time with Susan than with his family.

When Danny was in town, he worked late, and usually Darlene Jensen would have dinner with him. He decided she needed a larger apartment, and her salary was raised accordingly. Darlene seemed concerned about his long hours at work, the strain of decisions made and to be made, and she caressed his brow and massaged his neck. Danny stayed overnight when he had too many martinis. She fell in love with the boss. He taught her about sex, and she wanted him even more. The twenty-five-year disparity in age was no barrier. She spoiled him. She cried alone when he was gone for long weekends at the valley. She sensed that there had to be another woman there.

Lillian also knew that he was no longer hers alone, but she no longer missed him, no longer waited for his calls no longer asked where he had been. She made all the decisions at home. Chumley and Emily were in private school. Lillian was teaching and thinking of becoming more involved in academia. She attended the theater and occasionally was escorted by a graduate student.

Danny was spending the weekend at the valley. He had not been there for several weeks, and had not seen Frankie for two months. Frankie had been away in the city. Susan was continuing to meet him. But Danny also knew she was seeing an old college buddy, a friend of the family from home, divorced for two years. Roger's family owned the majority of the stock of the First National Bank. He was in banking and golf, and martinis. He played a better game of golf than Danny, but he was only a "so-so" lover, Susan quipped late one night after too much drinking.

It was at dinner that Friday night that he remarked that he had not seen Frankie for some time.

"Don't you know? He may have some problems, your old buddy," Susan said.

Casually, and only to make conversation, Danny retorted, "Working too hard? The pressure of the job too much?"

"Danny, Frankie could be heading for jail."

"What in the hell are you talking about, Susan? That's not a joking matter."

"Danny, your friend has been indicted by a federal grand jury, refusing to talk to the Crime Committee of the House. He took the 5th Amendment. You knew that, didn't you? It's been in the papers here for the past couple of weeks. Surely, Frankie must have talked to you about it."

Danny didn't respond. He took a deliberately long drink.

"The answer is 'no' to your questions. I told you, I haven't seen him for months. I haven't talked to him and I haven't seen the papers of this area for months. Where is he now?"

"Father said he's in the city awaiting the hearings. Father doesn't believe he'll cooperate — he's tight lipped — so he'll end up going to jail for a few years. You know he won't talk. Are you going to try to reach him, maybe go to the city and see him?"

Again, Danny cuddled his glass too long, held it to his lips too long, and took a long drink before he responded.

"What did they want to know?"

"Danny, don't give me that. You know damned well about his business. You know what he does for a living. We've all accepted him and his perks — my father, you Danny boy, and me. He's been good to all of us."

"What the hell can I do?" was Danny's only admission to the truth of her statement.

"Not much, except to let him know you're still friends. A note, a phone call, maybe a visit to the city. You could find him on The Avenue. Yes, I know about The Avenue, too, Danny."

It had been such a long time since Danny had visited the family. A good excuse to be in the area, to get back to The Avenue.

"I'm going home soon, I'll try to get in touch with him." Dinner later that evening was only eating, not much talk. Susan did remark, "You didn't do much better than Roger, dear friend. Was the news about our friend, Frankie, getting to you?"

Danny passed. Susan, once the martinis started flowing, had an oiled tongue, the needle was out, it was sharp, and she was not hesitant about using it. "So he does a few years, probably in one of those federal country club facilities. He can do his job from in there. Even help his friends, Danny. Daddy is unconcerned. He knows Frankie can be reached if necessary. Give him my love,

Danny, if you see him. Tell him I'll still expect the discounts when I come to the valley," she laughed.

The valley was losing its magnetic power. Home. Maybe that's where he should go.

Lillian was not at home. The children were gone, too. He watched television, dozed, and awoke in the dark house, wondering for a moment where he was. He recognized hunger, but found no relief in the refrigerator. Some wilted lettuce, a pepper that had lost its fiber, and a celery stalk that folded in half as he lifted it from the vegetable tray. There was cereal, but no milk. How long had they been gone? He called the Fosters. They were out to dinner at the club with his children. No, Lillian was not with them, was the report from the maid. They were expecting her for lunch the next day. Yes, they were expecting her to drive home after lunch.

Danny then drove the mile to the Pub. Beer and hamburger. He called Darlene, but there was no answer. And he remembered in talking to her on Friday, she said she would visit her family at the lake if he was not coming home for the weekend. It was then that he decided to drive over to the Fosters the next morning. He had not been there all summer. He would surprise them all. Two of the children could drive back with him, the other two with their mother.

The drive was effortless, like the wisps of clouds floating across the sky, aimlessly, without a flight pattern and with varying speeds. He had planned to arrive when they were at church, and he did. He was greeted by the maid, who expressed surprise, no one had told her that he would be there for lunch. But she recovered and assured Danny that she would find a place for him.

Danny parked in the rear and walked to the front porch. It was quiet. The grounds were beautiful, and he sat in the rocker looking out into the beauty of what God did best — the freshness of mid-morning in mid-summer. He heard the cars before he saw them, and he heard the children before the lead automobile pulled up in front of the house. The children saw him before he left the chair, and Anthony yelled, "Daddy, it's Daddy," as he ran up the stairs to be lifted high into the air.

Mother Foster whisked by, only pausing to say, "Hello, have to check with Mabel about lunch."

Mr. Foster stuck out his hand, "Didn't expect you, Dan. Lillian told us you were east on business. She should be here shortly. She and some friends went to the lake for some sailing yesterday."

Chumley was too grown up. "How are you Dad?"

Emily, always open, chipped in with, "A nice surprise, Daddy."

And his buddy, Brad, had to touch, to push up against his leg and await the touch on the head. "I'm glad you're here, Dad."

Lillian didn't arrive until well after lunch. Brad and Anthony were asleep. Chumley and Emily were glancing at the comics while lying on the living room floor. Lillian looked well, bounding up the front steps, saying, "Danny, what a surprise, we didn't expect you until next week."

Someone had delivered her to the door, he saw the sports car drive away. He couldn't see the driver, who appeared to be a man. She told her mother she wasn't hungry; she had eaten a late breakfast. The weekend had been super, she related to Mr. Foster. "The weather was perfect, Daddy, the sun was hot and the wind was anything but calm. *The Sea Winds* handled well."

And he wondered. Everything was in place — the scenery was the same, the players had not changed — but the atmosphere, the ambience had changed. Mr. Foster excused himself with the Sunday paper to read in the library. Mrs. Foster had to check with the kitchen.

Danny spoke softly to Lillian, "Let's take a stroll through the flower garden, I don't want to fall asleep, too." Lillian didn't answer, but stood and started down the stairs, Danny followed. Nothing was said until they reached a wrought iron bench near the rose arbor.

"What time shall we start for home, Lil? Brad and Emily can drive back with me, Chumley and Anthony can go with you. I'm ready to go anytime."

It was several moments before Lillian spoke. He waited. She didn't appear displeased or angry, but she was too self-controlled. Danny retreated into silence. Evidently, his passiveness encouraged her to speak, and she spoke softly, deliberately and calmly. It appeared as though she had rehearsed.

"Do you feel let down, Danny? Consider — your appearance was obviously unexpected by the children, my parents, and me. I had prepared them for your absence, with the magic words, 'away on business, not expected until the middle of next week,' and without a phone call, a notice of any kind, you stroll in awaiting to be fondly embraced."

When had she changed? Her demeanor was unrecognizable; it was too straightforward. He had to respond, but he was cautious.

"The meetings were canceled after I arrived on Friday afternoon. Williams' people had some problems and could not bring the right people down. Mr. Williams was apologetic and had to leave after a drink. Frankie was not there. I came on home and found the house deserted, the kitchen bare, and no note."

Danny paused and looked at Lil to see if the "old magic" was working. It did not appear to be, so he became more aggressive.

"I called your folks, your Mom and Dad and the kids were out to dinner, and you were, quote 'not expected until Sunday noon'."

Danny lowered his head as if hurt, and continued, "Lillian, your delicate and refined needle was recognized and felt."

"It was not my intention to be caustic or sarcastic, Danny. If there was a needle, it was not to hurt, but to awaken." She paused, as if she had taken the wrong road and, realizing her error, turned about. "That could be an untruth, Danny, perhaps I did want to do more than gain your attention, to rankle you. Maybe I wanted to hurt you."

Danny went on the offensive. "What in the hell for, Lil? I work my bottom off day in and day out to support you and the kids. Give me a break. What's turning you around?"

"Danny, you've always been selfish. I recognized and accepted that from the beginning. I loved you. And I ignored all of your evasions, your egoism. I didn't always understand why, but it made no difference, I loved you, Danny. However, it's gone far beyond a preoccupation with yourself and your needs. I cannot and shall not tolerate deceptiveness. You have not been honest."

She paused, and Danny answered, "I don't know what the hell you're talking about. Those psychology courses and readings have stirred up an ant hill of imagined hurts that have been kicked open by an inconsiderate husband who forgot to bring flowers after being away on a trip."

"Danny, please. Don't treat me like a sophomore."

And before she could continue, he responded rather forcefully, "Stop it, Lillian. When have I lied to you?"

"It's not that you deliberately lied. But I have to charge you with duplicity. You never told me the whole truth about Frankie. I now know what he does, how he made his business, or should I say, 'the business'. He is a mobster, a gangster, a damned crook."

Danny gazed at the ground, and folded his clasped hands between his legs, but remained silent.

Lillian raced ahead, knowing that if she stopped, she could not say it all, if ever.

"I read all the newspapers at the University library. I know all about his rise to fame. I'm not suggesting that you were associated with him. I am upset, and justly so, because you never told me."

Lillian rose and moved behind the bench. Danny turned to look up at her.

"You made yourself, me, and our family a part of his world by accepting his hospitality and accepting his friendship. Now, maybe I understand why you'd never permit me to visit The Avenue with you. Frankie probably owns all of The Avenue and most of the people."

And there was silence. Stillness. Danny was stunned. He could not align his defenses, so he struck clumsily. "Lillian, all your waspish prejudices are beginning to show."

No sooner had he finished, Lillian slapped at an overhanging branch of a willow tree shading the bench, narrowly missing Danny's head, and cried out, "Dammit, Danny, that's uncalled for and beneath even you."

Somberly, he answered, "I only found out this weekend. I told you Frankie was not there. Yes, I had heard rumors over the years about his involvement. But I never actually knew. And if he is, he never admitted it to me. We grew up together. What did you want me to do, forget my past?"

Lillian appeared more persistent with her attack. "Your recollections about your past have only been fragmentary, Danny. And I suspect that Susan probably was as much an attraction, an incentive to visit the valley, as was your home-town buddy."

Danny rose. "Are we going home? Which of the children do you want me to take back?"

"Danny, the children and I are going to spend a few more days with my parents. I have some time off from school. I need time alone, to think. I need some support. The environment here will sustain me while I try to think and feel my way through this matter."

"Have you discussed this with your folks, Lillian?"

"No, but they know I'm struggling with a problem, they suspect it's between us. No, I have not discussed Frankie or Susan with them."

"Will you call me when you're coming home?"

"Of course, but it should be some time near the end of the week. Say good-bye to the children before you leave. And if I may suggest, tell them your work calls."

The unraveling had evidently begun. But it was only a single strand, which had become untied. It could be put in place again, or snipped so that the missing thread would not be noticeable. On the journey home, his concern was not for Frankie and his predicament, but its possible affect on him. Perhaps the best course of action was to do nothing. There was nothing he could do which would in any manner relieve Frankie of his problems. Danny had never been intimate with the details of Frankie's position with the "boys", but Danny knew that Frankie was a player in the big league. Danny clung to the premise that all he knew was what was generally "understood" on The Avenue. What everyone knew on The Avenue was based on beliefs passed on by word of mouth, on inferences from associations, from opinions of those who had always lived on The Avenue.

There was nothing, which could implicate him. The only time he had been involved was when they were kids. There were no ties to him, Danny kept persuading his mind to accept. But Danny could have been seen with Frankie during the past several years. They had openly dined, gambled and played golf together. Certainly, Frankie would have been under surveillance during the past several years. They could have been photographed together. But generally there were others in attendance. Mr. Williams had shared time with them. Would Herb Williams now disassociate himself from the whole scene? Would the Williams firm look elsewhere for their supplies? It had become Danny's largest single account, the biggest profit lode. And the Senator, he surely would not step forward and proclaim a friendship.

Danny knew he couldn't write to Frankie, he couldn't say in writing what he could conceivably recite orally, the old buddy ritual. Surely Frankie's telephones had been tapped, especially since he was under indictment, and he wondered how long the tap had been in existence, as he frantically tried to recall when he had telephoned last. And he rationalized, that's all in the past, not much I can do about that, but what in the hell am I to do now? I can't ignore the situation. There may be a time when there could be a need for Frankie or the organization. The righteous and laudable answer would be to contact his friend and offer whatever help he could afford. But that was bullshit, plain and simple. Danny owed Frankie; he had a debt, which was due. Perhaps Danny's silence had been a pre-payment. He must go to the city, to The Avenue, and try to meet with Frankie.

He had not visited his family in some time. He should check in, see how they were doing, see if he could help in any way. And he would walk The Avenue again, by the library and Cooper's Hall. He would stop by and visit Dino, have a drink, pay a call on the Dutchman, inquire about his old friends. And they would surely meet, accidentally on purpose. It would work out. A pal, a school mate from The Avenue would offer to help. To Frankie, he would claim that he had come to ascertain if there was anything he could do, to the world, it was to visit his family.

Driving back to Pittsburgh evoked other remembrances, of Amy. And so he decided to stay at the Benjamin Franklin Hotel downtown, where they knew each other for the first and only time. Remembering only the past, and forgetting the present.

He ordered a cocktail and showered, indecisive about how to spend the evening. Maybe Amy would. But Amy's husband — suppose he answered. Danny called after the second scotch, and she answered, not immediately recognizing his voice, but seemingly elated when he admitted his identity. The lilting tone was still there.

After talk about their families, what else was there to say? Talking to her about Frankie would be strained, an effort, but he had to find an opening. He wanted to know what were the local rumors, the street news.

"Amy, what's happening on The Avenue? Any juicy gossip?"

"The people our age have or are in the process of moving out my way, where the grass is greener and we own our trees. Don't kid with me, Danny that's not what you want to know. Your old buddy, Frankie, will surely be spending some time in jail. You probably know he became a leader, a big shot. When did you talk to him last, Danny?"

Danny hesitated, then speaking slowly, said, "It's been some time since I've seen him," and then defensively, he continued, "I never realized that he had climbed so high up the ladder. Of course, I never was sure what his role was in the organization. I assumed he was just one of the boys, middle management."

He could almost hear her smile. "Tell me, Danny, are you going to see him while you're in town? They don't believe he'll be enjoying the freedom of The Avenue too much longer. The newspapers are of the opinion he'll be gone shortly, and for several years."

"There's some business that I need to take care of, and, of course, I want to see you, Amy, if possible, I must visit with my folks. I wonder what the neighborhood looks like."

She did not pursue it, either she understood his reluctance to answer directly, or that it was unimportant.

"Amy, can you have dinner with me tonight?"

"Sorry, Danny. The family's coming to Grandma's for dinner. Keep in touch, dear friend."

And so he ate alone.

The next day was cloudless, warm and windy as he drove down The Avenue toward the corner. It had changed. There were missing buildings, torn down, only loose bricks and blocks and cement remaining. Like viewing the missing teeth in the mouth of an old person one had not seen for years, the spell of what had been conjured over the intervening years was smashed, the unbroken mirror reflected the image as it was. Without viewing The Avenue again, it would have been consecrated in his mind, a holy place. The pavement was bumpy, patched many times, the gutters were covered with debris, which the shop owners no longer swept or removed. Windows were boarded, vines grew where they were not planted, grass was sparse. And the people walking down The Avenue were older; walking slower with heads looking downward. He saw no young people. There was no running, no shouting across The Avenue.

The house had been repainted again, distinguishing it from its neighbors, seemingly unrelated, yet all had been constructed at about the same time, some sixty-five years ago. The street seemed narrower, too, and had not been swept, except for the seventeen feet fronting the homestead. Papa still collected and removed the dirt from the gutter in front of his house.

Mama and Papa were sitting in the kitchen, both cuddling a cup of coffee in their hands. He walked in, the door was never locked. Mama's face lit up and a "figlio mio" poured forth, it was a joyous cry. If she could sing, she would have been an opera star. The expression was of surprise, with a joyful face, her eyes sparkling. Papa only looked, gaping. Mama stood and rushed to greet him, with tears flowing over the round smooth surface of her cheeks.

There had to be lunch. And questions about Lillian, about the children. How come you never bring them to see us? You got pictures? And Danny talked about how busy he was, Lillian was finishing school, the children were at summer camp. Life was "go, go, and go".

Papa nursed his coffee, saying very little, answering that he was well, and the garden in back kept him busy in the summer. It was harder in the winter, but he did visit The Avenue Social Club, playing some cards. He asked no questions, and seemed to have no interest in extending conversation, or the purpose of the visit. Mama shared some neighborhood gossip. She mentioned Frankie's trouble, and then Papa broke in.

"You keep in touch with your old friend? He going to go to jail, the big shot. It's a good thing you no stay on The Avenue, you be in the same trouble. He never was no good. You still friends?"

"It's been a long time since I've seen him, Papa. I can't remember when. You know how long it's been since I've been home, and I don't know if I saw him then."

Knowing her husband, Mama wanted to change the subject, so she began reciting all the families who had abandoned the neighborhood had moved out to the "country." She was going to die in her house, all her kids were born there. Little Donato, young Danny, who was Sal's boy and Danny's godson, was in summer school. He wanted to graduate early.

"It's stupid", Papa remarked, "He gonna have to go into service. And that fighting in the jungle; for what?"

Danny had not seen his nephew for two years, since young Danny had commenced college. There had been a few letters, several phone calls, Danny had visited him one time. He had grown tall and handsome and strong. And Danny thought, maybe he should stop and see him before he headed home.

Mama told him about Sal and Didi, that they had moved out to suburbia.

"Little Donato's sister is almost big as her Mama. Kids today, they grow like weeds in the garden. I call Salvatore and they come see us. OK?"

"Sure, Mama. I'm staying overnight. I have a room downtown in a hotel."

"You no stay here?" she broke in.

"Mama, I had to meet with some business customers yesterday and needed the room. There's a good chance I may have to see them again tomorrow, so I had to get a room. It's only a twenty-minute drive. We can all eat together tonight."

Danny was becoming uncomfortable and distressed. He had to get out. "Mama, I'm going for a walk down to the Clubyard, and then to The Avenue. I want to see what it looks like now. It's been such a long time. I need to get some fresh air. I'll be back in an hour or so."

He stopped at the corner. There were three men talking, but they were strangers, new arrivals, he was sure by their clothes and the cut of their hair. They spoke Italian only. None belonged to his generation, nor even the generation that followed.

There were three or four beer drinkers at the bar at Dino's. They stared. He recalled the faces, but not the names. Dino's son, Richie, came over. "Can I help you?"

"I used to live in the neighborhood and I was just looking for a face I know. And I know who you are; you look so much like your father. Incidentally, where is your old man? My name is Danny."

"Papa is down The Avenue at the Dutchman's, giving business to our competitor. Do you want me to call him?"

"No, no," Danny responded quickly. "I'll walk down there. Thanks."

There were more people in the Dutchman's Grille, the Dutchman's retired cronies, and twenty years older than Danny. They were seated at tables near the bar where the aproned

Dutchman was presiding. The apron rested higher on his stomach, which seemed to have grown more inches than the number of years, which had passed since Danny's last visit.

"Hey, Danny, good to see you. How is the world out there? How is it treating you?" He smiled. "Dammit, you look good. What can I get you? We got everything, even Scotch, Haig and Haig Pinch Bottle."

Dutchman, other than being stouter, looked good. "Is Frankie around?"

The Dutchman affectionately patted his ample lower chest, looked about the room, and speaking softly, almost whispering, stated, "He'll be here in half an hour. He wants to see you."

"Come off of it, Dutch, he doesn't know I'm in town. I only got in last night; stayed downtown. You mean you put a call in to him already?" was Danny's retort.

"No, not me, Danny. I don't call him; he calls me. And he knows every damned thing that happens in this burg, especially The Avenue. Nobody comes in or goes out that he don't know how and why. Capice?"

Danny, in fact, everyone in the bar, knew he was coming before he walked in. Two heavies, young, big and stern looking, and well dressed Spartans moved in, circulated throughout the joint, opening and closing all the doors to the restrooms, the kitchen and the cellar. No one spoke. Even the cigarette smoke seemed to hang listlessly, not moving, waiting for a command to continue its normal course. All talking had ceased, no one was even bringing a glass to their lips. The Dutchman did not remove the cigar from his mouth, but he had stopped puffing. On a signal from the taller of the two, the other tough moved toward the door, looked back and raised his arm upward. Within moments, Frankie had come striding through the door, preceded by large and determined men, and followed by two older and slower-moving men.

"Hello, Dutch, we got ourselves a visitor, a stranger from that world out there. He don't look like he comes from Mars, he ain't green; he ain't black neither, so he don't come from Africa. He ain't no foreigner, he dresses too good. Who is this mug anyway?" as he opened his arms to gather in and hold the standing Danny. They embraced, and Frankie led him to the private dining room, shouting over his shoulder, "Hey, Dutch, how about some coffee and those fancy pastries, and some Anisetta."

"Danny, you look like a fucking million bucks. Everything gotta be a hundred percent. Don't lie to me, you got the whole world by the nuts," Frankie spoke as he directed Danny to the table with the linen tablecloth, napkins, and silver ware.

"Everything's fine with me, Frankie. How about you? It seems you got some problems. The papers, they're roasting you good." Frankie raised his hand as Dutch and a couple of his lads came in with the coffee, trays of cookies, and the bottle.

"Now you don't got to worry about me. Everything's gonna be OK. Probably do some time. Maybe it'll be good, a vacation from everything. Sure, it'll be a little bother, but nothin I can't handle."

With such an attitude, Danny decided he could reach out more than he had expected. Seizing the moment, Danny, in a hushed and confidential tone, said, "Is there anything I can do, Frankie?"

And he was relieved as Frankie unhesitatingly patted his hand and said, "Nah, kid, everything's taken care of. But I appreciate you're wanting to help. You'se is a good boy, Danny, and I won't forget you neither. And I wancha to know if there's anything you need while I'm gone, talk to the Dutchman. Somebody will contact you. Now, one more drink, then I gotta go." All the words that Danny wanted to hear.

As they downed their shots of liquor, Frankie said, "Salute, per cento anno."

Danny, wishing to show he understood, said, "Frankie, I'm all for good health, but a hundred years would be too much. I hope to see you soon, buddy." And as he stood to shake hands, Frankie embraced him and kissed him on both cheeks.

Mama and Papa had fallen asleep in the living room, Mama on the sofa, Papa in the easy chair. He called the SAE house at the University, and left word for young Danny to have dinner with him at the hotel at about seven, to call and leave word if he could not make it. He had not seen him for such a long time.

Danny sat on the front porch until his parents woke. He wished that he could sleep. He had had several drinks, but it was not enough to close his eyes or his mind. One wondered if he had made any progress from the days when he played hockey with the smashed vegetable can as the puck, and the broken broom handle stick, slashing, kicking and pushing the can from the gutter through the sprawled legs of the goalie. Maybe it would have been better if he had stayed put. Maybe it would have been better if he had never found the opening when he fell through the ice on Beaver Lake, or had died with the others at the Rapido. The folks would have collected the ten thousand dollars from the GI insurance, and with that money they could have moved out of the neighborhood. Papa would have had a large vegetable garden in the summer time with lots of tomato and pepper plants.

It was easier excusing himself from dinner when he told them that young Danny was meeting him at the hotel for supper. They were pleased, they were concerned about their grandson, he was going to have to go into the Army, and there was that "stupido" war in Vietnam. Danny promised he would be back soon, a longer visit, when he would have more time to spend with them.

Chapter XXXII

He had finished showering and was watching the news when the phone rang; Danny could meet him about seven for dinner.

Young Danny had matured physically; he was about six feet two inches tall, with dark hair and broad shoulders. He looked solid. His pre-law studies would not defer him from active duty, nor would they alter his infantry classification in the Reserve Officers' Training Corp.

"Seriously, Uncle Dan, I believe I'm looking forward to a tour of duty in 'Nam'," was his opening remark after Danny initiated the discussion of what's after graduation.

Danny explained, "I report to Fort Bragg, North Carolina, two weeks after finishing school, then a six weeks training course for newly commissioned second lieutenants, and then the Far East."

The uncle looked into his glass of scotch, shook his head, and sipped slowly. He had never thought of that war, or of young Danny that much, or that his nephew would ever be involved.

The young man looked at his uncle and, sensing his reflection on the war, spoke out calmly, "What I meant, Unc', was I want to know if I can take it out there, will I be able to do my job, lead, while I'm out there? If I get through it satisfactorily, I'm confident I can make it out here, too, like you, Uncle Dan."

Danny responded carefully, deliberately. "I'm not so sure that you'll find the answers out there. Survival out there does not necessarily insure success or a long life on the outside. You will do fine, only don't be too anxious to prove how tough you are. You don't have to prove your manhood. Stay loose and think. You'll make it. Better still, knowing that, try to keep out of that hell hole."

And then he almost wished that he could have another go at it. So what? If he survived again, he would have to live again the intervening years until he died. Would it be worth it?

He would never see young Danny again, and a black man, with an earring and bandanna, later told Danny how it happened. It was almost a year after that dinner at Ben Franklin. Danny found the former Sergeant Wright living alone in a two-story house in a small college town in Indiana. He was working in a bank, not in maintenance and not as a bank clerk, although he would substitute for the regular clerks during vacations or in case of illness. He wore a business suit, shirt and tie, and made customers feel wanted and comfortable, when he was not moving between the main bank and the branches on the outskirts. He agreed to meet Danny for dinner at his hotel.

"Your nephew was an alright guy after he learned the territory, the V.C., and the people in his platoon," was his opening remark after ordering their drinks.

Danny immediately enjoyed being with the sergeant. "I feel like hell, he was my nephew, named after me, and I really never knew him, either as a youngster or a grown-up. I guess I was always too busy — the family, business, and where I was going," was Danny's contribution to the conversation during dinner.

After dinner, the sergeant finally spoke most forcibly. "Look, Mr. Castle, you been poking in all the corners, but you can't ask the question, 'How did my nephew get it, how did he get killed?' Well, let me tell you a little about him before he got it. As I told you, once he learned the ropes, he did all right."

Danny interrupted, "Before you get to that, tell me how he got along with his men, the fellows in the platoon?"

"The lieutenant never put on any airs, like he was a big shot, better than the grunts or the non-coms, and he could cuss better than most of them. We had about twenty-five black brothers in the platoon, and they weren't all nice kids. Well, hell, them white buggers, especially them from Dixie, were crude mothers, yes siree. You could hear them talking about that Dago, Lieutenant Castel Fart. But, like I said, they all respected him. And they moved when he ordered them to move out. He got them extra beer and liberty when we came back out of the jungle. He didn't baby them, he looked out after them."

Danny interrupted again, wanting to absorb and mentally review what he heard. "How long was he with you before he was hit?"

"About nine months.

The old Sarge paused momentarily, and then told the story.

"We had been in the swamps almost two days, and we was dirty and hungry and mad. We lost three, dead and seven wounded, four able to walk out and three on stretchers. The lieutenant had been all over the area, pushing, guiding, directing, moving to avoid the closing of the trap by a battalion of V.C. He was exposed all the time to incoming fire. He knocked one of the loud-mouthed sons of Dixie on his ass and saved that empty head from being blown away.

Danny was remembering the Rapido as the sergeant rose as if leaving, but only moved behind his chair, lowered his head as if in prayer, and continued.

"We inched our way toward the landing zone. But it wasn't cleared; the landing zone was under heavy machine gun and mortar fire. The Med-a-Vac helicopters flew high, circling above the firing, like crows scattering after every shout or clap of hands as they de-scended into a harvested cornfield. The lieutenant established a perimeter of defense along abandoned foxholes, and called for close-in air support. We lost another grunt, and had two others slightly wounded. The jets flew in, dropping bombs, rockets, and napalm; the surrounding hillside was on fire. We could see those monkeys in black pajamas running into the riverbed and we heard screaming, too. And we poured all the lead we could into their back-sides."

The sergeant backed away from the chair and in a gargled and barely audible voice could only say, "I gotta go. Be back."

Danny could not bring his glass to his lips as he tried to recre-ate what he had been told.

When the sergeant returned it was apparent that he had splashed cold water on his face. Now there was some brightness in his face.

"The smoke was heavy, like a brush fire on a hot August day at home. The Lieutenant was running about, encouraging every-one to keep their heads down, as he called in the Med-a-Vac hel-icopters. We got all the wounded and dead into the helicopters, and as the last took off, he radioed for the choppers to lift the rest of the platoon out of the area. They began landing, with the Hueys flying escort, firing into the valley whenever anything moved. The LZ seemed secure, and the Lieutenant was moving each squad out, one at a time. He yelled, 'keep low and run like hell'. The Lieutenant was urging that Alabama boy out of his hole. He was pushing him toward the helicopter when a single round exploded between that hillbilly's feet, and the dope fell to the ground. The Lieutenant turned and fired a volley in the direction of the fire, picked the kid up by his cartridge belt, crying, 'move, you fuck-head', and shoved him toward the hovering helicopter."

The sergeant stopped again, pushed his drink away, and low-ered his head into the palms of his huge hands. Silence. Danny looked at the hidden face, not knowing whether the sergeant could or would continue. Slowly, he removed is hands from his face, raised his face upward and looked at Danny.

"Now where in the hell was I?" A pause, then, "Now I remember. The lieutenant turned toward the perimeter, waving the remaining two or three troopers toward the helicopter. And there was that shot, like a twig breaking after a spring ice storm, and I saw the lieutenant fall. I was to his right. I dropped and saw Charley moving toward a hole. I sprayed the gook and blood spurted from the bastard's many holes, pouring out like from a sieve. I ran to the Lieutenant. The sniper had hit his mark, through the chest, through the heart. He died too fast. We carried him to the helicopter and lifted him aboard. He didn't look bad, he didn't look beat up; he didn't look unhappy, but, dammit all, he was dead; he weren't no more."

Danny could not talk. His larynx was clogged. And the sergeant realized he had to end with how he felt.

"A good man, the Lieutenant. He would have been helpful on the home front when we got back. Now it's only lip service. The people, they seem like they is ashamed of us. They'd like to hide us in some corner where nobody can see us, some place where the whites don't usually travel; hoping we'll kill each other or rot in our own filth. The ghetto was invented for the blacks, and they're going to keep the fences about us. If we're quiet and accept our lot, we can grow old before we die."

Danny could only think again of the black man before the church that Frankie had pummeled into unconsciousness. Sergeant Wright saw the pain in his face and assumed he was thinking of the death of his nephew. But all Danny could voice was, "Thank you. Is there anything I can do?" And he stuck out his hand and spoke softly, "Come back and see us again, Mr. Castle, maybe I'll become more humane as I grow older."

Chapter XXXIII

Driving home was almost good; things appeared to be clearer, like a cataract surgically removed. Everything was wrong and had been since his Army experience. Where he was, he was not secure, happy, or even satisfied. Adjustments would have to be made, beginning in his own home with Lillian and the children, and his parents and brothers and sister, too. Perhaps for the first time it became apparent that he could not change or alter or make new his life over the last two decades. He was irretrievably bound to them. And as he approached his home, the word "fairness" was circling the brain, trying to be verbalized.

It was almost five in the afternoon as he drove off the road into the driveway. He drove to the garage entrance and stopped, as a stranger would, inhibited by an unknown force that blocked the access to his parking stall. He almost rang the bell at the front door. He paused, and then opened the door and walked through the entrance hallway into the keeper room, the sanctuary for reading, music, and television. He spoke first, forgetting his pledge while driving home.

"Where are the children, Lillian? Are they going to be home for supper?" And then he remembered, before she could respond.

"How are you Lil, how was school today?" Lillian was teaching English Literature at the University.

She rejoined softly and conversationally, "Where have you been for the past week, Danny? We didn't have any idea when you would be getting back this way."

"Lillian, I'll give you a resume of my entire itinerary, but tell me where the children are," he responded quickly and with a hint of irritability.

"Daniel, you know Chumley is at Bexley, Brad plays golf with the high school team on Friday nights, and Mother picked up Emily and Anthony for the weekend. I am so glad that you made it home tonight. Oh, yes, Brad is having supper and spending the night with the Cliffords. The boys are playing golf at the club in the morning. May I get you a drink?"

Danny nodded, and Lillian rose. "A martini, or is it scotch and water? I can't remember your preference any longer," and she smiled. He had come ill prepared, he thought, as he waited for his drink. He sensed that she was ready, expecting and prepared for him. She had planned the agenda and he had had no advance copy. She had white wine, and his martini was extra dry. She was in control, speaking first after each had taken a swallow.

"Did you have a successful week?" she asked, pausing to take another sip. She went on, "Wherever you were and whatever you did, business or social."

Ignoring the implications that he perceived from her remarks, Danny more assertively said, "Yes, I made some important calls throughout the state, spent some time in Cleveland with Boxey, he's new in that territory. I had to go to Indiana afterwards."

Lillian interrupted, "And how do you meet them in Indiana, Danny? You really don't have to go that far."

The red began to creep up Danny's neck to his cheeks; inside he was becoming heated. Restrained, he replied, "I had to see and talk with the man who was with young Danny when he was killed in Viet Nam. I had to know how he lived out there, and how he died. I found this black sergeant, my nephew's platoon sergeant, living in a small town in Indiana. He was a great help to young Danny, and I learned so much in such a short visit about my namesake. Maybe I should have taken the time while he was alive to know Danny better."

"I'm sorry for what I've been saying, Danny. Those words must have sounded angry and flippant, as they were intended. I just assumed you were with Susan or someone like her. I apologize."

"Could I have another martini, Lil?" was all he could say until he could collect his thoughts and organize a defense for what now seemed so apparent. She obviously had hoped that he would return this evening, the children away, and her arguments rehearsed and ready to submit.

He took a drink from the fresh glass. "I must be tired, Lillian, I don't seem to understand what you're trying to say to me."

"Danny, we have a problem. In the last ten years you have not taken the time to know what I have become, or know how your children were growing up. Your only apparent concern about us was how we were making it each day. You were not aware of my struggles at school, or with our children. I'm sure that you did not know that Chumley was put on probation at school, drunk during Rush Week. He was not permitted to pledge a fraternity. Father and I spent several days at Bexley."

She reached for her glass, fingered the stem, and then took a sip before continuing. "Emily has become a woman, physically, emotionally and biologically. And she needed us, but I was the only one here most of the time. Brad and Tony know their grandfather better than they know you. And you and I? You awaken me about once a month, pull off my pajamas, and satisfy yourself, or maybe not, I don't know. You surely don't arouse me or satisfy me, or give me any pleasure. You groan when you finish, then roll over and continue your briefly interrupted sleep. Only an assignment."

Lillian could not remain seated. With glass in hand, she rose and stood behind her chair.

"I don't intend to review the litany of omissions and commissions that make our marriage now an untruth and, even more damaging, unimportant. That is it, Danny, we do not seem to need each other. We have traveled far from the time when we spoke of love and really meant it. I loved you passionately. I'm not certain that you ever had such a strong feeling for me, an unqualified devotion."

Lillian paused. She was as serious as he had ever seen her. Her eyes were moist, and her lips were drawn tight, almost quivering. She put her glass on the table and brought her handkerchief to her nose. Danny moved his head forward, preparing to respond.

Lillian, having replaced the hanky, lifted her head, put up her hand, saying, "Please wait, Danny."

She paused, as if recalling a rehearsed argument.

"You have a need which I have not been able to satisfy, neither have the children. My folks have been supportive. What is it? What more can we do for you?"

She gave him no opportunity to respond, and hurriedly continued, as if a break would deter her resolve.

"Nothing! So I have decided that it is necessary that I do what I believe is for the best interests of the children and me. It's unavoidable. We must separate, otherwise, what appears to be a failure could become tragic. Hopefully, there will be more of a focus on the children, giving them real time, more than ceremonial attention. And quite frankly, I need someone to pay attention to me, to pat me on the head or on the bum, and say to me, 'you is a good gal, Lil'. I need love and loving, Danny, and that I have not seen or received from you in years. Let's call it quits, before we do permanent damage to one another."

After she spoke, he knew that he had lost it all. "There must be someone else, Lillian. Is there?"

And he realized immediately that what he had said was not only sophomoric and defensive, but it gave Lillian the opening for her parting salvo.

"Danny, blaming it on another will not work. And, besides, you know better. The thought is too crude, too juvenile, even for you. There I go, saying things I wanted to avoid. Enough, it's over. Let's do it the most thoughtful way, especially for the children."

There was no more talking after that.

Lillian initiated the legal proceedings, and it was too easy. She was not forceful or demanding. Danny was contrite; inwardly, he acknowledged his shortcomings, but there was also that gnawing sense of guilt. There was regret and sorrow for what he lost, but without any appreciation of any wrongdoing toward Lillian or the children.

Danny's business prospered. He had more time. And he danced with one woman and then another. Never passion, ardor or devotion, only indifference and half-heartedness, and so the relationships never lasted. He felt he had no insides, that he was hollow. He was the mechanical man, the robot, performing the assigned chores, unemotionally. Except when he drove down The Avenue, for some reason there was gratification.

Frankie had done his time. And he remained in charge, never relinquishing any control. But he appeared to have subdued his devils. He was quieter, was at home most evenings, and he seemed to have learned how to listen. But above all, he appeared to be happy, or at least happy with his lot in life. So they had dinner several times at the Dutchman's and tried to recall some of the old days. There was some talk about business, and it always ended with Frankie saying, "You happy. I'm happy, Danny. It's good we can do business together. But I must go. Emma, she won't go to bed until I get home. Hey, stay loose, OK?"

Chumley graduated, and Danny attended the ceremony. Lillian was there with her parents, all of whom were formal and correct in their greetings. Danny had met with Chumley a week before graduation. They had dinner and he met afterwards with his girlfriend, Anne Powell. She was bright and comely. His son was lucky.

"What now, Chum, what do you want to do? Or, more importantly, what are you going to do? Anyhow, I want you to know there's a place for you in my business. I could use more time off, and I really don't want to spend as much time as I have in the office. I bought an old house on a small tract of land up in the mountains in northern Ohio. Nothing fancy, and not a place for a honeymoon. But you know me, I like to walk, plant trees and watch grass grow, and clouds move across the heavens. There's a large lake nearby, and I could do some fishing. And I want to read more, all the good books that I never had the time for."

Chumley only listened, and Danny continued to sell.

"It's a good profitable business. There's more than enough for you and your brothers, if you wanted to work together and grow."

Still no reaction from Chumley, so Danny pulled the keys to a new convertible from his pocket, handed them to Chumley, and added, "Good luck, son, but drive carefully, not only the automobile, but your life. Hopefully, we can become better acquainted."

"Dad, this is too generous of you, the car and the job offer. I really appreciate it. I don't know what I want to do, except maybe to get involved in business. Grandfather Foster has offered me a position with their company, and my uncles seem to agree. I don't know. It's too settled, too conservative. A good living, always, but no excitement. At least, your home office is in the city. I don't know. Gosh, Dad, can I think about it?"

Chapter XXXIV

Chumley went to work for Foster Furniture. It was the easy road. He married the slim, pretty Annie Powell within the year, and Danny was able to see Lil at the wedding. The distance between them had not closed. He was invited to the Foster compound some three years after the marriage when Annie gave birth to his first grandson, Brick. After that, there were only infrequent contacts between Danny and his family, only graduations and a few holidays.

About ten years after Brick was born, Lillian had called in panic, almost crying.

"Please, Dan, you must take Chumley with you. He's not making it with the Foster firm. He's spending too much time at the club, drinking, playing golf, the ponies, and some womanizing. Too many nights away from Anne and that beautiful grandson of ours, Brick. That child is so smart and so handsome. Chum needs direction and a steady hand on his back, or there could be some real trouble. Can we meet? I can come up to the city."

And they met for dinner. Lillian was aging beautifully. Her body was trim, more proportioned than he remembered. Her face had matured, resourceful and peaceful, with purity that he had never seen. He expected some bitterness, some tiredness. She was only anxious but not desperate.

Danny asked about her work, and the signs of apprehension disappeared. "Oh, Danny, I love my work. Teaching at the University must be what I was meant for. And I believe I'm very good at my job. But the last few months have tormented me. Chumley has been too much. I didn't want to tell you on the phone, but they told him not to return. Not only was he not doing his job, but he falsified his expense accounts. And he may have pocketed some payments from customers. My Dad made up the deficits, but my brothers will not keep him. And he needs some income."

So, Chumley went to work for Danny. He was bright and a good businessman. And it worked well for several years. And they were good years. Danny became a friend of his grandson, Brick. They became buddies. And they took a trip to Disney World together. The boy loved his grandfather. This was as close as the grandfather had been with anyone before.

Danny became less concerned with the business, and Chumley succeeded him as President. The firm was the exclusive distributor of Italian olive oils, Italian olives, and Italian cheeses, from the Mississippi to Harrisburg, Pennsylvania. The business was lucrative. Frankie had never forgotten his old buddy, although they had only seen each other sporadically at the Dutchman's after Frankie had done his tour in the Federal Penitentiary system.

And then he received the call.

"Danny, you know who this is? Long time, eh. You in good health? I know your boy, he runs the business, but we gotta talk. And I can't come out your way. Can you come to the city this next week? Settle in at the Ben Franklin. I'll know you're there and will contact you. Ciao." And he hung up.

Frankie came to Danny's suite at the hotel. Danny had been told to be in his room at seven p.m. Two men, unsmiling, searched the suite and then opened the door for Frankie. One stepped outside, and the other retreated to the bedroom. They embraced and Frankie kissed him on each cheek, stepped back, and looked at Danny for a moment, then exclaimed, "You look good, you old son-of-a-gun. Not too much of a breadbasket, neither. What's the matter, you not eating too good?"

Frankie was heavier, the paunch was further extended, and his hair had thinned. He looked darker and shorter. His clothes though, were impeccable, the successful CEO.

"Frankie, we don't see each other enough, but you continue to look well. Still prosperous, I see. And, of course, you're eating and drinking well," and he grinned.

"No complaints, Danny. Like I told you, even those thirty months in the slammer weren't so bad. Everyone there, even the warden, was nice to me. I had almost everything I wanted, except broads. Maybe I coulda had them, too, but I didn't want to push. I had my cigars and scotch. So it was OK," and Frankie continued, "So whatta you do now that your boy runs the business? They tell me you don't go to the office too much. Still chasing the pussy, Danny?"

Danny told him about the little farm, about his reading and traveling. "And there is my grandson, Brick. What a boy. We spend a lot of time together. He's only starting at the University. One smart boy, Frankie. He must have inherited the brains from his mother's side of the family. We've taken trips together. Last summer we had a month together in Italy, from Milan to Palermo. He loved it, and so did I. I never thought I'd see it again after the war. It's a great country, Frankie, and I love its people. I only wish that I would have found it sooner."

"Why didn't you tell me, you palooka. I could have had some friends there show you around. But, never mind, Danny. It's good you go back. Next time, you let me know, OK?"

Frankie re-lit his cigar, puffed and shook his head.

"I gotta tell about your son. Whatta name, 'Chumley'. That ain't Italian, no way. Anyhow, he must have a lotta of his Mama, too, because he's not like you. That boy got lotsa problems."

Danny sat up. "What's this about, Frankie?"

"First, he tried to hide the sales of our products, he wanna chisel on our deal. What a dumb guy, he try to steal on us. But the worst thing, he tried to use our people, our ships, our packaging, to ship coke into this country. We never dealt in dope, Danny. Never! And this schmuck wants to screw us up. I tell you, Danny, if he wasn't your boy, he'd be a goner. My people don't want no cokehead screwing up such a good moneymaker. So, whatta am I going to do? That's why I called you, Danny."

Danny had never felt so exhausted. His chin was resting on his chest when Frankie finished talking. He really had never known his son. He had hoped, and he had stayed away, he didn't want to know.

"Frankie, I'm so sorry. First things first. How much money did he stick you with, the total package?"

"My boys figure he clipped us for about two-hundred fifty G's, and he owes us for merchandise he got and ain't paid for, about one-hundred twenty- five big ones, somewhere about three seventy-five to four-hundred G's. And we gotta have that money. Our people don't want to, and ain't gonna lose that kinda dough. Sorry, Danny, but you know I got bosses, too."

Danny's head was nodding, acknowledging the debt, and the need to pay. "You'll get the money, Frankie, but I'll probably need about thirty days."

"I gotta your word and that's all I need, Danny. But about the coke, you'd better burn it. We don't want it; we want no connection to that stuff. We don't believe in that shit, it's for Niggers and Spics. You know we're in the business but not that kind. Find that crap and stop that goof ball or someone will kill him. Basta! Enough. No more."

Danny neither moved nor spoke.

Frankie saw it in his friend's face, failure, and filling the Stega glasses, pushed one toward Danny. "Now we have a drink, talk old times a little bit, then I go home to the ole lady. Salute."

"Oh, one more thing, Danny. My people says your boy likes the stuff, too, and he goes heavy sometimes. And he likes the crap tables, too, a high roller at Vegas. A loser there, too."

It was such a long ride home. Chumley was adamant in his denials at first, but became more open when Danny informed him he would be dead if the money was not paid and the coke route closed and sealed. And Chumley blamed it all on pressure.

Danny returned to work, and Chumley stayed away from the office. An old competitor, and friend, bought the business, for a little more than enough to pay off Frankie's people. Danny retreated to the farm with what remained.

Brick spent all the holidays with his grandfather. They fished and walked and talked. Brick attended the State University and had separated both from his father and mother. Lillian had tenure at the University.

Danny's other children were seldom seen. Emily married, running away with a farm boy and was now living in a cabin near the Everglades in Florida. Her husband was a fisherman and guide. Saturday night was their big night, dancing and drinking in the local pub. Emily had two children, a boy and a girl, who ran around without shoes most of the year. The Fosters would never have known her. Danny had visited the area only once, and an hour was the most he could endure of the heat and insects that were trapped in the four-room hut. Emily had not seen her mother since the birth of her last child five years before. She occasionally saw Anthony, who lived in West Palm Beach, and worked at the dog track. Bradford, she didn't know about. Danny gave Emily two hundred dollars. The squalidness would remain. No amount of money would change the lifestyle, which had trapped her into a feeling of happiness.

"Daddy, we're enjoying our life. The children are healthy and strong. And Thom and me are living the kind of life that's comfortable and exciting. We have so many friends here, and we all share. Good people."

And Dan could recall that sprightly redhead in her cotillion gown and patent leather shoes off to the high school ball.

Chapter XXV

He could not remember when he permanently moved back to the farm. He did remember the day he had stopped in town, grocery buying, book browsing, and glancing at the newsstand. His eyes stopped at the by-line on the left-hand column, puncturing the benign mood that had prevailed throughout the week. He had been overly pleasant to all the people he had come in contact with since arriving in town that morning. Earlier at the farm he had had winsome conversations with the birds, the rabbits and squirrels. The sun was bright and the sky was cloudless.

But a shadow passed in front of him as he pocketed his change after purchasing the paper. He walked to the corner and sat at an open table on the patio of "John's", the coffee shop. Danny ordered his coffee and roll, and only after he had been served did he re-open the newspaper and confirm what he thought he had seen at the newsstand.

"Crime Boss Dead." And Frankie's picture. A photocopy of a mug shot, which must have been taken years ago when Frankie had been questioned by the Crime Commission. This was a picture of a criminal, an animal on the prowl. Without reading the text, even a casual viewer, a passer-by, would have surmised that the photograph must have first appeared on the "Most Wanted" bulletin board in the post office.

His eyes remained focused on the photo; he could not lower them to read the story. Frankie was dead. And if what they had been taught by the church was true, Frankie had commenced paying his dues.

Slowly Danny lowered his eyes to the name in heavy print beneath the photo. "Francis 'Frankie' Collizio." The name, together with the photo, was a portrait of Cosa Nostra.

Danny's mind was racing ahead of his eyes, remembering when they were young. Frankie was dead. What else was there to be said? How he died was not important.

He sipped his coffee, but could not bite into the roll. His eyes moved across the street to the Methodist Church as the parishioners were hurrying up the concrete steps to the sanctuary. And he thought about The Avenue, the Clubyard, Cooper's Hall, and the church on The Avenue which he had never entered, but which had bonded them together, cementing a relationship which endured despite the turns in their lives.

Then slowly, patiently he read one sentence at a time. After finishing the last paragraph, Danny removed his glasses, wiped them with his handkerchief, and laid the hanky on his coffee cup, ready for use. When he had read the article in its entirety, he replaced his handkerchief in his pocket. There were no tears; no moisture dimmed the viewing of the page. He could not cry.

And he remembered he did not cry at his mother or father's funerals. He had appeared firm and stoic. The people of The Avenue thought of him as strong, keeping it all inside. Danny had not cried after the Rapido. He had never learned to cry. Strange. And he had never thought about it before. Was it physical, something wrong with his tear glands? Or was there something in the mind which was not functioning that surely was responsible for the opening and closing of the valve that caused the flow of the lubricating waters that washed out scenes that should not be retained. If he could not shed a tear for Frankie, would he ever, for anyone? Would he ever cry as a token of respect or affection? Evidently not. It was too late now.

The lead paragraph described it succinctly. Frankie had been shot, murdered, as he emerged from the Avenue Grille, by a young Black, who reached into a crude wooden shoeshine box and fired three rounds of forty-five caliber bullets into Frankie's stomach, screaming, "Die hard you, bastard." And just as he finished, Frankie's bodyguards poured at least thirty slugs into the head and body of the black man. Frankie died on the operating table at the hospital. He had been unconscious, in shock, from the moment the three shells had torn through his stomach wall and emerged through holes in the back the size of silver dollars.

No motive was known to the press. There was no immediate information available on the alleged gunman, except his name, Denzil Hopkins, Jr. No rivals had been known to covet Frankie's throne. Some Negroes were moving into houses on the extreme ends of The Avenue, some were writing numbers, running some girls, and operating some hidden gambling joints. Nothing big. Nothing challenging to the mob. The police were investigating. The story proceeded to name the potential contenders "for the mantle which had been worn by Collizio, the 'top dog' of the organization in the area for the past seven years". Danny remembered hearing the names of Frankie's possible successors, but he did not know any of them.

Danny, reading faster, noted that the article did report Frankie's age, sixty-nine, his birth in the neighborhood of The Avenue, his rise to power from numbers runner to bodyguard, protector to the leaders, promotion to under boss, and then Capo. Nothing was said of his military service. It recited Frankie's refusal to testify before the Crime Commission, he had taken the Fifth Amendment, and had been incarcerated for three years in a Federal penitentiary. The story said that it had been Frankie's only conviction, but went on to cite sources that attributed scores of crimes at Frankie's hands. The front-page story then described Frankie's predecessors in power, his present colleagues, their tenures, and how the careers had ended for those no longer at the helm. Violent deaths and incarcerations were highlighted.

Frankie was to be interred in the cemetery where his parents were buried, the cemetery that for the past three-quarters of a century had become the final resting place for most of the people of The Avenue. High Mass was to be conducted at the neighborhood sidewalk church where they had been baptized, received their first Holy Communion, and confirmed as members of the Church. Frankie had been its largest financial patron for many years.

Danny could visualize the banks of live flowers which would surround a carved mahogany casket at the public calling, with the blessed rosaries entwined in the hands that had no power, which rested upon the stilled heart. All authority, command, force, and strength, with its accompanying patronage, influence, and sway had passed by operation of death into the hands of another.

Danny had driven back to the Farm without really seeing the road he had driven on many thousands of times. Normally, during the drive, he had always found something new to program for future reference, additions to a house or barn, patching of the road, newcomers moving in, different automobiles parked in driveways, the condition of the crops, and the number of quail released from the Preserve. But today, everything was on automatic. And the film passing through his mind had no retentive powers.

The bagged groceries were placed on the counter in the kitchen. Taking the newspaper, Danny walked to the front patio, dropped into his wicker lounge, and looked toward the southeast. The hot sun was good.

He found the obituary page and his eyes stopped at Hopkins, Denzil, Jr. It was as if he had no choice. He had been drawn to that page, to that name. But there was not too much copy. Frankie's slayer lived with his grandfather, a retired steelworker. The young man's mother had remarried and carried a different surname. His father was deceased. Danny wanted to know more. But why? It was all that Danny could think about, that bloodied head in the gutter in front of The Avenue church, and he and Frankie racing home down The Avenue cursing a Black, and blaming it all on the advent of the night.

He had to go. To the city. He was not sure he should or wanted to see Frankie at the funeral home. Too many people; with too many faces for which he would not immediately be able to find a name. It had been more than forty years. But they would remember him, he had moved away, and there would be too many questions. Everyone there would know each other, except Danny and the representatives of the City, State and Federal law enforcement people. Maybe attending the Mass, if he arrived early and found a seat in the middle of the sanctuary, would shield him from The Avenue people and the strangers who were recording those in attendance. The heavy growth on his upper lip would not be trimmed or removed. He had never worn a mustache before.

Ever present throughout was the question, why. And after his second Scotch and soda, Danny had committed to himself to attend the wake or funeral of Denzil Hopkins, Jr. The grandfather had purchased a house two doors east of the house Danny had been born in. They were neighbors in distance, if not in time. And Danny wanted to see the old homestead.

The drive to the city was pleasant, easy. And having decided on what he was going to do, he was relaxed, enjoying the classical music emanating from the University station in the city. He drove to the Ben Franklin Hotel in time for a shower, a cocktail and dinner. Public calling for both dead was that day, from two to five p.m., and from seven to nine p.m.; different funeral homes.

After dinner, he drove to The Avenue and as he proceeded east toward the old homestead he began to notice the spaces where buildings and houses had been a part of the landscape, when as a youngster he walked up to The Avenue. The Avenue Church with its iron fence and gate appeared the same. Cooper's Hall was gone, the mainstay of the community no more. The windows and doors of the grocery stores and butcher shops were boarded. Lights showed under the swinging door of the Dutch-man's. No one was loafing on the corner. Danny turned off The Avenue toward the bridge. It was almost dark, and Blacks were walking on the street, sitting on the sidewalk porches, smoking, talking, and looking into the night.

Danny parked in front of the house where he had been born. It was now painted a robin-egg blue. And as he alighted from the car, a voice on the porch called out, "Whatcha looking for, part-ner?" A burning cigar located the speaker.

"I'm not quite certain. I was born in this house many years ago, passing through town and saw where a boy living on the street died, and I wondered whether his grandfolks would have known my parents. Too bad about the boy."

"Who you, man?" came the response as the cigar and then the man approached the porch wall fronting the sidewalk.

"My name is Daniel Castle. I moved away after high school, during the war."

"You ain't an Eyetalian, hell, I thought only Wops had lived on this here street before us. Of course, I only been here since about five years, don't know who was here in this house before, but they was Blacks, like me."

"My folks were Italian, my name changed after the war."

"Well, the Hopkins, the grandfather, they'd been here longer than any of us, maybe twenty years. When they came, everybuddy was white. I mean Eyetalian."

"Maybe it might not be a good time to visit Mr. Hopkins, his grandson only dead one day," Danny asked for guidance.

"No, I don't think it makes no difference. We know when you born, you're gonna die, some sooner, and some later. I sees him on the porch only ten minutes ago. If he ain't sleeping, he'll talk to you."

Danny thanked the unknown occupant of the house that Papa had claimed as one of his true accomplishments. He had owned a house during the great Depression and never missed a mortgage payment.

Walking those thirty-five feet to the Hopkins house, Danny remembered the Merlinos — three boys, and two girls, twins who were a year or two younger. They were hot stuff, teenyboppers, during his growing-up years. Oh, how he thought about them when he could not fall asleep in the attic cubicle.

The rocking chair was in motion, huge hands lay on the armrest, the eyes were closed, and a brown-stained, corncob pipe hung from joined, but not taut lips. He could not have been asleep; intermittent puffs of smoke spiraled around his white hair. There was a softness in his face that Danny had never seen in a human. The face was smooth, not a line of age, caramel brown in color, tranquil and composed. Danny stopped at the gate, and for a moment, he had forgotten where he was. All he could feel was the rapture of being alone in the Prado before Goya's self-portrait. "What a time and place to come face to face with humanness," he thought.

The chair became motionless, the hand removed the pipe from the mouth, and he spoke, "What can I do for you, mister?"

"I was born in that house two doors down, my folks lived there until they died. I wonder if you knew them. I'm just passing through", Danny responded.

"Your Mama was living there when we moved here. She was a nice lady, always smiling and always good for a 'hello'. Your Daddy was dead then. There's been lotsa changes in the past twenty years. The old people, we got along. The younguns wanna war most of the time. Would you care to set a spell? My name is Denzil Hopkins."

"I'm Dan. So nice to meet you, sir. I would like to sit here a moment. Sitting on the porch in the evening was something I did many summer evenings. We had a small radio, and we would listen to music when it was too hot to sleep. And people walked up and down the street all times of the night and day." Danny shook the old man's hand and sat in the other rocking chair.

Danny asked if the children used the playground very much, remembering to Mr. Hopkins the hours of joy he found in that clay arena.

"Yep, they use it. They got a section for real younguns, swings and climbing bars and slides, even supervisors during the summer months," Mr. Hopkins answered.

"During our time, the Depression, you know, we made up our own games," Danny reminisced, grinning.

"Say, did you know that gangster, Frankie Collizio, that was killed a couple days ago? About your age." was surprisingly thrust into the conversation, which until that moment had been so easy.

"We went to grade school together. He lived on the other side of The Avenue, never spent too much time on the playground, maybe he was a couple of years older. I knew him, everybody knew everyone in the neighborhood," Danny recited as if he were being questioned by the authorities.

"They say my grandson killed him, shot him dead," was the old man's curt remark.

Danny saw his opening and pursued it. "I read the newspapers, Mr. Hopkins. The stories are not too clear about why. Did the boy know him, did he mistreat the boy?"

"Little Denzy was a good straight kid until his father died about five years ago, brain tumor, they said. His father, my son, was named Denzil, too. The youngster was very close to his daddy. His daddy did odd jobs, couldn't keep a job, always had headaches. Nebber did get accepted in the Army. Denzil's wife ran off to California after their boy was two. I guess me and the Government supported my son during most of his life."

"When my son died, little Denzy began hanging out on The Avenue, doing favors for the mob guys, and they paid him good, he told me. He shined their shoes, picked up their dry cleaning, and swept out the Grille. Denzy bought himself a used Ford; got to dressing fancy and staying out late. He seemed to get along with all those guys, sez they treated him alright. Sure, Denzy knew all those dudes. I don't know what happened. That boy was not in them rackets. And I nebber knew him to have a gun. Maybe someone else did it, and they cover it up by shooting Denzy. Those people are bad ones."

Danny, unable to stop, pursued the opening. "How about your son, did he have any dealings with those people, with that Frankie fellow?"

"No way. My Denzil never amounted to much after he was sixteen or sebbenteen. How he got that young gal to marry him surprised me. She was sharp. But he got her in the family way. Then she leaves him with the baby. I guess she knowed me and my wife would take care of them both. And we shore did. We was living down in the Tunnel District, near downtown, when our son was a youngster. But he roamed all over the city. Had friends every place, he'd say. One time I member he come home with his head bandaged, his face was cut up some. Only thing he ever told me was he was 'ruffed up' by a couple of Dago dudes while he was walking along The Avenue. Police took him to the hospital. Nothin ebber happen about it."

Danny interrupted, "Did your son say who they were, did he know them?"

"No, he nebber told me nothin more. Nebber ever after talked to me about it."

"Do you know whether he ever talked about it with his son, little Denzy?" Danny anxiously asked.

"Don't rightly know, except they talked a lot. I hear them talk about them white dudes, the mob guys, living it up with lots of money, women, cars, and booze. My boys talked about them guys shacking up with some black gals."

Too hurriedly, Danny inquired, "Did you ever hear them mention Frankie Collizio's name, or the names of any people associated with him?"

Mr. Hopkins knocked the ashes from the cold pipe bowl, repacked some tobacco, struck a match, puffed, and when the pipe was well lighted, softly but clearly said, "You are what you say you are, ain't you? I hope you ain't a cop, or a reporter, or one of them mob boys, cause I ain't gonna say no more."

Immediately and firmly Danny responded, "I am who I told you. I am not with any cops, nor do I belong to that organization, or any such group. I am not a newspaperman. I am a retired businessman who was born two doors down the street. And I have not lived here for over forty years. I only wanted to know whether you knew my folks. I am sorry about your grandson. Really — is there anything I can do? I know how my mother would have felt if she were living. She would have surely wanted to do something."

"Nope, there ain't nothin nobody can do now. Denzy's OK now, no more hurt. I guess I gotta go in and wash up, gonna go to the funeral home in a little bit," and the old man rose and turned toward the screened door, without acknowledging Danny's extended hand.

Danny spoke to the back of his host, "Good night, sir, thank you for helping me to remember."

There was no response, only the sounds of the screen door striking against the doorframe.

Chapter XXXVI

No purpose would be served in going to the funeral home where Denzy Hopkins, Jr. had been prepared to receive and be viewed by family and friends. All would turn to watch the white stranger. The questions they would ask each other with their eyes and bodies would be the same as those posed by Grandfather Hopkins. This whitey is an interloper, a foreign body, infesting the occasion for organized anger for the mutilation of a black body by smoking guns held by white hands.

So, he drove back to the hotel downtown. Danny was tired, too much spent emotion. At his age, it had been too much for one day, now that the waking hours of his days had become shorter. He was exhausted, but not to the extent of being unable to re-run through his mind what he had learned, and from which he concluded that young Denzy had shot Frankie for having scrambled the brains of his father. Denzy knew who had been responsible; Frankie had been fingered by the young man's father.

For almost an hour, Danny sat in a pleasant, soft chair, looking out from the high windows of the hotel, focusing on the confluence of the rivers. For some time, he saw nothing but rushing water. Then the river became The Avenue and he could see

Frankie running backwards, laughing at the approaching night, at the day that had passed, and probably at life, too.

The Avenue made him think of Amy, the other tie that was binding. Impulsively, he telephoned. Her voice had not changed. It had not become tired or strained as her age might have demanded.

"What a pleasant surprise, Danny. How is my dear friend?" was Amy's immediate response. She had recognized his voice. Now that he was in voice contact with Amy, the river was no longer in view, The Avenue had faded, and he answered her as if he were calling from the farm.

"Older and slower, which makes me a wee bit sadder, that is until you answered the phone. What a pick-me-up! I arrived in town only this afternoon and have been sitting in this hotel room at the Ben Franklin looking at the traffic and the rivers flowing west, and remembering a time when there were hardly any automobiles, especially in our neighborhood. Come downtown, Amy, have dinner with me. Please. I must see you, talk to you. Take a cab. Please, my dearest friend."

Since Amy's husband had died, she was living in an apartment east of the city. And this was the night that she generally had dinner with her daughter's family. She laughingly told Danny it was not all fun anymore to be with the three teen-aged grandchildren for dinner. She would meet him at the hotel at about eight o'clock.

Then there was a pause, and speaking in measured and deliberate words, she said, "But aren't you going to the funeral home, Frankie's wake? I assumed that's what brought you into town."

Danny was taken aback momentarily. Recovering, he lightly remarked, "If only I could say that it was solely the thought of seeing you that was the designer of this trip, but you know that it had to have been Frankie. I had to come, not so much to see the present, but to feel the past. This much I am confident of — I cannot go to the wake, but I must talk about it with you. We can discuss it all at dinner. Thanks, Pretty Face. See you soon."

He hung up after her "Bye, looking forward to seeing you soon."

And she looked, as he wanted her to be — straight, upright on firm legs that rested comfortably on high-heeled shoes. Her hair coloring was a pictured maturity, not age. Her eyes were bright on a face, which was smooth, and with just enough color. Danny finally took her extended arms, looking from her ankles to the top of her head, pulled her to him and kissed her tenderly on the upper neck near her left ear. And she smelled young, too.

When he could speak, all that came out was "I thought we should have one drink in my room. Alone. I don't want to share you with anyone else for at least half an hour. You are so lovely, Amelia."

After the waiter had served the drinks and backed out of the room, she spoke of what both were thinking,

"Danny, I cannot for the life of me understand why you're not attending Frankie's wake. You were such close friends, especially early on. And there will be many old friends that you grew up with. The Avenue, the whole neighborhood, I suspect, will be there. And you knew Emma, she probably will be expecting you."

Danny took a swallow of his scotch and water, and without any preface, almost shouted, "I guess I'm a coward. A disciple who would have denied his existence."

Amy interrupted rather coldly, "Stop that kind of talk, Danny. I'm not going to listen to such mush. Now tell me the real reason, what you think is the problem with your attending the funeral calling of a long-time friend."

"Seriously, Amy, I'm concerned that the FBI, the State Police, and plainclothesmen of every law enforcement jurisdiction will be all over the area, video-taping all entrances and exits, and afterwards checking all the mourners unknown to them, seeking connections to the past or, more significantly, to the future. I don't need that kind of harassment, especially now."

Danny put his face in his hands, and talking through his stretched fingers trying to hold his face up, he spoke, "I probably would have denied knowing Frankie, if asked, admitting only that we might have been in grade school together. In all probability, I would have tried to pass myself off as a curious, inquisitive stranger."

"You had no connection with his business or associates, so why all the worry, Danny?" Amy asked.

"Old age has set in, Amy. No guts, that's me, even though it would make no difference now. There really is no way for them to hurt me, except they would trouble me by asking questions."

They drank in silence. Then Amy came over and sat next to him on the couch, patted his knee, kissed the side of his face, held his hand, and said, "Let's go to the Mass tomorrow, you and I, arm in arm, old friends from The Avenue, from the beginning, saying our good-byes. Danny, we must be there early, the church will be packed."

Noting acceptance by the look on his face, she laughed, "Say, when was the last time you attended Mass, when your mama died? You should see it now. It's been renovated inside and out since then. Frankie, the benefactor — he gave the parish all the money needed to restore our old church. Now, tell me where the restroom is, and then we shall go down to dinner, I'm starving."

Looking at her throughout dinner had given him a sense of well being, unalloyed happiness, and an emotion, which had long ago ceased to be a part of his life. He was so delighted; the trip was so much more joyous than he could have reasonably contemplated. What he had dreaded, what he had been so anxious about, had become an occasion for jubilation. Danny smiled broadly, more openly than he had for many years, he was aglow, and Amy's face responded radiantly. For a moment, he almost masked the flush that had caused his heart to pound with such a sustained beat. As he transported his mind back some forty years, Amy began talking about The Avenue, back when it had been all that they knew and understood. The smile on Danny's face, which had faded, reappeared then, which he tried to contain by covering his lips with a napkin.

"What's so funny, Danny, something you remembered about me?" was Amy's reaction to the napkin-in-mouth act.

"This is good, Amy. I was thinking about some of the characters we knew on the Avenue as we grew up. Do you remember 'Fatso'?

"Of course, I remember, Danny. There were a bunch of brothers weren't there, six of them, and all of them so fat?"

Responding quickly, Danny said, "They were about a year apart.

Amy reminded him that they were her neighbors. They lived in the flats, too.

"And what made you think about that goofball now, Danny?"

Danny nodded and remembered Fatso was one of a kind, unlike most of the guys. He marched to the beat of a different drummer.

Actually, I was thinking about the summer of 1941, my last summer on The Avenue, and the year of the 'streak'. To the boys on The Avenue, there was only one hero — Joe DiMaggio of the New York Yankees. It was difficult to believe that one of us, a son of an Italian immigrant, had made it to the top. He was wearing pin stripes! It was our adopted team; the Pirates had no Italians on their roster. You remember, don't you, Amy? And whenever the weather was favorable and New York was playing in Cleveland, only about one hundred land miles away, the guys gathered on our front porch to listen to the game. We had the only small radio and an extension cord to reach the outdoors."

Amy reminded him that the girls had never been invited, so why would she remember, and what was so important about listening to a baseball game.

"Anyhow, it was the middle of July, and I can still remember the date — July 16th. DiMaggio had hit in fifty-five consecutive games; he had beaten George Sisler's record of forty-one in the latter part of June, and the Yankees were playing in Cleveland where DiMaggio could extend his hitting streak to an unimaginable fifty-six consecutive games."

Amy interrupted, "That was important?"

"Sure. We were excited. There was no swimming or the Clubyard that day. Just before the first pitch, the static became over-powering; nothing understandable was being received. Generally the reception was good and Cleveland came in clear. Everyone took a turn at jiggling the dial, hoping to improve the reception. Just unintelligible noise.

Danny explained that not even cussing or pleading to the heavens helped. Everyone was down, awaiting a miracle. Every hit would be a new record for DiMaggio.

Danny stood, clapped his hands and laughed. Fatso jumped up from the floor and yelled, 'God-dammit, I got it. My brother got a radio at home, and it'll work."

One of the gang shouted, "Sit down, Jerko, what the hell makes you think that radio would work when this one doesn't?"

Fatso shouted back, "I know, cause I remember the tag on it. That radio was made in Cleveland, so it sure as hell can pick up a Cleveland station real good, no problem."

Danny took a seat beside Amy, and recalled how his dear buddy, Ronnie, slapped Fatso on the head with a resounding, "You must be the dumbest jack- off in the whole world."

Amy smiled. "And with all that build-up, did you hear the game?"

"We never heard that game, but bulletins on the local station came through. Some time later. DiMaggio had hit a single at his first at bat. The 'streak' had been extended to fifty-six consecutive games!"

They both laughed. And so the evening went. Two happy people in love with what could have been.

They walked arm in arm to the cabstand after making plans for the next day. He pressed her arm close to his body. He kissed her lips before she entered the cab, and he waved as the cab pulled away from the stand.

The next morning was clear, balmy, and the air carried little humidity. Weather-wise, it was going to be an exceptional day. Danny drove to Amy's home, arriving about an hour and fifteen minutes before the Mass was to commence. He could not believe how transcendently bright she was. Amy directed him to a side street a block from the church. As they approached the entrance to the church, he noticed that the crab grass still filled the cracks in the sidewalk pavements, but the outside walls of the church had been recently sandblasted, the color of sandstone shone.

There were some elderly couples mounting the concrete steps to the entrance. Danny and Amy followed, finding seats in the center pews, equidistant between the altar and the doors to the street. Many of the spaces had already been occupied. People of all ages were crowding into the sanctuary. Amy held Danny's hand. Candles were burning and music from the organ reverberated off the vaulted ceilings. They sat in silence. Danny had riveted his eyes to the altar and on the figure of the crucified Christ. Danny looked neither to his right nor left, until the casket was wheeled to the front of the altar, preceded by the young priest, and convoyed by six stalwart men, all of the same height and build, young and strong.

Danny rose, sat, and kneeled when Amy reacted to the commands of the Mass. He had forgotten after so many years, so many changes had been made. Danny waited for the homily. What would or should the priest say about Frankie? The priest was not new to the neighborhood; he had been born within blocks of the church. The boy who became a priest had attended The Avenue grade school and had run the bases in the playground, and even danced in Cooper's Hall before he went to the seminary. The father of the priest had been a contemporary of Frankie and of Danny, acquaintances, rather than buddies. Everyone knew everyone else on The Avenue. The priest's grandfather and Frankie's papa both spent all their working days in The Mill. Danny had never met the priest. The priest had been Frankie's confessor; Frankie had been the priest's financial benefactor.

Danny was enduring the Mass, uninterested, but not irreverent. He did not participate in the sacrament of Holy Communion, the taking of the bread and wine. He only lowered his head, as if in prayer, during that part of the service. Danny could feel no piety. He did become attentive as the mysterious segments of the services were ending and as he began contemplating the sermon. How would the local priest reflect on the passing of one of The Avenue boys who had reached such notoriety?

The sounds of the congregation preparing itself for the awaited homily were distinct, audible to the assembled and to the priest. Danny sat upright, adjusting himself comfortably against the back of the pew. Stillness followed, and the priest looked once more at his notes, and waited. When he was confident that each pair of eyes was focused on him, he commenced, smiling, "It is gratifying to be able to welcome such a large gathering to this humble parish church, who have gathered together in remembrance of our brother, Francis Collizio, who, during his entire life on earth, belonged to the community of The Avenue."

And as if there could have been those who did not know what was meant by The Avenue, he defined it. The Avenue was the Carnegie Library, Cooper's Hall, the Clubyard, and The Avenue grade school, each a thread woven into a tapestry of life which had bound him forever to his family, this community, and, most importantly, this church.

The priest paused, hoping to gather all those minds that might have wandered.

"The western terminus of The Avenue touched a part of the city which Frankie only learned about after he had passed his teens. His early excursions, and jaunts, and roving in that world beyond The Avenue only strengthened his decisions to live within its confines. And he did thereafter, never forsaking, disavowing or denying his heritage or his church."

Danny flinched, lowering his eyes to the level of his shoes. Could this young priest have picked him out from so many?

Continuing, the priest said, "Francis was born during the Roaring Twenties, the year was 1923. His parents had immigrated to our Country some fifteen years earlier. His father worked in The Mill, a day laborer, shoveling slag from the furnaces making steel to build towers for industry and commerce for the emerging super power of this earth.

After a professorial pause, the priest started again.

"Francis grew up on The Avenue during the Great Depression, cold usually, and hungry at times. Segregated, knowing only those landmarks along the two-mile length of The Avenue. He never forgot those days. And he did not forget his family or community, or this, his church."

Danny touched, then looked at Amy, indicating with his eyes that these remarks were directed at him.

And then the priest reminded the parishioners and informed the newcomers that, "The very physical foundation of this old structure and its present state of cleanliness and rehabilitation was attributable almost exclusively to this most generous man whose munificent gifts to this church cannot be ignored or forgotten."

Continuing, "And when war came in the 1940's, this citizen volunteered to serve his country, and he did so honorably."

The priest paused again, looked out at his audience, and slowly posed the question, which was uppermost in Danny's mind. "And so, you may ask, why has this parish priest, in the telling of his life, particularized only those attributes reflecting the goodness of this man? Let me assure you, my dear brothers and sisters, my purpose was not to justify nor condone his faults, misdeeds, or wrongdoing of which he was charged. To those who knew this man, such a recitation would not have been necessary. To those who knew him only through the press or radio, a more balanced and objective review necessitated such enumeration."

The priest spoke then of the contribution of the Catholic Church to civilization and that the church had been under-girded and sustained throughout history by those men who have remained faithful to God, to their family, and to the community in which they lived, concluding:

"And I say to you that our brother, Francis, was such a man."

The voice of the priest became stronger.

"And we must also remind ourselves that we have not assembled in this place on this day to judge this man, for it is our belief that at the time of death only the Creator has such power. Suffice it to say that in accordance with the teaching of our Church, our brother, Francis, having repented of his sins in his confession made to me before he drew his final breath, was absolved of all his transgressions against the laws of God, by the power vested in me, a priest ordained by Jesus Christ, the Son of God."

Having asserted his role, he reminded the congregation of the part they must play to assist their fallen friend.

"Because our prayers will assist him in attaining everlasting life, where he will be united together with all those who have gone before him in grace, I ask you to join me in a prayer for this man who was born as one of us, lived amongst us during his life, and died in our arms on The Avenue."

The priest waited until all heads were bowed, and more softly pled:

> "Most gracious and charitable God, the Creator of all things and all people, please embrace our brother, Francis, a practicing and participating member of this parish and Your Church throughout his life. He believed in You and Your Words. Comfort him with Your decision that he shall live in eternity with You in that Kingdom You have created for Your faithful followers. In the name of the Father, Son and Holy Ghost, Amen."

Danny had clasped his hands, lowered his chin to his chest and tried to selectively close the shutter in his mind as it resolved to recall all the times that he and Frankie had been together. Initially, he was successful in only exposing those pictures flashing the brightness and laughter of their youth together.

But he could not cover the interposing frames, in slow motion, of their encounter with Denzil Hopkins in front of the gate of The Avenue Church. The blood was still vividly red. The contorted features of a face in pain was indelible, probably never to be forgotten. And he wondered, had Frankie ever confessed that act to a priest? Had Frankie been forgiven for that most grievous sin, the destruction of a human mind? And, if Frankie had confessed and been forgiven, would it have only exonerated him, individually, or would there have been an inter-connection to the deed, forgiving the act and all its participants? No sooner had the latter thought formed than Danny recognized its absurdity. No god could be that forgiving. Absolution flowed only to repentant sinners. There could be no pardon without a plea for exculpation. Danny had not then and did not now believe. Danny could only wish that it had not happened.

Amy nudged him, her elbow into his side, and whispered, "Almost everyone's gone, we had better move. We would be too conspicuous as the last couple to leave".

Danny raised his head, turned his eyes toward her, smiled, and speaking softly, "You surely are the most beautiful of all the women on this earth."

Then Danny lowered his turned head on her shoulder, patted her hand, and momentarily forgetting who he was with, said, "There were too many missed opportunities, and everything was not black and white," and he kissed her on that spot where his lips met her cheek. The blush that covered her face went back fifty years.

The funeral coach had begun its trek to the cemetery. The procession of automobiles following the limousines carrying Emma and their children had started as Amy and Danny moved into the sunlight of the day from a side entrance. They slowly walked toward his parked automobile, two blocks away. As he looked back toward the church, people were still congregated on the steps of the church. But they did not appear to be outsiders, the press, or the police. They were locals, by their dress and expressions, talking the language of The Avenue with the accompanying hand and body movements.

Neither spoke during their slow walk, arm in arm, as they approached the first crossing away from the church. They stopped, awaiting the passing of an automobile through the intersection. A quaking male voice from behind caused them to turn. Danny noticed a resemblance from the past. The face was battered and scarred, the nose was flattened, the nostril openings were barely perceptible, and the ears were squashed against sides of a head that was hairless. But he could not put a name to that face, or to a face, which he could remember from his youth. And the man lisped.

"Say, ain't you, wait a minute. Don't tell me. Ain't you one time an Avenue boy? Oh, yes, I member her, too, still pretty. Younze married? Now don't tell me, I'll remember, it'll come to me."

Then, as if a rain-laden cloud had passed over the face that had caught too many gloved fists, the man shook his head, "I know you, but can't remember; your name is...."

Before the man finished, Danny spoke, too quickly, "Dan Castle, I am from out of state".

The beaten man, guessing wrong, and again a loser, mumbled what was meant to be an apology, and headed back toward the church.

Chapter XXXVII

It was Danny's last day to breathe, to think, and to endure, to exist. And he knew it. But the pictures of his remembrances were clearer than they had been since Brick had said his good-bye. Amy's face was now before him during all of his lucid waking moments. He especially recalled their last afternoon together. They had talked about the sermon as they drove back to the hotel. It was after they had that first taste of wine at lunch that Amy asked if he had recognized the shattered form of a man who had accosted them outside the church. Danny had shaken his head.

Amy smiled at his non-verbal response. Danny noticed that it was not the usual Amy smile. Not loving or approving, more like a question.

"Danny, you surely had to know who that was, he lived on your street. He learned to box at Cooper's Hall; as an amateur, he boxed throughout the city. He wanted to make it big, to fight in Madison Square Garden. You surely remember him. Everyone called him 'Tattoo'. He would brag that he would mark the faces of his opponents with the image of his fists. He was Petey Sena. His scrambled brain could not have translated the name 'Castle' into any name associated with his life on The Avenue. He might have recalled 'Castel Forte'. When did you change your name, Danny?"

And Danny told her. But he could not stop there. For the only time, he shared the hurts of his life with another human, with the only person he might have loved. Only after he had almost completely negated the evolution of his life, Amy interrupted, calmly but firmly, speaking tenderly, "Danny, I know this, you moved out and you made it outside The Avenue. Frankie, on the other hand, did not leave The Avenue. And he lived by the rules of the Organization, which made it's own rules for the benefit of a few thugs. Let's face it, Frankie was a bum, he died, face down on the pavement of The Avenue where he belonged, on concrete that was as hard and as dirty as he was."

"Amy, you're too good; still kind and loyal to this old friend. But we know differently. Too much of my life has been committed to denial, repudiation, and renunciation. The priest called that shot. I now know that I never completely understood The Avenue. I misread its role, its values, its very meaning, putting too much emphasis on a piece of concrete during a cold period in my life. On the other hand, I viewed the world beyond The Avenue through rose-colored glasses. That was wrong, too. The only thing that I'm halfway sure of is that it all may have worked with you — either on The Avenue or on the outside. You may have been the only person who could have helped me to learn how to cry; how to love; how to be human; to have been someone other than just a survivor."

And the last words he heard were from the nurse. "You keep thrashing about, knocking the covers off the bed. When I make my next rounds, I expect you to be sleeping."

There was half a smile on his face when the nurse returned and pulled the sheet over his head.